IN SEARCH OF
MAGIC FIRE

Amber Gabriel

Books in this series:

IN SEARCH OF MAGIC FIRE

by

Amber Gabriel

Book Three in *The Edge of the Sword* Series

This is a work of fiction.
Similarities to real people, places, or events are completely coincidental.
I don't know why people put this statement in books because normally it is a big fat lie. Novels set in our world all have real places like New York or Pennsylvania. This novel is in an imaginary world, so at least the places part is true. A more accurate statement would be that I have not deliberately patterned any of my characters after real people, and the things that happen to them are entirely of their own making, or mine.

To all who go to battle for the sake of others, on any front, this book is respectfully dedicated.

ACKNOWLEDGMENTS

"It's too cold out for this. Does it have to be done tonight?"

"Yes! C'mon!" I urge my husband.

"It's too windy."

"The wind will blow the sparks in front of the sword. That's how I want it to look."

Fortunately we are outside of city limits and not under a burn ban. I drive the sword into the earth by the edge of the driveway and tell Wayne to wait while I light the sparkler. The brisk, December wind does make it difficult to catch fire. After several failed attempts, I go inside and get a candle in a jar and light it. When I hold the end of the sparkler to the candle's flame, protected from the wind by the glass walls, it finally ignites.

"Ok, here. Hold it to the side of the sword."

He holds it. I take several pictures. The sparkler burns quickly, and I have to keep handing him new ones.

"Hold it closer."

Phone cameras don't go 'click' unless you have it

set to simulate the sound of a shutter. I miss that noise. The wind blows the sparks in a long stream, and the colored streaks reflect off of the polished metal blade.

"Oh, yes, that's good! Right there!"

Unprintable intimate comment and appropriate reply follow.

"Ok, I've got several good ones. We can go in now."

Back in the living room, I look through my photos and am very excited. "Look at this one! It's perfect! See!"

"You were right, it looks great."

I grin.

Thank you, Darling!

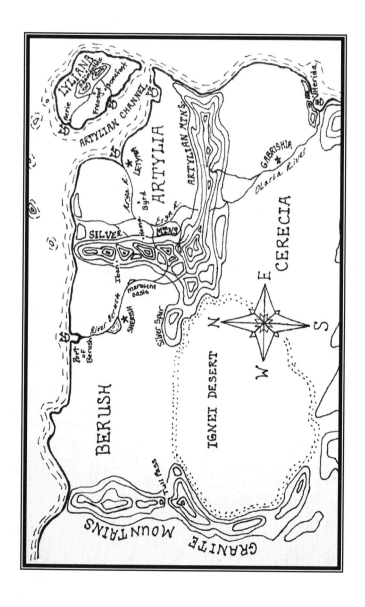

PROLOGUE

Eemya sat up straight in bed. Her sudden movement woke Darius, who was a light sleeper.

"What is it? Are you alright?" Darius asked, concerned.

Eemya lay back down, and he rested his hand on her belly. She had been having cramps as the new life growing inside of her began to ask for more room.

"I am fine. I had a terrible dream."

"What was it? The usual one?" Darius and Eemya both had trouble with dreams, less often now that they had each other to share their burdens with.

"No, I have never had a dream like this before."

"Come," he pulled her close. "Tell me about it."

"I saw Stelan. He was covered in blood. He was fighting off two other swordsmen. He killed one of them, but then the other raised his sword to strike a blow, and that is when I woke up."

Darius kissed the top of her head. "It is not an unreasonable fear considering the current tensions between us and Cerecia. You are relieved that he has not yet seen battle, but afraid the time will come."

"It felt so real."

"Cerecia will not have the capability of invading the

island again for some time."

"This was not on the island."

"Where was it?"

"It was somewhere I have never been."

"That could be almost anywhere," teased Darius.

Eemya smacked his shoulder playfully. She smiled, though he couldn't see it in the dark, and nestled into his chest. She became serious again. "I am worried."

"It is only a dream, my love."

"What if it is not?"

Darius did not believe that dreams could tell the future, but he didn't want to upset his pregnant wife. He remembered that his own captain had had a premonition recently that had been justified. His sister-in-law had midwifery skills that bordered on the magical. There were many things in the world that he did not understand. It wasn't necessary for him to understand them all, only to put Eemya's mind at ease. He cast around in his mind for something to say.

They had decided to stay in Sherish until Eemya delivered, and while they were here, Darius hadn't been idle. While Eemya had spent time with her sisters-in-law, playing with his nieces and nephews, and preparing baby things, in addition to copying scrolls from the library and discussing Berushese law with Cyrus, Darius and his brother had, with the help of Tomus, taken measures to defend against future attacks from Cerecia and put in place a spy network to give them advance warning of enemy movements.

"I really should visit Tomus. We have several things to discuss. If you can spare me for three weeks or so, I will go to Letyna. While I am there, I will find out how things are at Adamantine, even if I have to go to Lyliana myself."

"I will miss you, but I would feel better if I know for certain that all is well."

"What about Lydima? Do you want me to visit your holding for you?"

"I have received letters from Lydima. She is doing fine. I am not worried about her. If you visit, it will seem like I do not have confidence in her."

Darius smiled. "Alright." He closed his eyes and rested his cheek against her head. "As long as you love me, all is well with me."

Meanwhile, back in Lyliana . . .

CHAPTER ONE

Lydima awkwardly patted the squalling baby and tried to soothe it. "I know absolutely nothing about babies!" she protested with panic in her voice.

"The infirmary is overflowing with fever patients. I have no time for an infant," Yula responded crisply. The castle healer looked exhausted. The puffy circles under her eyes testified to the long hours she had labored battling against the illness.

"Is there no other family?"

"The parents succumbed last night. There is no one else that we know of. Now take the child out of here before the fever finds another victim."

Yula turned to the nearest sickbed, and Lydima was stuck with the wailing orphan. Eemya's ladies-in-waiting were assisting in the infirmary, or visiting the sick elsewhere, so there was no one who could help. She was utterly useless in a crisis of this sort, and she wondered, not for the first time, why cousin Eemya had asked her to stand in her place.

If she had known she'd be saddled with an infant, she would never have set foot in the infirmary. Before today, she had never even held a baby. She'd always been careful to minimize the chance of having any herself. There were special herbs for that kind of thing. If a woman knew her own body, she could also avoid men during certain times to lower the possibility of unwanted pregnancies.

There was nothing worse than being unwanted. She knew that from experience. Her parents had died when she was younger even than this baby, and she'd been passed around from one family to the next until she either wore out her welcome or ran away.

Cousin Eemya had taken her in for a while, but Lydima was so unruly and obstinate, and flirtatious, that Eemya had been obliged to ask her to move on. Lydima had done whatever was necessary to earn her keep since then, and there was only one occupation she'd found that she was highly skilled at. Men were always attracted to her, and she'd learned how to turn that to her advantage.

Now she and Eemya had mended their relationship, and Lydima was overseeing Eemya's domain while she and her new husband were visiting his family in Sherish, the capital of Berush. Eemya had just sent word that they were to be gone at least a year, for the birth of their first child, and had asked Lydima to stay at Freosyd until they returned.

Lydima was grateful for the opportunity, even though she was ill suited for it. Constantly trying to secure a man's attentions was tiring. She had hoped to persuade Lord Woldyn, a nearby land-owner, to ask her to marry him so she could have some security, but that had come to nothing.

The baby in her arms continued to cry. Lydima carried it out of the infirmary and into the sunny herb garden. The crisp, fall afternoon showed no respect for the suffering of the people living through it. It felt blatantly cheerful outside. The baby's wail broke the peace and tortured Lydima's ears.

One of Eemya's ladies, Nyla, came out and spoke to Lydima. "My lady, the child is most likely hungry. It has not been fed since the middle of the night."

Lydima held the baby out to Nyla, but Nyla shook her head.

"I have been nursing patients with fever for days. I cannot expose the child to the illness. You must go out to the barn and get some goat milk for it to drink."

Lydima sighed. Nyla and the rest of the ladies did their best to make her life difficult. They made their opinion of her clear, and gave her as little help as possible. Lydima knew it was only pity for the crying infant that moved Nyla to point her in the right direction.

Resigned, she made her way outside the castle to a barn and pen with various domestic animals, including a nanny goat. There she found the boy who took care of the animals and asked him if he could provide her with some goat milk.

"Lady Eemya could milk a goat herself," the boy chided with youthful honesty.

"Well, I am not Lady Eemya, but I am in charge in her absence. I need some milk for this baby, so please do your job, young man!"

"Sure," he replied cheerfully, "I can even show you how to do it."

Lydima rolled her eyes and held the baby as he showed her how to milk the goat. Eemya's subjects were far too independent for her taste. The boy put the nanny inside a special milking pen, sat on a stool, and pulled on one of the goat's teats, squirting the milk neatly into a bucket. Then he took the child, after informing Lydima that he had lots of experience

3

with his siblings, and motioned for Lydima to take a turn. Lydima looked at him with skepticism.

"Everyone should know how to milk a goat," he stated confidently. "You can do it. That way you can get milk even if I am not here."

Lydima sat gingerly at the stool and tried to maneuver herself into the proper position without getting her head too close to the stinky animal. She made a face as she went to pull on the nanny's teat, mimicking the boy's actions. Fortunately, the nanny was very tolerant and refrained from kicking her. She was concentrating so hard on what she was doing, that she didn't hear the horses until they had ridden right up to the pen.

"Well, this is a picture I never thought I would see."

Lydima looked up at the unexpected voice, lost her balance on the wobbly stool and tumbled backward onto the dirt. The boy quickly rescued the pail of milk so it didn't spill. The newcomer swiftly dismounted his horse and offered Lydima a hand up. He was lean and fit, with graying hair and twinkling blue eyes. His black tunic was impeccable, even after a long day's ride, and Lydima felt quite disheveled in comparison.

"Good day, Lord Yoused. Thank you for coming. I am sure you have many other demands on your time, and I appreciate the sacrifice."

Do not apologize or draw attention to anything you don't want a man to dwell on, she told herself, without even trying to dust off her dress. Her honey-colored curls were coming loose from her scarf, but she let them be, putting on her best smile. These were automatic thoughts by now, and she thought them even though she already knew Yoused had no interest in her that way.

"It is no trouble. As the interim governor, it is my

job to be sure that the tribute and additional loan are collected and sent to Artylia. Has Stelan arrived yet?"

"Not yet, but we expect him at any moment. Please follow me inside and the steward can show you to your room."

The goatherd took the opportunity to hand the baby back to Lydima, as well as the bucket, so he didn't get left with them.

"I will help see to Lord Yoused's men."

He bowed and hurried off before she could protest, and she frowned after him.

Yoused noticed her predicament and relieved her of the bucket. He motioned his men to take his horse and continue to the stables while he walked into the castle with Lydima. "And who is this?" He nodded toward the infant.

"A baby orphaned by the fever."

"Ah yes, we have many ill in my holding as well. Is it a boy or a girl?"

"I have not checked yet."

"Do you have a bottle to put the milk in?"

"I have no idea." Her shoulders slumped in weariness.

"If you can find some clean cloths, I can find something to put the milk in. I have raised three children of my own, so I have some experience." He smiled.

"I would be grateful."

"I will meet you in the study in a moment." He bowed his head toward her slightly and walked rapidly toward the stables after his men.

Lydima managed to locate some clean cloths and arrived at the study the same time as Yoused. He had found a small leather flask, and he filled it with the goat's milk. Then he took the baby from Lydima and held it gently, resting the narrow mouth of the flask on the child's lips until it began to suck.

Lydima was awed. "How do you know how to do that?"

"My wife was very ill after birthing our first child. I helped take care of him, and her. It was not something I wanted to leave solely to others."

After giving birth to two more sons, his wife had died tragically during an earthquake. She had thrown herself over their youngest son to save him from falling debris. Yoused had grieved deeply, and the son, who took after his mother, was sent to Lady Eemya for his upbringing. It was this son, Stelan, who was expected at the castle that evening. Lydima knew all this from her cousin, and didn't ask more questions about a painful subject.

Stelan had flourished at Freosyd, and Prince Darius, Eemya's husband, had made him lord of Adamantine, a holding on the other side of the island. Both he and Lydima were inexperienced in the economics involved in managing their holdings, and Yoused had come to review their separate accounts and advise them on what was required of them.

The baby finished the milk, and Yoused put one of the clean cloths over his shoulder. Then he turned the baby around, laid it over his shoulder, and patted its back.

"Why are you doing that?"

"Babies sometimes take in excess air while they are drinking, and they need assistance in expelling it." The infant took that moment to affirm Yoused's assertion by letting out a loud burp. "Good! Now we have to swaddle it in clean garments."

Yoused laid the baby down on a clean cloth on a nearby table. He removed the soiled garments, washed the child with water from a pitcher on the table, and swaddled it with clean cloths.

"It is a girl," he observed, handing the baby back to Lydima.

She looked down at the small baby, and a sudden, fierce determination came over her. This girl would not be left to fend for herself. She wouldn't let her go unwanted, as she had. The strength of her feelings took her by surprise, and she felt her eyes welling with tears.

"Thank you," she said with a hitch in her voice.

Youbed nodded. "You will need to feed her every three or four hours. Put the milk in the larder, or it will not keep long." Lydima was looking at the baby, so Youbed quietly slipped out of the room and went to find the steward himself.

The little girl had stopped crying and fallen asleep in her arms. Lydima sat in the study with turbulent emotions, afraid to move lest she wake her. She had responsibilities to see to, however, so eventually she got up, standing slowly so she didn't disturb the small child, and went to her room. There, she fashioned a type of sling out of a shawl and tucked the baby into it. The arrangement freed her hands and gave her a little more mobility. She removed her scarf, but was unable to redress her hair or change clothes. *Oh well*, she thought, it hardly mattered at this point.

In the hall, she discovered that Stelan had arrived, and dinner was ready to be served. Lydima gave the signal to begin, and she took her seat, maneuvering the sling so the baby rested in her lap.

"Welcome, Lord Stelan. I have not seen you since your appointment to the holding of Adamantine. Congratulations."

Eemya's young protégé still had his boyish smile, but his eyes looked more serious than Lydima remembered.

"Thank you. It is a huge responsibility, but Lady

7

Eemya's training has served me well. How are you managing here at Freosyd?"

"It is a position I am not well suited for, I am afraid." Lydima felt she could be honest with Stelan and not put on a false front. Eemya would kill her if she flirted with her young former captain.

"You will rise to the occasion, I am sure. We are all capable of more than we think."

Lydima attributed his cheerful optimism to her cousin's influence. He talked just like she did. Lord Yoused entered the hall and joined them at the high table, and they rose to greet him.

"Good evening, father."

"Son," Yoused nodded at Stelan and took his seat on Lydima's other side.

Lydima wondered if he blamed Stelan for his wife's death. Yoused hadn't seen his son for a couple of months, at least, and Stelan had suffered a grave injury during that time. She would have thought Yoused would be more demonstrative toward one of his own children, especially considering how tender he had been with the baby that afternoon.

With a baby in her lap, Lydima found that she wasn't able to be much of a conversationalist. It took most of her concentration to avoid spilling food on the child while leaning over her to reach her trencher. Hungry, she gave up talking and turned her attention to her dinner.

∞∞∞

Yoused watched Lydima with curiosity. It was a very different woman before him now than when he had seen her last. It was over five years since then, but he had never forgotten her. Her clear, creamy complexion, rich golden hair, and amber-colored eyes

8

were exactly as he remembered. But for once, she was not playing the coquette. Her unguarded expression when he had handed the baby back to her had been quite touching.

The infant began to fuss again.

"If you will excuse me, my lords, I must attend to the child. Can we conduct our business first thing in the morning?"

The men were agreeable, and she left the hall. Yoused and Stelan were left at the high table alone.

"How are you, father?"

"I am well." Yoused struggled with his emotions. "I am glad to see you. Are you fully recovered from . . . your injuries?" He could not bring himself to say 'earthquake.'

"Yes, thank you, father."

Stelan picked up a piece of bread but didn't raise it to his mouth. After some awkward silence which neither man could fill, they took leave of each other and left the hall. Both felt dissatisfied, but unsure of what to do about it.

∞∞∞

Lydima woke the next morning tired and cranky. She had been up several times in the night, trying to feed and change the baby as Yoused had shown her. The girl fussed incessantly until Lydima remembered to burp her. Then she wanted to be awake and gurgled and played with whatever she could grab hold of. Not having a crib or cradle, Lydima had made a little nest on one side of her bed and placed the baby there while she tried to catch a few hours of sleep. Afraid that she would roll over on her, Lydima found rest to be elusive.

While she dressed, she had to let the baby cry, or

she would never be able to change her clothes. She'd gone to bed in yesterday's dirty dress. The maid, Maygla, was one of those stricken with the fever, so Lydima was truly on her own.

Once she was ready to go downstairs, she had made two resolutions. One was that she needed to commission someone to build a cradle. Eemya and Darius would need one for their baby when they returned, so it would be well used.

The other was that she could not continue to call the child 'the baby.' She needed to have a name. A strong name. An inspiring name that would bolster her when tempted to repine. The first name that sprang to mind was that of her cousin, Eemya. A stronger, more noble name she could not find, but that name was already in use in this holding. It needed to be something unique. She would have to reflect on it a while.

In the meantime, there were records to be reviewed. Lydima put the baby back into her makeshift sling and went downstairs to meet Stelan and Yoused. Jayred, the steward of Freosyd, was there as well since he was more knowledgeable about the affairs of the holding than Lydima was.

Yoused went over the accounts of both holdings meticulously. He analyzed the amount of grain and vegetables harvested, the number of people in each holding, the amount of food it would take them to get through the winter, and the amount of grain they would need for seed. All the numbers and figures made Lydima's head swim. Somehow, she had managed to learn reading and writing, but calculations eluded her. She did notice, however, that the amount of people in Stelan's domain was nearly equal to Eemya's, but Yoused was requiring much less of a contribution from him for the loan to Artylia.

"Can you explain, Lord Yoused, why you are requiring less from Adamantine than Freosyd for the loan?"

"You have similar populations, but a large percentage of Stelan's people work in the mines and bloomeries. They produce a smaller amount of crops and will need most of it for themselves." Yoused explained patiently. He sounded unnecessarily pleased that she had asked a question. "They will also receive a smaller amount of interest than will Freosyd."

"Ah." Lydima felt silly for asking. She should have known there was a reasonable answer.

The baby whimpered, and Lydima took her out of the sling, laid her over her shoulder and patted her back absently while she continued to pour over the harvest data. A servant brought in lunch, and they ate while they worked.

"It will take several ships to carry it all," Yoused declared. "Lydima, your holding will need to bring your portion to my port for loading. Stelan, we will send some boats around the north of the island and you can row your grain out to them."

Stelan nodded. "My men and I will gather the necessary part of our harvest and be ready to meet the boats. If there is nothing else, I will return to Adamantine to make the final preparations."

"That is all. Safe journey, son." They bowed to each other.

"Goodbye, Lady Lydima. Thank you for your hospitality."

"It was good to see you, Lord Stelan." She dipped her head to him, and he left.

Yoused, Lydima, and Jayred continued to work on the details of the gathering and transport of goods from Freosyd. They figured how much each village

11

would need to contribute and decided on an efficient system to collect it. Jayred would see to its delivery at Youssed's castle, Sonefast, and Youssed would send it to the port from there.

When Jayred left the room to begin implementing their strategy, Lydima decided to tackle Lord Youssed with something that had been bothering her. It was none of her business, but she made a living on insinuating herself into situations where she did not belong. He was just gathering up his papers when she spoke.

"My lord, why are you so cold toward your son?"

"I beg your pardon?"

"You hardly speak to him. I can tell that he would like to hear some praise from you, or at least some show of affection, but you give him nothing."

"That is not something I wish to discuss with you, my lady," he said brusquely and moved toward the door.

Lydima shrugged. "It just seems out of character for you, that is all."

"What do you mean?" he said stiffly.

"I mean, you are very kind and patient with me, even though I know you disapprove of me, and you were so gentle and caring when you helped me with the baby. I also remember seeing you interact with your other sons, and you were very different with them than you are with Stelan."

"You know nothing about it," Youssed replied coolly. "If you will excuse me, Lady Lydima, I will see you at dinner." He bowed and left before she could say anything else.

∞∞∞

Youssed was angry. That impertinent young

12

woman had no right to speak to him about his son. She knew nothing about being truly in love with someone like he had been with his wife, Drayla. But he was angrier with himself than with Lydima. He had to admit, she was at least partially right. He'd pushed Stelan away rather than deal with his pain. His other two sons had stayed by his side, but he'd sent his youngest away to be raised by someone else. It was a common enough practice, but not a common reason. He almost turned around to apologize, but couldn't bring himself to do it.

It was too late in the day to set out for home, unless he wanted to be travelling all night, so he would have to wait and leave the next morning. Lydima's words rankled him. She had no room to talk when it came to personal deficiencies, but he had to acknowledge that his heart ached to know his son better.

He paced around the hall several times before returning to his room to write some letters of business. A messenger from Lord Kirdyn had brought some correspondence that needed his attention. Unsuccessfully, he tried to put Stelan, and Lydima, out of his mind.

∞∞∞

Meanwhile, Lydima had no trouble dismissing the interaction from her consciousness. The little girl had started cooing at her, and she felt her heart begin to warm toward the infant. She glanced at the map of the island on the wall, and suddenly she knew what she would call the child.

"Lyliana!" she exclaimed aloud. "I will call you Lyliana, after the island."

∞∞∞

While Lydima dressed for the evening meal, she smiled to herself and hummed. She was pleased with her inspiration for the girl's name. Lyliana was a beautiful island of strong, resilient people. This girl would grow up to be like her namesake.

In the passage outside of the hall, a man wearing Kirdyn's colors was leaning against the wall. When he saw her, he straightened and moved to block her way.

"Lady Lydima, it is a pleasure to finally meet you. I have heard much about you, and I am not disappointed." He looked her up and down, his eyes lingering over her figure.

"I cannot say the same." She kept her voice even and pleasant, but inside she was boiling. Normally she could stand a little playful banter, though a mere messenger was beneath her notice, but she simply didn't have time or energy for that right now.

"You will after we spend some time together." He leaned in closely while he spoke.

Lydima deliberately adjusted Lyliana in her sling, looking the man in the eye at the same time. "Let me be perfectly clear. Your only purpose here is to deliver Kirdyn's messages. That purpose is fulfilled, so you had best be gone, or I will have you thrown into the cesspool, which at this moment is full of the stinking vomit and filthy excrement of a dozen fever-stricken peasants. Now out of my way."

The man's mouth formed a nasty snarl, and he looked as though he would strike her, but he didn't dare, as she had the authority to carry out her words. Instead, he said through clenched teeth, "I cannot leave until I receive my reply from Lord Yoused."

At that moment, Lord Yoused himself appeared at

the other end of the passage.

"Well, there he is. I suggest you retrieve it and ensure that I do not see your face again."

The messenger bowed stiffly and turned to Yoused who held a letter out to him. He took it and departed without speaking.

Yoused lifted an eyebrow and looked at Lydima. "Is everything all right?"

"Perfectly fine, my lord."

"If that man was bothering you . . ."

"I can handle myself!" Lydima snapped at him, though she hadn't meant to. Secretly, she'd been relieved to see him, but she would never admit it. She didn't need to be rescued by anyone.

Yoused appeared taken aback, but recovered himself quickly. "I did not mean to imply otherwise, but just because you can does not mean you have to. If you ever need anything, please do not hesitate to ask."

Lydima was truly perplexed. Men never offered anything to her unless they expected something in return, but Yoused had made it clear years ago that he wanted nothing from her. The only time she had dared to flirt with Lord Yoused, he'd set her on a horse and sent her on her way.

She tried to fathom his motives but was unsuccessful. Finally she decided that Stelan must have inherited some of his purity and integrity from his father, not just acquired it from Eemya. She quit thinking about it.

"Thank you. Shall we go in to dinner?"

He bowed and followed her into the hall.

∞∞∞

The next morning, Yoused headed back to

Sonefast, but not before he had interviewed Jayred and the sergeant-at-arms, Byden, to ensure that Lydima was receiving their full support. He expressed some veiled concern that her reputation might cause others to try and take advantage of her, and the men assured him that they would stay attuned to the possibility and try to prevent any further problems.

Still, Yoused felt uncomfortable leaving her, and he looked back more than once as he and his men rode south toward home.

CHAPTER TWO

Stelan stood on the deck of the sailing boat and felt the sea air in his face. It was the first time he had ever left the island. He had missed the battle in the channel while recovering from cracked ribs, a broken arm and a collapsed lung. An earthquake had caused a mine shaft to collapse on top of him. It had been immensely disappointing to be left at home while others went to battle, and he relished every moment of this new experience, tame as it might be.

Now he was accompanying the shipment of grain from the northeastern side of the island to Letyna. Kirdyn and Yoused would be supervising the transport of the rest of the island's contributions. Stelan and his small fleet of merchant vessels sailed around the northern end of the island to avoid entering into Cerecian waters. The Cerecian navy had been soundly defeated, and their losses were immense, but that would only make them anxious to even the score.

"Letyna off the starboard side!" shouted one of the sailors.

After four days of sailing, they were finally in sight of the Artylian capital. Stelan watched excitedly as they sailed into Letyna. The harbor was wide and deep, and merchant vessels, fishing boats, and warships sailed in and out and were tied up at the piers.

"Shipping traffic has increased greatly since Berush assumed control," remarked the captain.

"You are pleased with the change?"

"The new harbor master and customs officers have everything running smoothly and fairly. All the captains are pleased."

Cyrus, the King of Berush, had taken over the rule of Artylia by force, and repelled a naval invasion from Cerecia shortly afterward. So far, everyone agreed that the abdication of Uriya to Cyrus had turned out for the best. It had certainly worked out well for Stelan. Cyrus' brother, Darius, had appointed him lord of his own holding.

As a third son, he had expected to remain a captain of the guard for most of his life. Not that that would have been bad. Lady Eemya was gracious, kind, intelligent, and fair, and he had learned a great deal from her, but now he was enjoying the challenge of leadership and responsibility his promotion to Lord of Adamantine afforded.

The merchant boats he led were directed to a dock near the customs office, and Stelan spent the rest of the day supervising the unloading of the cargo and making sure it was properly documented. When everything was safely stowed in the warehouses, he ensured that the custom clerk's records matched his own before making preparations to return to the island.

When he exited the customs house, Stelan heard his name called.

"Stelan!"

It was his father calling to him. Yoused quickly caught up with him.

"Son, I wanted to speak with you."

"Yes, father?"

"I know this is not the best time or place, but I wanted to let you know how proud I am of you, and congratulate you formally on your appointment to Adamantine."

"Thank you, father." Stelan was surprised, and felt a frozen piece of his heart begin to thaw. He was suddenly emotional, and didn't know how to act.

Yoused put a hand on Stelan's shoulder. "This is very hard for me to say, but . . . I regret sending you away. I know things turned out well for you, but it was not your fault . . . what happened . . . and that I could not deal with it. I am sorry."

Stelan blinked back tears. He felt like a little boy again. He felt all the emotions he had bottled up when his mother had died. When she had died saving him. He had blamed himself, not his father for sending him away. His younger self had thought it was what he deserved. He knew otherwise now. Lady Eemya had disabused him of that notion immediately, but it was still a wound that had never healed. He threw his arms around his father and embraced him, and after a moment's hesitation, Yoused hugged him back.

"I am so sorry," he repeated.

"It is alright, father. I forgive you."

"Thank you, son." They stepped back from each other and smiled, unconscious of the stares of passersby. "I would like to come and visit you, at your castle, if I may?"

"Of course! You are always welcome."

Yoused smiled again. "Well then, I shall see you soon." He gave a nod and continued on his way to go over his own records with the customs agent.

Stelan headed toward the docks with a light heart and an even lighter step. He felt like he was floating. His father's approbation was something he had not known he was missing. It seemed like a great weight had been lifted off of his shoulders.

He was still puzzling over his father's unexpected expression of sentiment when he returned to the boat that was scheduled to carry him home. There he found an emissary from the palace awaiting him.

"Lord Tomus requests a conference with you, Lord Stelan," announced the messenger.

Stelan directed him to lead the way, and followed him curiously. He was glad for an excuse to see the town more closely. They wound their way through the crowded streets and up to the palace. Stelan looked at everything with wonder. He had never seen a town so large. All the streets were paved, and tightly-packed houses lined both sides. People even lived inside the town walls.

Once they reached the palace, Stelan was led into the most lavish hall he had ever seen. There were two rows of pillars, and tapestries hanging between windows of colored glass. At the end of the hall, the dais held no throne, but a row of equal-sized seats. Prince Darius had explained to him that Cyrus had decided Artylia would be run by a council of lords, with a representative of the Berushese throne as facilitator. Tomus, son-in-law to King Cyrus, now filled that role.

Two people stood in front of the dais, talking in hushed tones. They ceased speaking when he approached.

"Lord Stelan, it is a pleasure to meet you. I am Lord Tomus."

A young man in his early twenties, not much older

than Stelan himself, thrust out his hand. Stelan clasped his forearm firmly.

"The pleasure is mine, my lord."

"I am told you speak Berushese," Tomus stated, switching to that language.

"Passably, my lord. I am still learning," he answered in the same tongue.

"Yarin has told me you have quite a gift for language."

"I certainly would not accuse your advisor of an untruth."

Tomus smiled. "Let me introduce Captain Talia," and he motioned to the other occupant of the hall.

Stelan turned his attention to the captain, and had a hard time not showing surprise at the title, since Talia was a woman. She was dressed as a Berushese soldier, but wore a longer than normal tunic, with loose trousers underneath, and a leather cuirass and bracers. Other than her pretty face, long braid, and slim waist, everything else about her was the same as every other soldier. Except that her sword might be a little shorter.

She stood at attention, with her feet apart and hands behind her back. Her expression was impassive, and she merely inclined her head to him when her name was spoken. Stelan imagined she was approximately the same age as Tomus, and she had very similar features. Perhaps they were characteristics common to most Berushese.

"We have no Berushese captains in port at the moment," continued Tomus. "After the battle of the Channel, we sent them home since we did not have enough ships left for them. Captain Talia does not speak Artylian yet, and she needs transportation to the island. Since you speak Berushese, I thought it would be convenient for her to sail with you. When you arrive, she will need to be put in touch with Halem."

"That will be easy, as he is currently supervising my holding while I am gone," replied Stelan.

"Perfect. When do you plan to leave?"

"I expect to set sail this evening, with the tide."

Tomus turned to Talia. "Can you be ready?"

"I am ready now. My bag is packed."

"Then it is settled." Tomus motioned to a servant to fetch the captain's pack. Then he looked hard at her. "Be careful."

"I will." She returned his earnest gaze.

If Stelan hadn't known that Tomus was married to one of Cyrus' daughters, he would have thought something was going on between him and the captain. The Berushese did occasionally take more than one wife, but that was not his business. The servant returned with Talia's bag, and she threw it over her shoulder. Stelan instinctively knew better than to offer to carry it for her. She turned to him with eyes at a height level to his own.

"After you, my lord."

∞∞∞

After two days at sea, Stelan began to wonder why Tomus thought it important that Captain Talia had someone with her who spoke Berushese. The captain hardly spoke enough words to matter. She stood silent and straight as a cedar, a few stray tendrils of hair waving in the wind, looking out to sea or pacing the deck.

Stelan tried to make polite conversation, but didn't get very far. "So where were you stationed before this?"

"I was patrolling the southern border with Prince

Varus."

"Were you with him during the invasion of the Artylian mountains?"

"Yes."

"Did you fight in the battle of the Channel or stay with Varus?"

"I fought on the *Restia*."

Talia definitely had more battle experience than he did. His experience amounted to zero. He had received some swordsmanship training from Prince Darius, and then from Halem, but Stelan was sure that was nothing compared to the training Talia had had. It would have been interesting to hear more about the battles from her, but she showed no interest in talking to him. He gave up trying to converse with her and strolled away to speak with the boat captain.

∞∞∞

Captain Talia was busy with her own thoughts. Foremost among them was how handsome Lord Stelan was. Most Berushese were dark complected, and until the last few months, she hadn't had much interaction with Artylians. Stelan's blond hair, kind blue eyes, and tall, muscular physique were traits she found highly attractive.

She had worked long and hard to be regarded the equal of a male soldier, and now, for the first time, she had to fight to maintain that persona. Lord Stelan was treating her as an equal, like she was a man, but part of her wished he would recognize that she was a woman. She tried to limit her interactions with him so she wouldn't be tempted to give way to these feelings. Her mission was vitally important, and she must not allow anything to sidetrack her.

They rounded the northern end of the island, and the boat had to zig-zag forward at angles since the wind was coming from the east. This slowed their progress, and they wouldn't arrive at Adamantine for at least another day. When they were finally able to turn south, they were able to cover the distance more swiftly.

Suddenly someone started yelling and pointing off the port side toward the open ocean. There were sails in the distance. It appeared to be a much larger ship, possibly an Artylian warship. Running with the wind, it closed the distance between them rapidly. Talia sought out Stelan to learn what was happening.

"It appears to be Artylian," Stelan confirmed, "but I have no idea what they would be doing on this side of the island." The boat captain, on Stelan's other side spoke and gesticulated excitedly. Stelan frowned.

"What did he say?"

"The captain thinks it is the missing Artylian warship, the *Sea Star*. It never returned to port after Berush took control of Artylia and was presumed lost or turned pirate."

Talia gripped her sword. "So it is an unknown. We should run."

Stelan spoke with the captain again. "He says it is impossible. The *Sea Star* is sailing with the wind, and is a much faster ship than ours. The island itself blocks our escape, and the coastline here is too rocky for us to put in. We are armed with nothing but our swords, so we are at their mercy and will have to hope for the best."

Talia set her mouth in a grim line, and they both drew their swords, as did the few guards Stelan had brought with him. In moments, the *Sea Star* had caught up with them. Their ballista shot a warning over the boat's bow, and someone yelled out instructions in Artylian. The sailors reefed the sails, and grappling hooks were thrown over the railing to keep the ships together. The crew of the *Sea Star* easily clambered down onto the deck of the smaller boat and quickly surrounded the small band of people on board.

A rough-looking man swaggered over to Stelan and glared at him. His expression was intimidating, but his clothes were filthy and his beard long and matted. He issued a demand, and Stelan replied in a firm negative. This prompted the pirate to yell and wave his sword fiercely.

"What does he want?" Talia asked Stelan urgently.

"He wants us to hand over the payment we received for our goods, but we received none. It was a loan. He says I am lying and threatened to slit our throats. Do you have a recommendation?"

While Talia considered their options, one of the invading seamen spoke a few words to another sailor. She was sure this man had spoken Cerecian. Rapidly she scanned the *Sea Star's* crew and perceived over half of them to be in Cerecian garb.

"Who is actually the captain here?" she asked in that language. Her tone implied that none of them appeared to have the necessary authority to be recognized as such in hopes that one of them would put himself forward to claim the title.

The Artylian turned to a man standing at his shoulder for an interpretation.

"I am the captain!" he roared loudly in Artylian.

The Cerecian interpreted the captain's words, but his shrewd eyes belied them. Talia suspected that he was really the one in charge, manipulating the captain into doing what he wanted most of the time. This may have been one instance when he was unable to control him.

"And whom do you serve?"

"We serve ourselves!"

"Are you sure that you are not here on a mission to retrieve a Cerecian spy?"

The Cerecian hesitated to translate this, and the Artylian punched him in the shoulder. He interpreted. The captain of the *Sea Star* narrowed his eyes at Talia.

"What do you know of it?"

"You fools!" She let out a string of curses at them. "You are early! Thought you could make an extra score while you were waiting, did you? Well, I am the one you were supposed to retrieve, and I have not yet fulfilled my mission!"

Before Stelan could hear the interpretation of this statement, she jammed the pommel of her sword into his hand, making him drop his weapon. She took him by surprise, and he was unprepared. Her sword was at his throat before he could blink.

"Back up!" she yelled to Stelan's men, who had stepped forward uncertainly. They didn't speak Cerecian, but they gathered her meaning from her tone.

"What is going on?" hissed Stelan in Berushese, but she ignored him.

Turning to the pirates she yelled, "You will take me now. Back in the ship, quickly!"

"What is the password?" asked the Cerecian.

"Windwolf."

The Cerecian nodded and spoke to the captain. The captain's face turned red with anger. Without warning he took his sword and thrust it through the heart of the captain of the merchant boat. He waved his crew toward Stelan's men, and they ran at them with swords. The men resisted, but they were outnumbered, and it was soon over.

The captain stomped over to Talia and motioned to Stelan.

The Cerecian interpreted, "What about this one?"

"Since you have interrupted my mission before it was completed, he is the only source of information I have. He comes with us."

CHAPTER THREE

Lydima and Lyliana were settling into a routine. It was not easy, but it was the new normal. Milk the goat, feed the baby, burp the baby, change the baby, let the baby nap, repeat. Between these required actions, there were sweet baby sounds and movements that Lydima came to look forward to. In caring for the infant, Lydima felt a sense of purpose she had never experienced before.

Some things she had to figure out for herself, like how to keep Lyliana from scratching herself with her fingernails while she slept, or what to give her to play with. The cold goat milk from the larder was vomited back up, and she figured out through trial and error that the milk needed to be warm, the temperature it was when it came out of the goat. She also learned to let her spend time lying on a soft blanket on the floor, tentatively kicking her feet or flailing her arms.

There were other things that demanded her attention, however. The infirmary continued to receive victims of the fever. Many who fell ill were able to recover in their own homes, but the elderly and the very young, or those with chronic conditions were particularly susceptible, and the worst cases were sent to the castle for treatment. Maygla, at least, was better, and could help Lydima with the baby.

One afternoon, Lydima returned from a conference with Jayred to find Maygla rocking Lyliana in her cradle, and she was struck with a thought. Maygla was the only inhabitant of the castle itself who had become sick. All the other cases of fever had been contracted in outlying villages. "Maygla, did you leave the castle at all before you became ill?"

"I went to visit my sister for a couple of days, remember? She had just had a baby."

"Oh, yes." A theory was beginning to form in her mind. "Was anyone in her village sick?"

"There were a few families down with fever, yes, my lady."

Lydima sat in a chair and thought for a moment. The only people, then, who were ill, were those who lived in villages or visited them. What could it mean? Something about how people lived in a castle and how they lived in a town must be different.

"Can you watch Lylie for me today? I think I need to go out."

"Certainly."

Maygla looked at Lyliana and smiled as she continued to rock her. The maid truly seemed to enjoy caring for the infant now that she was over her illness.

Lydima put on a light cloak and set out in search of Byden. On her way, she stopped in at the infirmary to speak to Yula, who was overseeing the care of several sick farmers and villagers. Yula was carrying out buckets of waste from the chamber pots, and Lydima could hardly refrain from holding her nose. The healer had previously informed her that the waste had to be taken outside of the castle to the cesspool under the south tower. The toilets were located in that tower, two on each level, and they all drained into the cesspool through narrow shafts.

"Yula, can you tell me exactly which villages your patients are from?"

Yula named a couple of nearby villages. "The one where Maygla's sister lives has had the worst outbreak."

"Why do you think that is?"

The healer shrugged her shoulders. "Who knows? If I knew why, I could stop them from becoming sick."

Lydima nodded and Yula went on her way. Next, she tracked Byden down and asked him to choose a couple of men to ride out with her as she visited the villages. She was not much of a horsewoman, so she had a cart hitched up instead. Two of Lady Eemya's workers had invented a cart seat with special springs, so the rider didn't feel the bumps and ruts as hard as they would on a normal cart. Lydima felt it was a much more comfortable way to ride.

A servant departed with her as a driver, and two other guards rode on either side of the cart as she set off down the road. It took an hour to reach the first of the villages Yula had mentioned. Lydima's cart rolled into the green, and a number of smells immediately assailed her. A small inn was brewing beer, and the air smelled yeasty. Overpowering that smell was one of sewage in the street. The smells brought memories to the surface of Lydima's mind that she had not dwelled on for a long time. She had stayed in a village like this for a short time, and it wasn't a pleasant experience.

Her mother had died in childbirth, and she had never known her father. She was told he had died in a raid by Cerecian pirates, but she'd also heard that it was a pirate who had forcibly sired her on one of these raids. Neighbors took turns caring for her as an infant, and as a young child, she ran practically wild, not feeling like she belonged to anyone.

When she was five, an aunt, who was a lady-in-waiting to the dowager Lady Kirdyn, had sent for her and cared for her until she was twelve. It was this aunt who had taught her to read and write, and tried to teach her numbers.

When the aunt died of a cancer, she was sent to stay with yet another aunt in a small village. The small, thatch hut had been like a living nightmare. Even now, Lydima couldn't think of her aunt's husband without her flesh creeping. Everyone had always told her she was a beautiful child, but this man had told her things that no child should ever hear. He had touched her in ways that a child should not be touched.

Lydima blinked and tried to erase the thoughts from her mind. She had finally run away from that terrible house and found work at a castle two holdings away. Even there her beauty had made her prey to the appetites of errant men. After a miscarriage at fourteen, she had sought out a healer to learn what could be done to lower the possibility of bearing a child in the future. The healer had instructed her in the use of several herbs and the workings of her female body. This had given her the feeling that she had some measure of control over her life.

Eventually, her cousin Eemya had found her, and though she was only two years older than Lydima, and recently married, she had taken her in. Eemya had cleaned her up, tried to round out her education and instill some confidence and morality into her, but it was too late. Lydima's character was formed, and she had found it easier to profit from her looks rather than make an honest living doing handiwork or manual labor. She was much too precocious for a lady's maid, and too encouraging with the men. Eemya reached a point where she could no longer put up with her and arranged for her to take a position as a lady-in-waiting at another castle.

Lydima could not blame her cousin. Eemya had just taken charge of Stelan, and she knew her cousin thought she would be a bad influence. Lydima took the position, but ran off with a merchant not long after, only to find out the man was already married. After that, there was a long list of men with whom she kept company in order to keep herself. Most recent was Lord Woldyn, and she had hoped he might propose marriage, but it had not come to pass.

Disappointed, she had jumped at the chance to come to Freosyd again and take a break from the pressures of her lifestyle. It had given her some time to reflect and consider what she would do next. Her current feelings favored throwing herself at Eemya's mercy and asking her to reinstate her as a lady-in-waiting again. Eemya had indeed already offered her the position, but she felt uncomfortable horning in on her newly remarried cousin's life.

No matter what happened, she had to find some occupation that would secure her a future. Being tossed around at the whim of others was no longer palatable to her. And now, she had a baby's welfare to think about. She wouldn't subject a child to that kind of life.

Getting out of the cart was the last thing she wanted to do, but she made herself do it. She climbed out, with the help of the driver, and stepped carefully onto the stones placed in the road for that purpose.

"Has not Lady Eemya directed every village to have a cesspit rather than throw the refuse in the street?"

"Yes, my lady," replied her driver. He frowned. "We must find out the reason for this negligence."

The village headman came hurrying over to the cart to welcome the visitors. "My lady, how honored we are to see you. Unfortunately, we have many who are ill, and we cannot welcome you as we ought. Has anything been discovered that can stem the tide of this fever?"

"That is what we are looking into," replied Lydima. "Why is there sewage in the street? Do you not have a cesspit?"

"We do, my lady, but it is leaking." He pointed to a shed on one side of the ring of houses. The land where it was located was elevated slightly above the surrounding village.

"So does not that mean that you should empty it?"

"It is not overflowing the top, but leaking through the sides."

"Then why did you not build another?"

Lydima thought this would have been the obvious thing to do. The ground around the cesspit was damp, and small rivulets of brown liquid flowed into the center of the green. A putrid stench wafted from the soil. The man obfuscated with great skill, but Lydima perceived that it boiled down to the fact that no one wanted to do the work.

"You will dig another cesspit, within the week, and I will send men to help." Lydima ordered firmly.

The headman bowed repeatedly and assured her it would be done. The driver assisted Lydima back into the cart, and they continued on to the next village on the list. Lydima vowed to burn her shoes when she returned to the castle.

The next stop was really more of a small town. It

had a large number of houses, an inn, a windmill, and a blacksmith. In the center of the town was a well where everyone drew their water. The driver offered to fetch some water for her, but she had been rationing the liquid in her flask and refused to drink anything else. A fresh, mountain stream flowed right by the castle, and that was where its residents procured their water.

Lydima looked around the town square and tried to fathom what the source of the illness in this area could be. Again, she followed her nose, and discovered the cesspit located on one side of the square.

"How deep is the well here?" She was beginning to sense a pattern.

Several residents had come out to meet them. One, a middle-aged, female tavern keeper, looked at Lydima with a mixture of curiosity and disdain. Lydima was used to that look and paid her no attention.

"It is only twenty feet deep," the miller answered her. "There is an underground spring that flows through here."

The volcanic origins of the island left much evidence behind, including mineral springs, hot springs and a wealth of igneous rock. Lydima looked at the mountain and saw that the cesspit and the well lined up with it almost exactly.

"You must cease using that cesspit immediately and empty it! Build a new one on the opposite side of the town, out of the path of the stream. In the meantime, fetch water from another well."

"You think the refuse is contaminating the water?" asked the blacksmith.

"It seems likely." She explained her reasoning and the residents of the town reacted with gratitude and excitement that they might be able to prevent more illness. Lydima reflected that if she hadn't visited the previous village first, where the leakage was obvious, she might not have been able to recognize the problem.

There was one more village to visit. This was the one that had been the hardest hit. Here, the water source was a clean, mountain stream, like at the castle, and the cesspit was downstream from it on the opposite side of town. Lydima had no idea how far away it would need to be from the water source to mitigate the risk of contamination, but if they fetched their water upstream, she couldn't see how it would be an issue.

She walked around the village with her guards. The headman had died in the channel, so his widow guided them instead. After they had completely circumnavigated it, Lydima was perplexed and on the brink of giving up. There was a little hill on the northeast side, and she headed toward it. On the hill were many piles of stones. Some older, larger ones were carved and etched, but the ones toward the front of the site appeared to be freshly laid. It was a graveyard.

All the new graves made Lydima's eyes sting, and she blinked back tears. She had suffered a lot of things in her life, many of them of her own making, but these people had suffered as well. Letting out a sigh, she turned to walk back to the cart. As she turned, her eyes travelled down the hill from the graveyard to the stream, and she was enlightened.

"You have buried the victims of the fever here, yes?"

"Yes, my lady," choked the headwoman.

Lydima didn't know much about soil or farming, but she had overheard many times about the rich, shallow, sandy soil on the island. Farmers on Lyliana were able to grow many crops in the fertile earth. The large amount of rainfall the crops received made up for the lack of depth, and plants grew exponentially.

If her theory was correct, and the fever was spread through human waste, then the decaying bodies might be releasing fluids into the soil that were contaminating the stream. But they couldn't possibly dig up and move all the graves and surrounding earth. They would have to use their rainwater cisterns or hike further upstream to collect their water.

Lydima gave them directions about the drinking water as well as a new graveyard in a better location. Then she listened to the people recount stories of the illness and the lives it had taken. Coming on the heels of the battle of the channel, it had taken a devastating toll.

"My lady," one particularly weary and depressed woman pleaded. "What am I to do? My husband and my sister's husband died in the channel when their boat was attacked by a Cerecian galley. Then my sister died of the fever and left her two children. I have four of my own. I cannot care for them all."

The woman motioned to two small waifs, a girl of six and a boy of three years. The children gazed at her solemnly with hollow eyes.

Lydima's heart went out to them. "I will take them with me," she said decisively, then amended, "If you would like to go."

She looked at the two siblings. The girl nodded slowly, and Lydima smiled at her.

"What is your name?"

The girl cast her eyes downward and didn't reply.

"She is called Katya, and the boy is Dzhon." Their aunt answered for them.

"We will take care of them, I promise. You do not need to worry."

"Thank you, my lady." The woman stood straighter and seemed lighter already, her burden eased slightly.

Lydima lifted the children into the cart herself, giving them her cloak as a blanket. They were thin and weighed hardly anything. They must have been ill as well, but survived. She wondered if, besides their mother, they had had siblings who had been taken by the fever.

The ride home was silent except for the occasional fussing of the young boy. His sister tried to shush him. Lydima pulled him into her lap and kissed his head.

"You can cry if you want to."

She held the boy with one arm and put the other around the girl. Little Katya tried to be brave, but tears poured rebelliously down her cheeks.

It was late when they finally arrived at Freosyd. Jayred had fulfilled his role as steward by beginning the meal in Lydima's place. Having learned a few things from baby Lyliana, she first showed the children the toilets, and then took them into the hall for dinner. At first, the two youngsters were awed by the greatness of the room and the plentiful food, but their shyness was soon overtaken by hunger, and they ate ravenously. Jayred looked somewhat shocked by their table manners, but Lydima glared at him and gave the children a few gentle instructions. She didn't want to overwhelm or shame them for their ignorance. They had been through enough already.

Maygla entered with Lyliana and handed her to Lydima. "She missed you, my lady. She has been fussy today."

Lydima held out her arms and took the baby who looked at her and flailed her arms. She held her close and the infant calmed and nuzzled against her breast. Maygla handed her the leather bottle and Lyliana began to drink. It was amazing to Lydima that the child could tell the difference between her and someone else. She was her mother now.

Lydima was suddenly shaken by the enormity of the task in front of her. How was she going to take care of these three children?

Dzhon spilled his water, distracting Lydima from her thoughts. She barely had time to eat anything before the boy was finished with his food and started climbing down from the bench. Maygla had just started eating, so Lydima called one of the other ladies to help her with the youngsters.

"I have been nursing the sick all day. I do not have any strength left to wrangle children," protested the lady.

"And yet it must be done. Dig deep, Aylria." She handed the baby to her, picked up a squirming Dzhon, and held out a hand to Katya. She took the children up to her room.

"Should they not have a room of their own?"

"No."

Lydima didn't know much about young children, but she knew at least that. There was no way she was going to let these children sleep alone in a strange room, and none of the other women would want to serve as nanny.

Aylria helped Lydima to bathe them all. A servant gathered a few spare items of clothing from those workers who had families living in the castle, and soon everyone was clean, dry and warm.

"Ugh!" Aylria held up Katya's worn dress. "Should we just burn these?"

"No. Send them to be washed. They are the only things they have to remember where they came from."

"Very well." She wrinkled her nose and gathered up the soiled garments.

Lydima showed the newcomers how to use the chamber pot. They were used to just running outside, and Lydima didn't want them to get lost trying to use the toilets at night.

Katya tugged on Lydima's skirts, and she had to bend down close to hear her whisper, "Dzhon does not wake up. He just goes."

"Oh."

Lydima had to stop and think about this. She wrapped him up in a diaper similar to Lyliana's, and put him to bed in the baby's cradle, which was fortunately a large one, and he was just able to fit. Tomorrow she would have to have another bed made up for him. Being woken by warm liquid soaking the sheets was not an idea she relished.

She dismissed Aylria and tucked Katya into bed on the side next to Dzhon. Then she climbed in on the other side and put Lyliana in the middle. Lydima was so tired that she fell to sleep almost immediately. Even the nagging doubts and fears swirling around in her mind couldn't keep her awake and merely plagued her dreams.

CHAPTER FOUR

Down in the belly of the ship, Stelan sat seething with anger. Not only was he stinging from Captain Talia's betrayal and the death of his men, but he had been unable to strike even a single blow. It was humiliating. The pirates had dragged him aboard the *Sea Star* and thrown him in the brig, which was little more than an iron cage. At least it was tall enough so he could stand up and stretch, and there was a bucket for refuse, so he didn't have to sit in it.

With his fingers, he had explored the door and the lock to see if there were any weaknesses, but it was Artylian in design, and very well-made. It was impossible to remove the hinges without tools, and he had nothing with which he could pick the lock.

The only light was a faint glow around the bottom of the door to the hold and the outline of a hatch above him. He could hear scratching and chewing sounds, and he imagined hundreds of tiny rat teeth gnawing on the barrels of food, but he could see nothing. He didn't speak Cerecian, and no one had bothered to explain to him what was going on. A man had brought him a bowl of some kind of tasteless stew and some water, but he had not been able to eat.

The outline of the hatch had disappeared and reappeared, so he knew one day had gone by. Sleep fled the first time he felt something skitter across his feet. The door to the hold opened, and a lamp shone into the dark space.

Stelan stood up, and saw Talia descend the stairs. She hung the lantern from a hook in the ceiling, and turned to face him. In one hand she carried a withered apple and a biscuit which she held out to him. He wanted to refuse, but his stomach growled in spite of himself. They looked more palatable than the stew.

"Take the food," she instructed as he hesitated. "It would be foolish to starve yourself."

He extended his hand through the bars, and she placed the items in his open palm. Resisting the urge to hurl them back at her, he took a bite of the still juicy apple, and the tart taste awakened his hunger even more. They stared at each other silently while he ate. Not wanting to appear too eager, he chewed slowly and savored each morsel. Figuring any simpleton could guess how someone in his situation would be feeling, he made no outbursts or demands for information. He would not condescend to be the first to speak only to be denied satisfaction.

Talia waited until he had finished eating, and then she simply left. Stelan couldn't understand her at all. Tomus had obviously trusted her. Could she truly have fooled the young Berushese representative? Or were they both traitors working against Cyrus, or just against him for some unfathomable reason? None of these possibilities made any sense to him.

It was not until she had been gone for some time that he noticed she had left the lamp. Had she left it on purpose, or merely forgotten it? Either way, he was grateful for the illumination and took the opportunity to observe his surroundings more closely. The rats, who must be used to near complete darkness, had fled the light, and after seeing nothing useful within reach, Stelan leaned against the bars and took advantage of their absence to catch some sleep.

∞∞∞

Above decks, Talia was under constant strain to remain alert. She couldn't understand the words of the Artylian sailors, but she understood their tone and lewd gestures. Even being on a special mission for the general of the Cerecian army might not protect her from this rough crew if they took it into their heads to remind her of her womanhood. The Cerecians were a little more restrained. They knew she would understand them, and they were in more awe of their general than their foreign companions.

Shortly after her visit to Lord Stelan, the florid captain accosted her with a barrage of forceful Artylian, his face close enough that she felt spittle land on her chin. She stared back at him with steely eyes as the Cerecian first mate came over to interpret.

"The captain wonders why you are treating the prisoner with special favor." The mate wore an expression of curious amusement, as if this were all a game that he enjoyed watching.

"I am sure that is exactly what he said," Talia replied caustically. "Tell him that General Riash prefers his prisoners to be healthy. It makes the torture all the more entertaining."

The captain narrowed his eyes at her, muttered

something and stalked off. The mate did not bother to interpret.

"Why do you put up with that imbecile?" The mate was obviously more intelligent than the blustering Artylian, and it would have been more typical for the Cerecians to take over the entire ship.

"He has his uses," replied the mate placidly. "We do not always want to advertise that the ship is under Cerecian control."

"I see."

"If you want to take the night watch, you can use my cot to sleep in during the day. The officer's cabin has a lock."

"Thank you." Talia was surprised at his thoughtfulness, but decided to take advantage of the offer. She might not get much sleep otherwise.

∞∞∞

After a few hours of unmolested slumber, Talia rose and paced the decks. When the sun appeared and the watch changed, she found some extra food and took it to Stelan. The lamp had gone out, so she refilled the oil. She wondered that Lord Stelan neither asked questions nor railed accusations at her. He possessed either an appalling lack of curiosity or an unusual abundance of restraint. The intelligence in his eyes indicated the latter.

Again, she left him without speaking, wishing she could say something to reassure him, but she did not dare. She didn't know if anyone on the ship spoke Berushese, and there was no way she could guarantee anything once they arrived in Cerecia anyway. When she had eaten her own breakfast, Talia retired to the officer's cabin.

The sun had only traversed halfway through its

circuit when she was roused by a commotion. She hurried onto the deck to discover the cause and saw that the captain had brought Stelan up and tied him to the mizzen mast. His shirt had been torn off and his back was exposed.

Talia strode swiftly over to the captain, who had a whip in his hands, and planted herself firmly in front of him, hands on her hips. "What is going on here?"

Her eyes never left the captain's as he sneered at her and spoke in a deprecating tone.

"The captain says he does not take orders from little girls, and prisoners are not to be coddled on his ship."

"Tell him again that the orders are not from me, but from the general. The captain's blundering has already prevented me from gathering the information I was sent to gather. He will not interfere with my prisoner. If he has an issue with that, I will be only too happy to explain it more fully with the point of my sword."

The Cerecian interpreted this with a twinkle in his eye, and the captain responded with a loud guffaw. He made to shove her out of the way, but Talia grabbed his arm, used his own momentum to spin him toward the railing, and drew her weapon before he could regain his balance.

"Draw your sword!"

The authority in her voice was compelling and the captain's eyes flickered.

"What, are you afraid to fight a girl? Defend yourself, for I have no scruples against running you through, armed or not! The world would be better off supporting one less idiot."

The Cerecian contingent tittered, and the captain's face turned red as he listened to the interpretation. He roared and cracked his whip at her instead of the prisoner. Talia deftly sliced it in half in midair which only infuriated the ruffian more. Giving in to his rage, he drew his sword and attacked with strong but untrained swings.

Talia was the taller of the two, and faster, but the sea captain had the advantage of weight and muscle. Fighting aboard ship was also more difficult than land. The opponents had to move with the rolling of the waves. Talia met the captain's onslaught with her own blade, but used leverage to deflect him rather than completely absorb the impact.

The Artylian attempted to crush her under his heavy blows, but his wide, sweeping movements also left him vulnerable. Even though it was only leather, Talia's armor was better than nothing. The pirate captain wore only an open shirt and breeches. As he lifted his sword over his head to strike, Talia was able to cut a gash in his side and spin away unscathed. This only made the pirate angrier, and he swung at her ferociously.

A typical sword only weighed three or four pounds. Talia's was slightly smaller. It was made especially for her and the weight was just what she could handle. Unfortunately, it made her reach a little shorter than that of a longer sword. She had to keep that in mind and stay out of her opponent's range until she was sure of scoring a hit. Letting the captain expend some energy, she circled just out of his reach while she waited for an opening. The crew stood well back, watching with intense interest.

The ship hit a wave, and Talia lost her footing and fell to the deck. She rolled away, and the plank where her head had been suffered a deep gouge. Quickly, she sprang to her feet and blocked another blow just in time. Unable to deflect the impact of this blow, Talia was pushed back against the railing, and the captain pinned her sword against her chest with the flat of his own blade.

Using all of his strength, he strained to push her backwards into the sea. Feeling like her back was going to break, Talia kneed the captain in the groin. He let up just enough to allow her to push him off.

Her enemy now showed signs of panic. Afraid he might give in to fear and suffer the humiliation of asking his men for assistance, she took the lead and attacked with fervor, keeping him too busy parrying her blows to call out. A couple of the Artylian seamen stepped forward to intervene, but the mate held them back.

Talia was used to practicing for hours at a time, while the worthless example of humanity pitted against her probably never practiced at all. As he attempted to give another crushing blow, she angled her sword and slid it up the side of the captain's as he brought it down. The tip of her blade reached in and cut a gash in the side of his throat. He put his hand up to it, and he staggered as blood gushed from the wound.

Without hesitation, Talia plunged her sword through his heart and finished him off. She tore the scarf from his head as she kicked him in the chest, removing her blade, and he toppled over backward. Using the scarf, she wiped her sword off and nonchalantly replaced it in her scabbard.

As the captain's body thudded against the deck, the Cerecian seamen erupted in cheers mixed with laughter. The Artylian sailors shifted their feet and looked uncomfortable, afraid that they might now be resented. They returned quickly to work, and the mate, now the acting captain, directed the body to be thrown overboard.

Talia turned to the mate. "It seems the captain is

no longer useful. I assume that you will not be questioning the general's orders?"

"Not at all." He grinned widely. "Take the prisoner back to the brig," he directed two of his men.

Deliberately avoiding looking in Stelan's direction, Talia returned to the officer's berth. There she sat on a cot with shaking hands, and took slow, deep breaths while she waited for the heat of battle to wear off.

∞∞∞

Stelan suffered no more than a kink in his neck from craning to watch the fight. He had to strain himself in order to see from his position at the mast. During the brief conversation at the beginning, he learned some interesting facts. Most importantly that Talia had been sent on a mission to spy out the island for the Cerecians.

She had also been sent to the island by Tomus, so either she was spying for both sides, or Tomus was in on it. He really couldn't see Tomus betraying his father-in-law, but such things had happened before. Perhaps Talia had seduced him into it.

Stelan rejected the thought as soon as it entered his head. Talia didn't seem like the type of woman to do that. For some strange reason he found himself fervently hoping she was not.

But what type was she? He had no idea. Strong. Beautiful. Ruthless. She had put her own life in danger to save him from a flogging, even if it was only because she considered him a prize for some Cerecian general. He wondered if she would still bring him breakfast the next morning. He found himself looking forward to it.

CHAPTER FIVE

My Lord Yoused,

You told me to ask you if I ever needed assistance. I believe I have discovered a way to stem the spread of the fever, but I worry that I will not be taken seriously if I share this information with the other land-holders directly. I know that you are a man of integrity, and if the news were to come from you instead of me, action might be taken more swiftly.

For the sake of the island's inhabitants, I ask you to send letters to all the lords outlining the steps that must be taken to stop the spread of the illness. In case you are in doubt, or suspect me of another motive, I am sending representatives from the villages in question to explain my findings firsthand. Please, look into this matter, and once you are convinced of the veracity of my theory, I beg you to act on it.

Yoused smiled as he reread Lydima's letter. She had gone on to explain what she had seen in the villages and the conclusion she had come to. The truth of her reasoning was immediately plain to him, and the words of those who accompanied the letter merely reinforced it.

When he received her missive, Youssed had been absurdly gratified that she had requested his help. He had promptly dictated a letter to his scribe giving directions to the other island lords and had the letter copied and sent out without delay.

Not for a moment did he suspect that Lydima had any ulterior motive for reaching out to him. She had never shown any tendency toward vindictiveness, in spite of her many other faults, and had never tried to humiliate anyone by causing them to spread false information. He was also pretty certain that she wasn't scheming to win his favor. Instead of trying to improve her own lot in life, she was showing initiative and trying to help people other than herself.

The villagers she sent told him of more than just the means by which the disease was spreading. They also told him how she had taken in a pair of orphans. If helping the sick and caring for orphans was scheming, he could not fault it. It was working. He was sorely tempted to return to Freosyd and ask her to show him the sites personally, just so he could see her again. His heart quickened at the thought.

Almost, he was at the point of giving in and ordering his horse when another messenger arrived. The man was one he recognized, Halem, a Berushese soldier who was supposed to be governing Adamantine in Stelan's absence. Perhaps Stelan had returned and sent Halem with a message from the capital. Halem had been chosen to stay on the island primarily to provide training in sword fighting, and he spoke fluent Artylian.

"My lord," Halem bowed.

When he straightened, his face was grim, and Yoused's chest tightened with worry.

"An island merchant vessel was sighted floating listlessly off the eastern shore with reefed sails. I sent men to investigate, and the boat was full of dead bodies."

"Fever?"

"Sword."

"Stelan?" Yoused spoke his son's name hoarsely.

"I do not believe he was among them. The bodies had lain exposed to the elements for a couple of days, and the gulls had pecked at them. Several wore the colors of Adamantine, but none of them had the yellow hair of Lord Stelan. His sword was found on the deck."

Halem held it out and Yoused took it somberly.

"There was no other sign of him?"

"There was not." Halem looked like there was more he wanted to say, but he stopped himself.

"What else?" prodded Yoused.

"My lord, I was also expecting a captain of the Berushese army to be aboard, but she was not there either."

"She?"

"No women were aboard the boat."

That wasn't what Yoused meant, but then he remembered Berushese women were allowed to serve as soldiers in that country and let it alone. "The time of the attack would coincide with the time Stelan could be expected to return," Yoused mused aloud. "Since you found his sword, he and your captain must have been on that boat. Either they were killed and their bodies thrown overboard, or they were captured."

"Why throw two bodies over, but not the rest?"

"Indeed, so most likely captured. So he is probably

still alive." Yoused let out a sigh of relief. "But for how long? And who could have attacked them?"

Halem shook his head. "I do not know, but I must return to Letyna at once to inform Tomus of the incident."

"I will send out ships to look for them, but they have quite a head start. If they headed for Cerecia, they are long gone. You must ask Tomus to inform every ship he has to be on the alert. If it was a pirate ship, perhaps they will ransom them."

Halem bowed and took his leave.

There was no possibility of going to Freosyd now. Yoused wrote Lydima a reply, and prepared to ride to the port.

∞∞∞

Lydima had been surprised the last couple of mornings when Maygla had brought in the breakfast accompanied by Aylria. When the woman began helping with the children, Lydima didn't argue. She gulped down her breakfast while the other two ladies changed diapers. Then she fed Lyliana, Lylie as she was now calling her, while Aylria helped Dzhon eat without making too much of a mess.

After breakfast was finished, Aylria had returned to the infirmary without speaking directly to Lydima, but the unasked assistance was enough. It gave Lydima some hope that people might change their thinking toward her eventually if they saw her working with them.

The letter that she had received from Lord Yoused also boosted her morale:

My dear Lady Lydima,
    I was most pleased to receive your request for

assistance, and I desire to assure you that I acted on it immediately. Your theory on the spread of the fever is most sound, and I believe that your recommended actions will prove to be of great effect in preventing further cases of it. Thank you for entrusting me with this information. I was grateful to be of help.

I must also confess that you were entirely in the right about my relationship with my son, Stelan. When I arrived in Letyna, I sought him out and spoke to him, as you suggested. Happily, I report that he has forgiven me for my lapses as a parent. I am thankful that you had the courage to speak your mind.

This means even more to me as I have just received news that his boat has been attacked, and he is now missing. I am sending out ships to search for him and have hope that he will be found. But should that not be the case, I have peace in my heart now that we have made amends. This is entirely due to your influence, and I am forever in your debt.

Your Servant,
Lord Yoused

Lydima had blushed when she first read it. She wasn't used to receiving praise for her ideas, only compliments on her appearance or capacity for giving men pleasure. Certainly she had never been thanked for speaking her mind.

The news about Stelan was shocking, and she was sorry for Yoused's pain. Eemya would be sorry too, if he was lost forever. In spite of the dire news, Yoused's gratitude warmed her heart, and she tucked the letter away to read again later.

Now that the collection of the loan was finished,

and the fall crops were planted, there were less official demands on Lydima's time, and she was able to spend most of the day caring for and playing with the children. It was something she had never done in her life, but she found herself enjoying it immensely.

Katya was a great help with Lylie, and she played with her like a doll. Lylie lay on the floor exercising her limbs in baby fashion, and Katya held toys up for her while she batted at them. Dzhon and Lydima invented a game with a stuffed fabric ball, and they rolled it back and forth. He tried throwing it, and she missed. The boy shrieked delightedly. He had been silent and sullen the first day, but gradually warmed up to his new surroundings and started talking. There were quite a few words in his vocabulary, and he could even form a few simple sentences.

Many fall days on the island were rainy, but there had been a couple of fine days in a row, and Lydima decided to take her new young charges to see the goats while Lylie was napping. She could get more milk at the same time. Dzhon squealed at the sight of the goats, and chased them around the pen. Katya was more reserved and gently patted a placid nanny. One of the billy goats butted Dzhon in the chest, and he fell back with an "oof" and started crying. Lydima picked him up quickly, before he could get stepped on. Maybe she hadn't thought this through carefully enough.

"Are you alright, Dzhon?"

He sniffed. "Mmm hmm."

"Come with me and I will let you feed them some carrots," offered the stable boy who had come over to help.

Dzhon squirmed to be let down and eagerly followed the older boy.

"Let me show you how to milk the nanny, Katya,"

Lydima proposed. She fetched a bucket and began to explain the process to the girl.

Though it was a skill Lydima had only recently acquired, she enjoyed teaching it to someone else. Maybe Katya could be responsible for milking the goat. Was she too young for a chore like that?

Lydima tried to remember what she had done at that age in Kirdyn's court. It was so long ago. Doubts assailed her again. What was she doing, trying to raise children? She knew nothing about it. What would she do when Eemya returned? That was still a long way away, but would Eemya continue to let her and the children stay at the castle? Her cousin loved children, and she was sure she wouldn't mind, but was that what a new wife and mother would want, someone else's children constantly underfoot?

Lydima's own aunt had taught her not to be a nuisance. To be seen and not heard. This attitude was partly to blame for making her an easy prey to men like her uncle.

Katya brought her back to the present. "There's no more."

"Then we are done. Good job, Katya! You are an excellent helper."

The girl smiled at Lydima's praise. Lydima remembered that the girl had been considered a burden and realized that being found useful was important. She smiled back at Katya, and thought that they had a lot in common. Maybe Lydima could be useful to the children after all.

"Say goodbye to the goats, Dzhon."

"Bye goats! Bye!" He waved enthusiastically, over his fright.

Katya took her brother's hand while Lydima carried the bucket. The little girl was still shy, but Dzhon, once he started speaking, was impossible to keep quiet. He waved at everyone they passed. He also wanted to throw everything that resembled a ball.

"Hewo! Wanna see me trow?" He asked the guard at the gate, and picked up a round rock.

Lydima caught it just as he was about to let it fly toward the unsuspecting occupants of the courtyard.

"No, Dzhon, this is a rock. It might hurt someone. Let's go inside and find your ball."

The boy raced ahead to find his ball. Lydima remembered too late that Lylie might still be napping. *Oh well.*

Fortunately, Maygla was with Lylie and kept Dzhon from waking her up. He threw the ball a couple of times and then crawled into the small cot that had been set up for him. Worn out from the excursion to the barnyard, he fell asleep. Lydima wanted to take a nap too, but Lylie chose that moment to wake. After feeding the baby, she handed her off to Maygla who took her for a walk.

Aylria came by to fetch Katya to help her make an alphabet book for Dzhon out of fabric. It was a creative way to learn embroidery and make something fun at the same time. Aylria had lovely stitching, as well as patience for the tedious work. There were fewer patients in the infirmary now, so she had extra time to help with the children.

Once the ladies and their charges were gone, Lydima plopped down on her bed and was soon fast asleep.

∞∞∞∞

An hour later, Lydima was startled awake by what felt like an earthquake. Instead, it was Dzhon jumping on the bed.

"Goats! Goats! I wanna see goats!"

"How about you lay down here in the big bed and try and sleep a little more?"

"No! Goats!"

Lydima sighed. Taking care of small humans was exhausting. Though more demanding, it was also more rewarding than entertaining adults. It felt like she was doing something important, giving herself freely for their good, not selling herself out of need. She sat up and contemplated the boy.

"We already saw the goats today. We can see them again tomorrow. How about we play with your blocks?"

The castle carpenter had cut a small limb into relatively equal-sized sections that could be stacked on top of each other.

"No! Goats!" insisted Dzhon, and he climbed off the bed and started to run for the door.

Lydima caught him before he could open it and set him firmly on the bed in front of her. He squirmed and slid off the bed, but she picked him up and put him right back. She knew how important boundaries were.

Others might not believe it, but she did have personal boundaries. Things she would do and things she would not do. Letting this child get the best of her was something she would not do. In a test of wills, she could be as stubborn as anyone. It wasn't a trait that came naturally to her; she had had to learn it in order to survive.

"We will see the goats again tomorrow if it is not raining. We can play with your blocks or the ball."

"Goats!" He squirmed down again, and she returned him to the bed.

"No goats. Blocks or ball."

Dzhon hugged himself tightly and screwed his face

57

up into a deep frown. He began to turn red and kicked his feet against the bed. Lydima figured that throwing a tantrum would wear him out as well as anything would. She folded her arms and waited for him to tire of fussing.

It took much longer than she expected. The boy seemed to have an inexhaustible supply of energy. He was still kicking the bed when Katya returned. Tantrums must have been a normal thing for him because Katya ignored her brother and skipped over to show Lydima her needlework.

In a blue square of fabric, she had stitched a letter 'B' in orange thread. It was wobbly, but recognizable.

"Oh, that is lovely, Katya. You worked so hard on this!"

She handed the square back to Aylria, who had accompanied Katya back to the room. Aylria put it in her sewing basket with the rest of the squares. Katya trotted over to the blocks and started playing with them. Dzhon slipped off the bed and joined her. Lydima let out a breath. The storm was over, for now.

"You are doing a good job with them, my lady."

"Thank you, Aylria," Lydima replied, surprised at the admission. "Your help has been invaluable."

Aylria curtsied and left. Maygla returned with Lylie, and they all played together happily until dinner time.

Meals were gradually becoming easier. Lydima made sure Lylie was fed and changed before going down since she still refused to be fed by anyone else. Maygla and Aylria took turns watching her while the other ate, and Lydima supervised the older two children. She made Dzhon sit for a little longer each time before he could be excused from the table. Now that they knew their way around the castle, Lydima let Katya take her brother back to the bedroom to play as long as one of the other ladies was there. That gave Lydima enough time to finish her own food.

Then came the bedtime rituals. All faces were washed, hair was combed, and everyone was dressed in nightclothes. Katya had requested a bedtime song her second night in the castle, and it became part of the routine. Lydima would sing a traditional Artylian lullaby, and Dzhon would be asleep by the end of it. Katya would fall asleep next to Lydima shortly afterward.

Tonight, however, she was still awake and wanted to talk. "Lady Lydima, are you married?"

Lydima thought this a funny question since there was obviously not a man in the room, but she supposed the child knew couples might sometimes have to be apart. "No, I am not."

"Do you want to be married?"

"I do not know."

Lydima was surprised at her own response. She had wanted the security marriage offered, but Eemya assured her she had a home at Freosyd as long as she needed it. Now, she didn't think she wanted to be married unless she fell in love with someone who loved her in return. With her history, that was highly unlikely.

"I do not want to be married," stated Katya with uncharacteristic vehemence.

"Why is that?"

"Because everyone you love dies."

Lydima was silent for a moment. She could not refute that fact. "Yes, everyone dies sooner or later. People you love die whether you are married or not."

Katya's angst was palatable. Lydima sat up and pulled her into a hug.

"You know, my parents are dead too. I never even met them."

"Never?"

"No."

"That's sad."

"Yes."

"At least I knew mine."

"Tell me about them."

Katya told her about her father and how he loved to tell jokes. He tickled her and made her laugh. She talked about her mother and how she could sing. She had a beautiful voice and would sing at festivals and celebrations. Her mother had a long, brown braid that reached to her knees. Katya told Lydima about the fragile baby sister who had died of fever with their mother. Lydima found herself wiping tears from her eyes.

The little girl looked up at her and patted her wet cheek. "How about I can be your mother now, and you can be mine?"

Lydima thought her heart would burst. "That is a lovely idea, sweetheart." She could hardly keep her voice from breaking. She kissed the adorable child's forehead and squeezed her tightly. Lydima knew she would have to get up and feed Lylie in a few hours, but after their heart-to-heart discussion, she and Katya finally fell fast asleep.

CHAPTER SIX

Anxiously, Stelan waited for Talia to visit him again. He rehearsed several questions he thought would be most likely to receive an answer from her. When the door opened, he was disappointed to see one of the Cerecian sailors bringing his breakfast. At least the man brought the customary apple and biscuit, fresh water, and oil for the lamp.

With nothing else to look forward to, Stelan felt extremely depressed. He thought about his father and their last conversation. For the first time, he had felt like his father loved him, and now he might never have another chance to get to know him.

Another day passed, and then another, and still Captain Talia did not appear. To help fight against the feelings of hopelessness that tore at his mind, Stelan exercised his body by pulling up on the bars at the top of his cage, doing squats, and anything else he could to stay fit inside the small space. He thought about overpowering the guards when they came to empty the refuse bucket, but then what? There was a whole ship-full of men above deck, and he had no idea how far they were from land. If land was close enough to swim to, it was probably hostile. They must be in Cerecian waters by now. He would have to bide his time and wait for a good opportunity to escape.

Nearly a week after his capture, Stelan felt a change in the movement of the ship, and he assumed it was now tied up to a dock. It wasn't long after that when the door to the hold opened and Captain Talia descended. Several sailors followed her. In addition to her sword, she also carried a quiver of arrows and a bow.

Talia gave a brief order in Cerecian.

The sailors grabbed him and pulled him roughly out of his iron prison. They tied his wrists tightly, and Stelan couldn't keep from wincing. Talia looked him in the eye.

"Try to escape, and I will shoot you. Do you understand?"

He nodded. The sailors shoved him forward, and he fell against the stairs, bruising his knee. They picked him up by the elbows and practically dragged him onto the deck. There, he managed to walk across to the gangplank without slipping. Talia uttered some directions to the sailors, and they more gently helped him down the ramp so he didn't fall into the water.

Once he was on the pier, he tried to take a better look at his surroundings, but he was continually prodded forward, and he had to concentrate on where he was walking. The docks were like an immense maze, and the majority of the slips were empty.

The Cerecians had lost most of their fleet in the battle of the channel. Stelan remembered Talia saying she had fought on the *Restia*, an Artylian warship. Had that been a lie? It would explain why she hadn't elaborated. Either that, or she'd been spying for Cerecia for some time.

They walked for what felt like miles. Once they had left the docks, they wandered past rows of large storage barns and empty warehouses. Everything looked neglected and dilapidated. The lords of this land had put all of their resources into warmongering and thievery instead of improving their own country.

Eventually, the small party drew up outside a large, stone fortress. Talia was in the lead with the acting captain of the *Sea Star*, and four other sailors had come along to transport the prisoner. After speaking with the guards at the gate, they were allowed to enter, and Talia strode across the courtyard like she had been here many times before. Stelan was escorted right behind her, and they entered a passage where Talia knocked loudly on a door.

∞∞∞

"Enter."

Talia pushed open the door and stood at attention in front of General Riash. The general was a tall, middle-aged man with greying temples. His muscles were hard and thick, and he was known for still being able to best his soldiers in any contest of fitness. He rose from his chair behind a desk full of papers and frowned at Talia. "You are earlier than scheduled."

"The *Sea Star* intercepted my transport before I was able to complete the mission."

"What is this?" The general looked at the Cerecian mate for confirmation. Anger showed plainly on his face as he listened to the explanation of the Artylian captain's actions. "Get out! I will deal with you later. Take your men with you. We can handle it from here."

The sailors scurried away gladly. One of the general's own men took a post inside the door to keep an eye on the prisoner who had been shoved against a wall. The general narrowed his eyes at Talia.

"I would have expected someone of your resourcefulness to find another way onto the island."

"I was supposed to arrive with the Artylian." She jerked her thumb at Stelan. "If I came without him, I would be immediately suspect."

"You could have told the truth. Your ship was attacked."

"Then either the *Sea Star* would have been discovered, or they would have been unable to retrieve me if the whole Artylian navy was out looking for them."

"I see you have an answer for everything."

Talia stood impassively and did not reply as this was not a statement that required a response.

"Who is this?" Riash waved at Stelan.

"This is Stelan, Lord of Adamantine, who was my escort to the island. He grew up there, and is intimately acquainted with its defenses. He also recently returned from a conference with Governor Tomus, and is a close friend of Prince Darius. Hopefully we can get some information out of him that will make up for my incomplete mission."

∞∞∞

The general walked over to Stelan and looked him up and down. "Who are you?" he asked in Artylian.

"Lord Stelan of Adamantine on the island of Lyliana."

"Who is that?" he nodded at Captain Talia. Stelan was taken off guard by this question.

64

"You must know better than I."

The general backhanded him and he staggered, narrowly avoiding falling to the floor. "I am asking you."

Stelan straightened and looked at Talia who stared impassively back at him. "I was told she was a Captain in the Berushese army, but it appears she is a Cerecian spy."

The general barked a laugh and turned to say something to Talia, and she smiled placidly in reply. He faced Stelan again and switched back to Artylian.

"As I am sure you know, our resources have recently been severely depleted. We will have to augment them with supplies from elsewhere. Your island will have more than enough to go around. It was Cerecia who first settled it, after all, and the Artylians took it away from us. It is only right that they pay us back. Just how much do you consider your life is worth?"

Stelan made no reply to these lies. They were obviously meant to rile him up.

"Paying a ransom would be the simplest and least painful way out of this for you. We get your fall harvest, and no one has to get hurt."

Silence.

The general walked over to his desk and gestured to a blank sheet of paper and an ink pen. "All you have to do is write out a letter. We will deliver it and collect the payment. Then you may return home."

Stelan still didn't answer. He would never sacrifice his people's well-being to save his own life. The Cerecians didn't have the ships or the manpower to implement a successful invasion of the island after their recent defeat. The general knew this as well as he did.

"Tell me about your defenses, then. Artylia was

ripe for invasion, but Cyrus beat us to it. Berush has not sent a large force to the island, though, have they? How many soldiers are currently stationed there?" The general paused. "You still refuse to cooperate? Very well, we will do this the hard way."

He spoke to the guard at the door who called in another soldier. Each took one of Stelan's arms and dragged him out of the room and down the passage. Talia and Riash followed.

∞∞∞

The guards took the prisoner into an interrogation room, stripped him down to his loincloth, and chained him wrist and ankle to manacles hanging from the wall. His arms and legs were spread tightly so he couldn't move.

General Riash gave directions to a hardened-looking man stirring coals in a pit. "Give him something to think about, Cush. I will return later to see if he is ready to answer my questions."

The general stalked out of the room, and the two guards took positions outside the door. Only Talia and the interrogation expert remained. She subconsciously registered an appreciation for Stelan's well-toned body, but her mind was busy trying to find a way to help him.

The room was stifling, even with the open door. The man stirring the coals was shirtless and sweaty. Grime covered his face, and he looked like he had been a victim of torture himself on numerous occasions. Maybe he even practiced on himself. One ear was missing and he was covered in a grotesque pattern of scars, burns and tattoos.

He grinned at Talia. "I do not think you will want to stay here for this."

"Why not?" she countered in a teasing tone. "You are not the only one with scars. I might learn something."

Cush raised his eyebrows at her. "You will be sick."

"What will you wager?"

The scarred man walked around the fire pit and stood with his arms akimbo as he studied her figure lasciviously. He circled around her until he was quite close and could speak almost in her ear. "I do not have many willing female companions."

"Leave this man his pretty face and manly parts so I can play with him later, and you have a bet."

"Looks like you will be getting some action either way. I am not certain that is fair."

"I am sure you would love to give me a scar," she traced his stubbly chin seductively with her finger. "I will let you do that for free."

"You are crazy!"

"Now you understand."

"Where do you want it?" he asked with gaping mouth, still not believing her, but his sadistic mind was tantalized by the thought of a willing torture recipient.

Talia rolled up one sleeve to show a long, thin burn mark on her right bicep. "Give me one on the other side to match." She rolled up the other sleeve and stuck her arm out.

Cush's eyes were about to bug out of his face, and he was practically drooling as he readied the poker. Stelan could not understand their conversation, but Talia saw the expression of abject horror on his face as the inhuman creature drew the thin, hot iron along her arm and scored it with red blisters. She didn't flinch. She did not even blink. The muscles around her jaw tensed slightly, but that was all.

When Cush withdrew the poker, Talia rolled her

sleeves down. "So, do we have a wager?"

He nodded slowly. "We do, but I think I will lose."

∞∞∞

Watching Stelan be tortured was the hardest thing Talia had ever done in her life. She knew it was impossible to rescue him yet, so the best she could do was try and keep him from suffering any irreparable damage. She had seen eyes put out, teeth extracted and jaws broken in rooms similar to this one.

Cush was true to his word and avoided the face and groin, but he burned, cut, whipped, and beat almost every other part of his body. Stelan gritted his teeth and tried not to cry out, but a loud groan still escaped from him every so often. He lasted an admirable length of time, but finally he gave in to the pain and fainted. Talia went over to check that he was still breathing.

"He will be fine. Nothing is broken, and nothing is too deep. I know my job. He should be ready to answer the general's questions when he returns. I can do more then, if he still refuses to talk."

"And I have won our wager, but he has passed out," she complained and looked at Cush accusingly.

"You did not stipulate he had to be conscious."

Talia tsked. "How long 'til he wakes up?"

"Hard to say. Half an hour? Maybe more."

"I will come back later when he is awake."

Cush shrugged. "Up to you. If I am not here, you will have to make another deal with the guards."

"I can handle them," she replied dismissively.

"I am sure you can," Cush chuckled. "If you ever need another scar, look me up."

She winked at him and left the room. Outside, she filled her lungs with fresh air to clear them of the smell of sweat and singed flesh. It was nearly evening, and the general would be having his dinner. If he was enjoying himself, he might not return to question Stelan until the next day. He was a patient strategist and might expect the prolonged imprisonment would loosen the subject's tongue. That gave her a few precious hours to work, and she had much to accomplish. Her real mission was just beginning.

With utter confidence, she strode down the passage back to the general's office. The guards were gone, and the room was unlocked. Swiftly she opened the door and stole into the room, shutting the door behind her. She took the blank sheet of paper, dipped the pen into the ink and wrote out a brief directive. Then she used the general's seal to sign it.

Not wanting to leave any signs of her presence, she declined to blot the paper with sand and waited valuable moments for it to dry. When she was sure the ink wouldn't smear, she rolled up the parchment and stuck it inside her pouch. Finding more blank sheets in a drawer, she replaced the one she had used.

Then she left the room, walked across the courtyard and out the gate into the town. Still in her Berushese armor, she garnered some strange looks, but no one dared question her. All the way back to the docks she marched, stopping only when she reached a series of three large, connected warehouses. One of them belched black smoke through several chimneys. The second one was smaller. Both of these had been infiltrated by others. It was the third warehouse with which she was concerned.

Outside this building, even at this time of night, there were a few people in line with steaming buckets of urine. They poured it into a funnel in the side of the building, and a man at a window gave them each a small coin. Two guards stood by the entrance, and others patrolled the grounds around all three warehouses. Workers were active here every hour of the day.

Talia walked up to the entrance. "I need to speak to the officer in charge."

"That would be Captain Shal. There he is now." The guard pointed to a soldier just coming around the building toward them.

Talia walked over to intercept him. "Captain Shal, I am on an urgent mission from General Riash." She handed him the parchment from her pouch, and he held it up to a lamp hanging by the door.

When he finished reading, he looked sharply at Talia. "And how do you expect to uncover this spy?"

"That you may see for yourself, as I will need you to arrest him if I find him," she replied grimly.

"Come with me."

Captain Shal opened the door to the warehouse, and an unbelievable stench filled her nostrils. She stepped inside after him and could hardly breathe. In spite of the high, open windows, noxious gases filled the air.

The urine poured into the funnel on the outside was piped into a series of large beds of sand. Workers turned the sand with shovels making sure they were evenly saturated. Others poured buckets of ashes into the mix. More rows of beds were disconnected from the urine pipes and instead were being sprinkled with water. A third section of sand beds were being shoveled into special filters where it was watered down and left to soak.

As Talia watched, a worker removed a stopper from one of the filters and the liquid then entered a vat where potash was added. Liquid was being poured off of a vat further down the line into one of several large iron boilers. All of this Talia had to observe unobtrusively while appearing to scrutinize the laborers.

"Introduce me to the workers," she whispered to Shal. "Tell them I am here to conduct an inspection."

Shal did as she asked, and the workers looked up at her furtively. She scanned the warehouse looking for a particular face while wending her way to the back of the building. It was hot near the boilers, and steam filled the air as the liquid from one of the boilers was poured into a large tray.

One of the trays was cool, and white crystals filled the bottom of it. A man removed the crystals and piled them in a basket where another man dried them off. The man removing the crystals was the one she was looking for. The last time she was in the Cerecian city, he had been specifically pointed out to her by another spy in her network. She approached him, apparently to observe his work.

"Have you been working here long?"

"A year, my lady."

"Captain."

"A year, Captain."

"And what is your name?" Talia asked this in Berushese.

"Kayus," the man replied, and then snapped his mouth shut as he realized what language she had spoken in.

"Here is your spy," she turned to Captain Shal. "Take him away."

The man shoved past her and ran down the aisle between the sand beds, but another guard blocked his way. They towed the man away as he screamed and protested his innocence.

Talia knew he was innocent of this current accusation, but he was not innocent of wrongdoing. He had sold Berushese secrets to the Cerecians. Now he had paid for that betrayal by giving Talia the excuse she needed to enter the warehouse.

She thanked Captain Shal and left the building carrying a secret far greater than the ones the traitor had sold. She knew the process for producing the final ingredient needed to create 'magic fire.'

∞∞∞

Just before dawn, Talia reentered General Riash's fortress and made her way back to the torture chamber. She hoped fervently that Riash had not yet returned to interrogate Stelan. There was still a guard at the door, which must mean that he remained inside, alive.

She was taking a huge risk in returning for him. If they were caught, and she did not escape with the recipe for 'magic fire,' months of effort by a network of spies would all be for nothing. The contact at the safe house had been reluctant to help, but had finally agreed.

Talia strolled purposefully up to the guard. "I am here to relieve you. The general will be here to interrogate the prisoner as soon as he finishes his breakfast."

It was a little early for his shift to be relieved, but the guard nodded gratefully and headed toward the barracks.

Talia opened the door and saw Stelan still slumped against the wall, but as she entered, he straightened slowly and lifted his head. She rushed over to him, but stopped short as she looked over his wounds.

Dozens of purple bruises had begun to appear, and some of the blisters had burst and were oozing. His cheek had a mark where Riash had struck him. Talia's breath caught in her throat, and her hands reached tentatively toward his face.

∞∞∞

Stelan had woken a few hours earlier. His entire body ached, and every nerve ending screamed with pain. But he could breathe. That was at least better than he had felt after his lung had been punctured in a cave-in a few months ago. It felt like all of his bones were intact. His condition was, overall, better than he would have expected.

When Talia entered the room with the first rays of morning sun behind her, he thought at first she was some kind of apparition. Then she stepped closer, and he saw the tears in her eyes and forgot about his pain. She placed her hands on either side of his head and leaned forward and kissed him gently. Her lips tasted both sweet and salty from the tears, and he felt strength surge through his being.

"What was that for?" he asked softly.

"Because once I free you, I would think kissing me is the last thing you would want to do," she sobbed.

"You have no idea what I want to do to you." He leaned forward as far as he could and kissed her back.

Talia froze in surprise, then responded passionately, caressing his face and fondling his short, blond curls.

Stelan grasped the chains at his wrists and strained at his shackles, yanking one of them loose from the mortar. The anchor hit him in the shoulder, but he didn't even feel it. Now he had one arm free, and he drew her closer and held her tightly around the waist, in spite of his wounds, as he continued to kiss her.

Too soon, Talia pulled away. "We do not have much time."

Stelan released her reluctantly, and she snatched the keys Cush had carelessly left on the table holding the rest of his morbid instruments. There were many means of torture available that he had not yet used. Perhaps he was saving them for the actual interview.

Swiftly Talia unlocked the manacles, and Stelan rubbed his sore, bleeding wrists. She tugged a length of fabric out from under her cuirass, and held it out.

"Here, put this on. It was all I could hide on me."

It was a simple tunic and he threw it on quickly. It only reached mid-thigh, but it was better than nothing. Talia grabbed a length of rope and motioned for him to turn around. She wrapped the rope loosely around his wrists and tucked the ends into his hands.

"Just until we get to the end of the passage." Instead of drawing her sword, she unslung her bow and nocked an arrow in it. "Let's go."

They stepped out of the door into the empty passage.

"Turn left."

They walked to the end of the corridor and stopped at an archway leading into another passage to the right. They had not yet been seen, so at Talia's direction, Stelan rid himself of the rope.

Talia glanced through the arch and jerked back rapidly. She raised her bow, stepped into the opening, and quickly loosed an arrow. She ran forward with Stelan following just as a guard thudded to the floor in front of the postern gate. Noiselessly, she raised the bar and drew back the bolt on the door. Rolling the dead soldier out of the way, she pulled the door open and stepped into the long, early morning shadows.

CHAPTER SEVEN

Every time Lydima thought she had a routine established, something happened to throw it off. They visited the goats almost every day, and Dzhon regularly fell asleep afterwards. Katya continued her sewing and embroidery lessons with Aylria, and Lydima was adding reading and spelling on top of that. Lylie was definitely heavier than she was a couple of weeks earlier, while Lydima felt that she herself had slimmed down slightly from chasing after the children and carrying the baby. She was not overly plump, but she was definitely curvy.

Katya had also gotten her started singing. It had begun with the lullaby at night, but now they sang as they worked and sang as they played. Katya liked to compose her own songs, and she sang an ode to goats that made Lydima smile. She found that she enjoyed singing, and it made her happy to hear the young girl's voice mingled with hers.

Today, the hiccough in the schedule came, strangely, from the docile Katya. She absolutely refused to study her reading lesson. Lydima was at a loss to understand the reason. Most peasants on the island never learned to read, but Eemya thought it was important for everyone to learn. Lydima knew from experience that the more knowledge you had, the more power you had, and she agreed that reading and writing were good skills to possess. It gave a person more options for occupations than ignorance. But Katya cried and stomped and would not comply or be cajoled into reading today.

Lydima suspected the reason for Katya's fit had nothing to do with the reading. She put the book aside. "What would you like to do? Shall we sing?"

"I never want to sing again!"

Now Lydima knew there was really something wrong, but she didn't want to push too hard. "Why not?"

"Because I cannot sing with mama! Her face is going away!"

"Oh, honey, you mean you are starting to forget her?" Katya nodded through her tears.

Lydima knelt next to her and hugged her. The little girl threw her arms around Lydima's neck.

"How about we draw a picture of her?"

"I have never drawn anything before."

Lydima easily forgot the differences in their stations. Paper was a rare thing in most households. "It is easy. I will show you." She readied some paper and, after a short search, found some charcoal pencils in a cupboard in Eemya's study.

Lydima wished she had some paint, but she didn't know if there was even a portrait artist on the island. That was something she would have to look into. Possibly she could order some paint if she could find an artist to make it. The pencils were wrapped in string so the charcoal wouldn't get all over the artist's fingers. It could be unwrapped as the pencil became shorter.

"You should draw something simple first, for practice, to see how the pencils work." Lydima set an inkwell in front of Katya. "This is an easy shape. Look at the lines and follow them with your eyes while your hand draws what you see onto the paper."

Katya followed Lydima's instructions with utter concentration. She was actually quite good for a beginner. Lydima showed her how to smudge the lines to create shadows. Katya seemed to enjoy the drawing process. Lydima put her first exercise aside.

"Now think of your mother and draw what you remember."

The girl bit her lip and thought for a while, then started to draw. Lydima could easily pick out the features on the face of the woman in the drawing, but Katya was not satisfied with it.

"My drawing does not look anything like her." The girl's voice wobbled and tears threatened again.

"You are doing very well for your first try, but I can take a turn if you want. Tell me what she looked like, and I will try to see her in your face and memories." Lydima took the pencil and a paper and turned to study Katya's facial features. Her aunt had taught her drawing in addition to reading and writing.

Katya stood up straight and tried to describe what her mother looked like. The child's description was helpful mostly for distracting her while Lydima worked. Instead of listening to Katya's words, Lydima looked at the little girl's face and tried to imagine what she would look like as a woman, and that is what she drew. She hoped Katya would be satisfied with it.

When she was finished, she turned it around for the girl to see. Katya took it without speaking and studied it. She looked up with shining eyes. "It is beautiful. Thank you!"

"Be careful, the charcoal can smear," Lydima warned just in time as Katya prepared to hug the drawing. Instead, she bent and kissed the face in the picture. "Do you know, I think your mother would be happy to know you were still singing." She wouldn't bring up the reading now.

"I will sing to her picture," and Katya got up and started singing to the drawing and dancing around the room.

Lydima was happy that she had been able to figure out what was bothering Katya and help her feel better. It made her strangely sad to see the girl so happy about her mother's drawing. Lydima knew she could never replace the girl's real mother, and she tried to be content with the knowledge that she was at least able to provide a small part of the love the girl needed.

And she did love her. She loved Lylie and Dzhon. Lydima couldn't remember ever loving anyone before this. She hadn't even fancied herself in love with the merchant she had run off with. She had only hoped he could provide her with an escape from the life she had been living. That had not turned out to be the case. Now she felt such strong emotions that it hurt.

Katya finished her song and ran over to Lydima and hugged her. "Lydima, I am sorry I was bad."

Tears sprang to Lydima's eyes. "Oh honey, it is not bad to miss your mother."

"But I was mean to you when I would not read. Mothers are not supposed to be mean or make a fuss about their chores."

"It might be too much to expect yourself to be my mother. Maybe you could just be like my sister? Why do we not try that?" Lydima hoped this suggestion would not offend her.

"Alright."

Lydima kissed the girl's cheek. "We had better check on Lylie and your brother."

∞∞∞

"We are almost there. You can come out now."

The old, gray-bearded man driving the rickety cart turned and spoke to a lumpy brown blanket. Out from under it crawled a bedraggled young girl of ten or eleven years. She glanced around furtively. Seeing no one on the road, she climbed over the seat and sat next to the driver. Pots and pans rattled around as the mule pulling the cart stepped over the uneven ruts in the road.

The man was a tinker, and as such, he travelled all over the island trading things people needed for things that needed to be repaired. They paid him for their upgraded goods with a plate of food, or occasionally with a small coin. Because he journeyed constantly, he saw a lot of people and places and always had an ear out for gossip. Sometimes this was a more valuable trade than a new pot and had earned him many a meal.

Recently he had heard that the interim overseer of Freosyd was taking in orphans. When he found the fugitive hiding in his cart, he had taken pity on her and decided to help. This seemed like the best place to take her. Lady Lydima was reportedly making a fresh start, and she might be the ideal person to deal with this situation. She would certainly have a better idea of what to do with a young girl than he would.

The cart lumbered up to the castle barbican, and the guard waved the driver through. He took a few pots and motioned for the girl to follow him. The tinker did not want his true purpose immediately advertised, so he headed to the kitchen to see the cook, which was his normal routine.

"Hello, Naythan," smiled the cook. "I do not need any new pots right now, but you are welcome to have a seat and refresh yourself. I might be able to find something that needs mending, but you will have to wait until we are done preparing for dinner."

"I have something that needs mending this time."

The cook noticed the small girl peeking from behind the tinker and quivering like a scared rabbit.

"Who is this?"

The cook expected to hear a good story, but the tinker shook his head.

"I need to speak with Lady Lydima. Can you persuade her to see me?"

"I'll try."

She called for one of the maids to go and look for the lady, impressing on her that it was important. The cook arched her eyebrows at the tinker for confirmation as she gave her directions, and he nodded his assurance that it was indeed urgent. When the maid left, the cook set out a few pieces of bread.

"Pour yourself some beer. You know where it is. I have work to do," and she walked over to check a pot of stew.

As soon as the cook turned her back, the girl snatched a slice of bread and ate it ravenously. The tinker poured himself some beer, and then mixed a little of it with some water for the girl. She drank it quickly.

They didn't have to wait too long before the lady of the castle entered the kitchen. She was holding a tiny baby, maybe eight weeks old at most, and looked slightly annoyed. Her impatience vanished when she saw the young girl at the table. The girl shrank back and tried to make herself as small as possible. "How can I help you?" she addressed herself to the tinker.

"My lady," he bowed deeply. "I need to speak to you about a very sensitive matter."

∞∞∞

Lydima glanced around and tipped her head toward the larder. They ducked in there, out of hearing of the cook, but still able to see the girl through the open doorway.

"I found her in my cart two nights ago. Naked. She had been beaten."

Lydima's face hardened as she listened.

"I took her to my sister, who cleaned her up and gave her a dress to wear, but she dared not keep the girl. She has a large family of her own, and the girl does not appear to trust anyone. I have been afraid to turn my back on her for fear she will run off." The tinker looked uncomfortable, and his eyes were evasive, like he was hiding something.

"Tell me everything," Lydima urged. "I will help if I can."

"There is an inn at the port of Sonefast where men can go . . ."

"I know of it."

"Yes, well, she is from there."

Lydima looked at the girl. "So young?"

The man shrugged. "She is probably the daughter of one of the . . . women who are employed there. When they are old enough, they are put to work too. This girl will be looked for. That is why neither my sister nor I can keep her. I was hoping she might be safe here."

This was a serious problem. Lydima's lips formed a thin line. She had never been inside the inn, but she had been offered employment there. When Yoused had refused to let her stay at his castle, someone had met her on the road to attempt to recruit her. Fortunately, she had already heard about that establishment and had the sense to refuse. Once a woman went to work at The White Lily Inn, she never left. Lydima had enjoyed her freedom more than the promise of regular meals.

For a while, she had resented Lord Yoused for leaving her vulnerable, but he had not taken advantage of her, and for that she now respected him. However, he let this inn continue to exist.

"What is Lord Yoused's opinion on the situation? This is really his jurisdiction."

The tinker shook his head. "Yoused's eldest son runs the port, and as long as the business of the inn stays in the inn, he leaves it alone. The owner pays a stiff license fee."

Lydima scoffed. License fee indeed. More like a bribe to look the other way. They didn't think about the children these women would inevitably have and how they would be born into a life of bondage no one would choose. Lydima's lips formed into a determined line. As if she hadn't taken on enough already, she found herself saying to the tinker, "I will keep her. She will be safe here."

The tinker nodded in relief. "I will explain it to her."

They walked over toward the girl. She cowered against the wall.

"This is the Lady Lydima. She is going to take care of you. I will come and check on you when I can."

The girl gave no response, but looked at him blankly. He threw a sad smile at Lydima and left.

Lydima shifted Lylie to one arm and held her hand out to the girl. She didn't move.

Over her shoulder, Lydima spoke to one of the maids, "Reyla, bring a plate of food and come with us." She turned back to the girl once the maid had the food ready. "You must be hungry still. Come with me and you can have some dinner."

The girl slowly rose to follow Lydima and the maid with the steaming stew. Lydima took her to an empty guest room and had Reyla set the food down on the table. As the girl began to shovel the food into her mouth greedily, Lydima took a closer look at her. Was something moving in her hair? Gently she moved aside one of the girl's tangled locks. Lice. She held the baby out to Reyla.

"Here, take Lylie to Maygla, then get Aylria and a couple of the other ladies and bring a washtub, several pitchers of warm water and a large bottle of vinegar."

While she waited for the maid to return, Lydima tried to extract some more information from her new guest. "What is your name?"

The girl cast her eyes down, and kept eating.

"I will need to call you something. Is it all right if I call you Saley?" This had been her favorite aunt's name.

The girl's eyes flicked up and then back down.

"So, Saley, is your mother still alive?"

The child swallowed, blinked, and a couple of tears ran down her face. She hung her head and put down her spoon.

"Do you have any other siblings at the inn?"

Saley started twisting the fabric of her skirt nervously.

"How many? Can you show me with your fingers?"

The girl stretched out two shaky fingers.

"Older," Lydima held her hand up high, "or younger?" she lowered her hand.

Saley slowly lowered her hand to indicate that they were younger.

Lydima's heart ached for the girl. It must have been difficult to leave her siblings, especially if their mother was dead. She must have had no other choice. They were still in danger, and Saley would never have peace knowing they were still there. Lydima knew that if she had had siblings, she would never have had the courage to leave her uncle's house. Something must be done for Saley and her family, but this battle seemed bigger than she could handle.

Reyla returned with the washtub, and Aylria and two other ladies followed in her wake. As they began to set up the bath, Lydima explained to Saley what they were going to do.

"Saley, we are going to give you a special bath to get rid of the lice in your hair."

The girl looked suspiciously at the bath.

"I have had lice before myself, and I know it can be very uncomfortable. We will use some vinegar to help clean your hair and loosen the nits. Here," she reached out for the vinegar and Reyla handed it to her. "Smell it."

The girl sniffed timidly and jerked back.

"I know, it smells nasty, but it will make your hair feel soft and look shiny. It will also wash out all the lice. Come, let us help you."

Saley pointed to Lydima's hair.

Lydima smiled. "Yes, I use vinegar in my hair sometimes. I like the result."

Saley rose slowly and appeared ready to submit to the washing. Lydima talked her through the entire process, not doing anything without telling the girl first. They removed her dress, and Lydima consented to let this one go to the burn pile since it was one she had only just received and would have no attachment to it.

The ladies clucked over the bruises on the girl's back and shoulders. She had some red stripes across her back that indicated she had been caned as well. Aylria rubbed liniment into the bruises while Lydima poured the vinegar-water over the girl's head and into the washtub. She directed Saley to lower her head into the tub so the hair could soak.

Lydima scrubbed her scalp and continued to pour more of the vinegar over her hair. She noticed there was a crude tattoo of a lily at the base of the girl's neck. That must have been how the tinker and his sister learned her origins. Her mind revolted at the thought that someone had marked the child as a man marks his cattle to show ownership.

"Keep your eyes closed, or the vinegar will sting them," she directed.

Finally, they rinsed her hair with clean water and patted it dry with a towel. Then Lydima poured some scented oil onto her head, after letting her smell it, and rubbed it into her scalp. One of the other ladies held up a clean nightdress and Lydima helped Saley into it. She motioned her into a chair and started combing her hair carefully. This had the dual result of removing nits and working the oil through the hair.

Reyla removed the washtub of lousy water, and when she had finished combing, Lydima braided the girl's hair tightly. She showed her where the chamber pot was and then helped her into bed.

"I will be back to check on you in a few minutes," she assured her, and then she motioned the ladies out of the room.

Lydima looked at the women before her. She had asked Reyla to summon the rest of the ladies so she could give them instructions, and all five ladies-in-waiting were now assembled in the passage.

"We cannot leave her alone. Someone must be with her, watching, at all times, or she will try to run away."

"Why would she run away? There is nowhere she can go."

"She would go back to try and rescue her siblings, and she would be caught."

"What are we going to do?"

Lydima's heart warmed at the 'we.' "Keeping Saley safe is our first priority. We will take shifts to watch her day and night. Her handler will come looking for her. If he comes here, Byden will deal with him. I will send word to Lord Yoused that I need to speak with him, and we will see what can be done about the others."

"I can stay with her first," volunteered one lady. "I never fall asleep until after midnight anyway."

"Wake me next," said one of the older ladies. "I usually get up to go to relieve myself around that time."

The ladies soon had a schedule all sorted out. They insisted that Lydima not take a night shift. "You have the baby to look after. You will have to get up with her."

Lydima nodded gratefully. She dismissed all the ladies except the one who would take the first turn and went in to introduce her to Saley.

"This is Udmyla. She will stay with you tonight in case you need anything."

Saley gave a slow nod.

"I will see you in the morning," Lydima forced a cheerful smile and a wave. Then she went to find Byden and Jayred to apprise them of the situation.

"Under no circumstances are we going to allow

that monster who runs The White Lily Inn to retrieve this child. Jayred, what legal recourse do we have?"

Jayred outlined the Artylian laws about slavery, indentured servitude, paternal rights, and debt collection until Lydima began to feel overwhelmed and had trouble keeping everything straight. She made him go through everything again slowly, and she wrote down a summary of the information so she could memorize it.

"Byden, I need you to send a reliable scout to track down Lord Yoused wherever he is and impress upon him that I need to speak to him urgently. I am also worried that the owner of the inn may resort to violence to gain information on the girl's whereabouts. We should send messengers to all the villages to be on the alert for strangers. The garrison here should be prepared to make a show of force, if needed."

"You will not defy Lord Yoused?" Byden asked incredulously.

"No, I do not believe that will be necessary, but anyone who comes searching for the girl may not back down easily. I hope that Lord Yoused and I can come to an acceptable solution when I speak to him. I know my cousin would not want us to stand by while injustice occurred inside our own walls."

The men voiced their agreement, and Byden went off to fulfill Lydima's instructions while Jayred retired for the night.

Lydima frowned. Eemya would have had no trouble persuading Yoused to resolve the issue in the girl's favor. After all, he had asked Eemya to marry him once. She had refused, but Lydima was sure he continued to have a soft spot for her cousin. Still, he had acknowledged her contributions toward the well-being of the islanders and his own relationship with his son, so she hoped he would listen to her in spite of his views on her style of living.

When she finally returned to her own bedroom, Maygla had already put the other children to bed. Lydima kissed them all lightly as they slept, reflecting on what a strange turn her life had taken. She quickly changed into her nightclothes and crawled into bed. In spite of all her worries, she fell into a deep slumber.

CHAPTER EIGHT

Long shadows stretched across the ground and moved in unison with the guards on the wall above.

"Follow me," Talia ordered Stelan, and she set off across the clearing that surrounded the fortress.

As he stepped past the dead soldier, Stelan shuddered. He had never had cause to kill anyone, and he regretted that this man had been shot in cold blood. There didn't seem to be any other option, however, so he followed after Talia as quickly as he could.

Running in a crouched position, they made it to a stand of scrubby pines before the soldier on watch turned to retrace his steps. A man beckoned to them from behind a tree.

"Well done."

"You doubted me, Ashur?"

"I am merely relieved that I neither have to attempt to describe the complex process you tried to get me to memorize when you woke me in the middle of the night, nor explain to your brother your capture or death."

"Brother?" queried Stelan, panting not from exertion but from the pain he felt every time he moved.

"Tomus is my twin brother." Talia hardly gave him time to absorb this information before she continued, "We have to move before we are discovered. You brought the clothes?"

Ashur threw a large pack at her. Swiftly she pulled the garments out of it and sorted them between her and Stelan. "I only brought you sandals, since I did not know your boot size," Ashur explained apologetically to Stelan.

"These will do fine. Thank you." He pulled them on and laced them up. Thankfully, Cush had not bothered to score his feet, but the shackles had cut into his ankles. The sandals rubbed against the raw skin. Loose Cerecian trousers and a vest completed his disguise.

Talia appraised him skeptically. "You will stick out like a swan in a flock of ravens with that hair." She took Ashur's hat and placed it on Stelan's head. "That will have to do for now. You will be less remarkable with a sword than I, so you had better wear it." She handed him her sword and he buckled it on. "I guess I will have to leave the bow."

Regretfully, she shoved the bow and quiver under some bushes and covered them with leaves. A small dagger was the only weapon she kept for herself. Removing her armor, she stripped down to nothing but a short shift and pulled a plain homespun dress over her head.

"Sorry, I was unable to procure the proper female undergarments on such short notice."

"The weather is still warm. I can get by with these. Here, help me lace this up." She tossed her braid over her shoulder and turned her back to

Stelan.

Stelan had been distracted by the brief glimpse of her naked limbs and had to shake himself. By the time it occurred to him to look away, she had already finished.

Never having assisted a woman dress, he fumbled with the laces, but eventually got them tied satisfactorily. She thrust her clothes and armor into the pack and shrugged it onto her back.

"Should you not get rid of those?" asked Ashur.

"I might need my armor again. If we are stopped, they will know who we are without bothering to search us." Talia looked at Ashur. "You cannot be seen with us. We cannot risk them finding you out. We dare not even go to the safe house. From here, we will have to find our own way out of the city."

"Your friend's wounds will need treatment."

"Do you know of anywhere else we can go?"

Ashur thought for a moment. "There is a healer near the tannery who does not ask questions. Her name is Janis."

"Thanks, Ashur. I probably will not see you again."

He nodded. "Good luck." He faded into the trees, and Talia set off in another direction.

Stelan hurried after her as well as he could. There were so many questions he wanted to ask, but talking would be too dangerous. They could only communicate in Berushese and couldn't risk being overheard. Before anyone noticed they were missing, they needed to be as far away as possible.

Talia headed down a slope through the trees where they encountered a shallow creek. She pulled off her boots, hiked up her skirt, and waded downstream. Stelan sloshed through the water in his sandals. The cool water soothed his feet and ankles. Standing all night had made them hot and puffy. The pleasant view of Talia's bare calves helped to sustain him. He could hardly look anywhere else; he had to follow her.

Several huts could be seen through the trees, but they met no one. They walked downstream through the woods for some distance to obscure the direction of their escape. Several times, Talia stopped and made Stelan take a drink.

"Weeping sores can cause a person to become dehydrated. You must drink plenty of water."

Though she spoke close to his ear, he could barely hear her. Finally, she signaled it was safe to exit the water, and they cautiously made their way back toward more densely populated areas.

There had been no sound of pursuit, and Stelan had to assume the general hadn't returned to the interrogation room yet. If the dead guard at the gate had been found, it might be a while before they put two and two together and checked on their prisoner.

Talia stopped and sat on a rock to pull her boots back on, then glanced at Stelan with concern. He followed her gaze and noticed several spots of blood and plasma soaking into his shirt.

"Are you able to continue?"

"I will make it," he grimaced.

Talia nodded and started off again.

In more ways than one, it was good that his face was not scarred. The rest of the wounds could be covered up and wouldn't draw attention as easily. One bruise was easily explained; dozens were not. Why had that part of his body been spared?

"It is about an hour's walk to the tannery district," Talia informed him, interrupting his thoughts.

Stelan steeled himself to persevere. Only an hour. Putting one foot in front of the other, he forced his body to move forward.

Talia took him through a maze of side streets and alleys, avoiding the main thoroughfares. Outside of a food bazaar, she made Stelan wait in the shade of a deserted stall while she bought some breakfast. She returned with a type of fried bread stuffed with some kind of meat. Stelan knew he was hungry, and ate mechanically, but his body was so tired and numb that he couldn't even taste it.

"Drink this."

She handed him a flask containing a hot, bitter liquid. It helped to clear the fog in his mind, and he drank it all. He handed it back, and they continued on.

Close to the tannery, they passed a patrol. "Stop and check the laces on your sandals," Talia whispered.

As he bent over, she moved in front of him to block him from their view. The patrol marched down the street without giving them a second glance. Talia put her hand on Stelan's shoulder to signal all was well.

"News of our escape must not have reached them yet."

"My escape. You could have stayed."

She shook her head. "You do not know everything yet."

∞∞∞

Talia held up her hand to warn Stelan to keep silent as they entered a street with heavier pedestrian traffic. Most of the people on the street were going in the opposite direction. The putrid smell in the air indicated that the tannery was close.

Located along the eastern edge of the peninsula, the proximity of the ocean was conducive to brine-curing. In an alley next to the tannery, a healer's shingle hung over the door of one of a small series of houses that were little more than shacks.

With a sigh of relief, Stelan leaned against the doorframe as Talia knocked. A panel slid back from a hole in the door, and a wizened old lady peered through it suspiciously.

"Yes?" she rasped.

"My friend has wounds in need of attention."

"Can you pay?"

"I can pay well. Especially well if you can give us a room for a day." Talia retrieved a gold coin from her pouch and held it up.

The woman opened the door, took the coin and studied it. Satisfied with what she saw, she stepped aside and let them in. "Over there." The healer motioned to a cot on one side of the room next to a shelf of small pots and vials.

Talia guided Stelan over to the cot. He was so tired and sore he could barely move. She helped him off with his shirt like he was a child, removed his sword belt, and bent down to untie his sandals for him.

Janis looked him over. "Torture?"

"I was told you asked no questions."

The healer chuckled. "Merely rhetorical." She poked around on her shelf until she found what she wanted and held one of the pots out to Talia. "You can rub this gently into the bruises. It will take several different salves to deal with each type of wound. I will work on the cuts and burns while you do that."

Stelan was barely conscious, and he closed his eyes and rested his chin on his chest while they worked. On a couple of the larger burns, Janis affixed a thin piece of beaten silver and covered it with a paste.

"This will help it to heal faster and keep it from becoming septic," she explained at Talia's look of curiosity.

Once they were done with his upper body, Talia made him lie down while she pulled off his trousers. His eyes were still closed, but he groaned in pain. Carefully they treated all the wounds on his legs and bandaged him up, and then Janis covered him with a blanket. His breaths were slow and even. He was asleep.

"They did a thorough job on him," Janis remarked. "Strange they left the face alone."

Talia wiped her sleeve across her eyes and sniffed. "Which salve is for burns?"

"This one," she pointed to a small clay jar.

Talia rolled up the sleeve of her left arm and put a little salve on her own blistering burn. The first layer of skin had cracked and parted, and her wound was now weeping as well. Janis raised her eyebrows, but Talia did not satisfy her curiosity. Her emotions were much rawer than that small scorch mark.

"It looks like you could use some rest too." Janis handed her a blanket. "Feel free to sleep on the floor. I have work to do in my kitchen."

"Thank you," Talia replied gratefully. She spread the blanket on the floor and lay down, using her pack as a pillow.

When Janis left, she listened to Stelan's steady breathing and sat up and studied him. He had returned her kiss, without knowing who she really was or what side she was on, after being imprisoned and tortured because of her. She still couldn't believe it. Softly, she kissed his lips, overwhelmed by the strength of her feelings, and lay down again to bittersweet dreams.

∞∞∞

Stelan slept for hours. It was dark before he awoke. Some of his abrasions had started to dry, and every movement he made pulled at his skin and strained the fresh joins his body was attempting to make. Talia was still asleep, and he tried to turn on his side to improve his view of her, but he felt even more sore than he had the day before. He had to be content with just knowing she was there.

His stomach growled. Janis had left some food and wine on a table, but it was more than he could accomplish to sit up and walk over to it.

Somehow, Talia sensed he was awake and she opened her eyes. Sitting up, she saw the food on the table and got up to fetch some for Stelan. She helped him sit up and propped her pack behind him so he could eat. Then she sat on the floor next to his cot.

He ate a little, but he really wanted to talk to Talia. He needed to find out what was going on. He needed to kiss her again. Her hand was out of reach, but he extended his arm and stroked her cheek gently with one finger. "Why did you come back for me? You did not have to."

Talia looked at the floor. "You were not meant to get mixed up in this. I am sorry." She turned her dark eyes toward his. Her long, black lashes were wet. "For everything."

"I am not," he said softly.

"How can you say that?"

"I have felt closer to death before than this, but never as alive as I did when you kissed me. Kiss me again," he pleaded.

Talia got up and sat on the edge of the cot. She placed her hands on the wall on either side of his head and leaned forward to kiss him without irritating his sores. Her mouth covered his carefully and tenderly, but Stelan devoured her lips hungrily. A low moan escaped her.

Stelan moved his arms as much as the pain would allow him, and he ran his hands along her back, her waist, and her hips. Without her leather cuirass, she felt softer, and he could feel her curves under the dress and thin shift. Her breaths came faster, and he hoped her emotions were as intense as his.

Suddenly, she drew back with a startled expression. Stelan saw confusion in her eyes, and it worried him. He really knew so little about her and how her mind worked.

"What is it?"

She slipped away from him and walked to the other side of the tiny room. What had he done wrong?

∞∞∞

Janis entered at that moment and saved Talia from having to answer.

"Well, you are finally up!" She looked from one to the other of them and obviously knew something was going on, but didn't remark on it. She walked over to her cabinet and picked up a jar of ointment. "Let's see how you are looking."

The healer folded the blanket down to inspect her patient's arms and chest. Looking him over, she nodded to herself and seemed satisfied with what she saw. She changed several bandages and reapplied the salve. Then she did the same for his legs.

"Well, how is he doing?" asked Talia impatiently.

"So far, all is looking well. There is no festering, and the wounds are clean. They are, for the most part, not as deep as many I have seen." Janis looked sideways at Talia as she said this. "Let me see yours."

Talia rolled up her sleeve obligingly. She hadn't

bandaged her burn, and the raw skin had stuck to her sleeve as it dried. She pulled the fabric free without wincing. Janis dabbed some more ointment on it and put a bandage over it for her.

"How soon will he be well enough to travel?"

"The longer he can wait, the better, but a week at the least. Two would be best."

"We cannot wait that long."

"For his sake, you should. As long as you were not followed, you are safe here. The tanning community is close-knit, and no one comes this way if they do not have to."

Talia hesitated and looked at Stelan.

"I will do whatever you say," he assured her, guessing at the substance of their conversation. He was starting to pick up a few Cerecian words here and there.

Talia felt conflicted. She needed to report her discovery to her superiors as soon as possible, but she could not leave Stelan. Forcing him to leave too soon would inhibit his healing and could cause the wounds to suppurate. On the other hand, the prospect of spending several days in the same room with him offered its own complications.

"We will take it one day at a time," she stated grimly. "Can you acquire a few items for me?"

"What do you need?"

"Some accurate maps of Cerecia. That may be the most difficult thing to procure without suspicion. Boots for him," she canted her head toward Stelan thinking it best not to give the healer any names. "A couple of water flasks. I do not suppose it would be possible to purchase another sword?"

"I will see what I can do," Janis' mouth twitched in a smile.

Talia handed her several Cerecian coins of various

denominations.

"Do you want to dye his hair?"

"Yes, that would be very helpful."

"Too bad we cannot do anything about his blue eyes," Janis suggested slyly.

Talia made a half-smile. "I would not want to change those."

Both women looked at Stelan, and even though he couldn't understand what they were saying, he assumed he was their subject and gave them a rakish grin.

Talia couldn't help grinning back. Janis stepped out after assuring her female guest that she would begin assembling the required items first thing in the morning.

When she left, Talia sighed and leaned her head against the wall.

∞∞∞

Stelan ached to know what was wrong. He longed to hold her, reassure her that he didn't blame her for anything. Looking back, he could see how Talia had tried to protect him at every turn. It was clear now that she was only pretending to spy for Cerecia while really spying for Berush.

She was amazingly talented. He had never seen anyone play a role so convincingly. And what a soldier she was! So brave and strong. Twice he had seen her kill a man, she had defied an entire crew of pirates, and she had withstood a hot poker. He still did not understand that part.

"Talia." He began to have an inkling of the reason for her exchange with the man in the torture chamber.

She turned and faced him.

"Did you take that burn to spare me from worse torture?"

She looked away.

"Talia . . ." he called her name softly, caressing it with his voice.

"It was nothing. It was the least I could do," she muttered.

"It was far from nothing."

"Why do you not hate me?" She burst out vehemently. "It would be so much easier!" With long, swift strides she strode to the door, yanked it open, and walked out into the night leaving Stelan gaping after her.

∞∞∞

Crying vexed tears of frustration mixed with longing, Talia walked through the dark, stinking alleys near the tannery. She needed to clear her head.

When she had kissed Stelan the first time, she had not expected him to reciprocate. She had thought it would be safe to kiss him, to be attracted to someone who would not, could not, possibly be attracted to her. It would have been more natural for him to be enraged with her for getting him into this situation and for not saving him sooner, even though she didn't see how it could have been possible.

Maybe she had anticipated he would be angry only because she was furious with herself for being unable to spare him the torture. In spite of all he had experienced, he was unexpectedly grateful to her. He had figured out why she had let Cush scar her, though she had hoped he wouldn't. She didn't want him to feel indebted to her. It did not *appear* like he felt indebted to her, but rather that he hoped her attraction to him was her motivation. Was it? Would she have made the effort to rescue just anyone who had been caught up in her mission unwillingly? She didn't know.

Surprisingly, her attraction to him had not been repelled; it was mutual. He obviously felt something for her as well. Now, instead of just being a part of her mission, he was of personal interest to her, and that could affect her focus and her judgment. It could affect his judgment if he was concerned about her. The mission was more important than either one of them. It had to be.

When she and Tomus had planned it all out, they had expected Talia to be able to leave the Cerecian capital immediately after infiltrating the warehouse, before her deception had been discovered. She would have set out on horseback toward the southern end of the Berushese mountains and met up with one of Varus's patrols. Rescuing Stelan had changed everything.

Now, she would have to figure out another way to get them both safely out of the city, and if they didn't escape in time, she might miss the rendezvous. The roads and docks would be sure to be watched. She no longer had access to the stables at the fortress, and she didn't have enough money to buy horses. Most of her money was going to be used to pay Janis and purchase supplies.

If they were able to get away safely and return home without capture, what then? She had planned on being a career soldier. To her, that meant she had to stay away from romantic entanglements. If she had a love affair, or married, and became pregnant, she could not fight. You couldn't carry a child into battle. At least, she would not. She had vowed that she would remain celibate, but she didn't know if she could resist Stelan if he tried to make love to her.

Talia wanted to ignore the future implications of the situation, but she knew things could not continue in the direction they were going now. She would have to explain her feelings to Stelan so that the relationship would not progress further. It would be easier to stop it now than it would be later.

She also realized that he still knew nothing about her true mission. He really didn't know anything other than the fact that she was Tomus' sister. He needed to understand the full situation. After all he had been through, she owed him that much. She turned her feet back toward the healer's house.

Aside from a few rats scurrying through the shadows, Talia encountered no one in the streets. Even criminals stayed away from this part of town. There was nothing to steal, and if you didn't live here, the smell was one to avoid. It was a good thing, since she had stalked out without strapping on her sword.

When she opened the door and stepped back into Janis' receiving room, Stelan was visibly relieved. He exhaled slowly and relaxed back into his pillow as he watched her pace the floor. Had he been worried she would leave without him, or was he worried about her safety alone in the streets at night? Regardless, she had things that needed to be said. She prepared herself to say them.

From underneath the small table, she picked up a stool and set it in front of the cot. She sat near him, but deliberately out of his reach. Refusing to be a coward, she looked into his eyes, though she risked drowning in them and forgetting her resolve.

With her back straight and her hands on her knees, she announced, "There are some things that need to be made clear."

CHAPTER NINE

The morning was gray and drizzly, and Lydima and all the children slept late without the bright sun to wake them. When Lylie's cry finally roused them, Lydima was grateful for the damp, rainy weather. It meant that no one would be likely to come looking for Saley today. She fed the baby and handed her off to Maygla when she arrived with breakfast for Katya and Dzhon.

Grabbing a slice of bread with cheese, Lydima hurried down to check on Saley. Aylria was there, and they were eating a hot meal.

"Good morning Saley. Did you sleep well?"

The girl looked at her and swung her legs in her chair while swallowing a spoonful of porridge.

"Would you like to come and meet the other children staying here?"

Saley spooned up the last of her porridge and stood up. Lydima held out her hand with a smile, and the girl took it shyly. They headed upstairs to Lydima's room. She thought that other children might be the best tonic she could offer Saley. Probably, she had never been able to just play.

When they entered the room, Katya and Dzhon looked up from their breakfast.

"Children, this is Saley. She will be staying with us now. Saley, this is Katya and Dzhon, and the baby you saw last night is Lylie."

Dzhon slid out of his chair and looked up at Saley. "Wan to pway bwocks?" He didn't wait for an answer, but took her hand and dragged her over to the blocks. "Guess what! We have goats! But weo not see dem today, 'cause it waining. Maybe tomowow. Hewe," he handed her a block, "you 'tack dis one."

Saley inspected the block and set it carefully on the top of the stack. Dzhon put another one on top. Then he took his stuffed ball and threw it at the tower. It toppled over nicely, and he let out a whoop. "Do again! You trow da ball!"

While they restacked the blocks, Katya came over to Lydima. "Can we draw again today? I can show Saley how to do it."

"Certainly."

Lydima wondered how Eemya would feel if they used up all her paper. If it helped the girls to get to know one another, it would be worth it. She knew she couldn't leave them alone together, however. Even though Katya and Dzhon had already experienced their share of grief, they were still ignorant of many things that Saley had likely been exposed to. Saley would have a more difficult time adjusting to being a normal child. Lydima herself had been unable to go back, but she had been a little older than Saley appeared to be.

The children took turns with the blocks and the ball, and Lydima sat and watched them play. She couldn't remember ever playing like this with other children. Their activity was so simple, but they enjoyed it immensely. Lylie started fussing, so Lydima picked her up and laid her in her lap. Lylie began to coo and make happy noises, and Lydima did also. They passed the morning pleasantly this way.

Maygla brought their lunch, and after everyone had eaten, Lylie went down for a nap. Saley put a few crusts of bread that the others had left into her pockets, glancing around guiltily as she did so. Lydima noticed.

"You can have as much bread as you like, dear. Here, I am not going to have this one either," and she handed her another slice. Saley took it slowly and put it in her pocket.

Dzhon wasn't quite ready for his nap yet, so Lydima suggested they take a tour of the castle while Maygla watched Lylie. Dzhon and Katya were eager to guide Saley around, and they ran up and down the corridors excitedly. Even Saley's eyes showed some interest in her new surroundings. Saley hadn't seen the great hall yet, and the other children were happy to show her.

Jayred was giving instructions to servants in the hall, and while the children raced around, she stopped and spoke with him.

"Do you think Eemya would mind if I showed the children the cavern?"

The steward reflected for a moment. "I suppose not. It is not something she wants generally known, though. Some of the rocks are sharp. They should be careful." He called one of the servants over and asked him to fetch a lantern. "Kyel can go with you. He is one of the few who has complete knowledge of it."

Lydima expressed her thanks and called the children over. "We are going to get to see something really special. I think you will like it."

They exited the hall and followed Kyel down a

passage to what appeared to be a dead end.

Kyel pressed in on the wall, and a solid rock door swung away from them into complete darkness. Cool, stale air wafted toward them.

"Stay close to me," he cautioned, "so you can see where you are going."

"Katya, hold Dzhon's hand. Saley, hold my hand."

The children showed some reluctance to enter the dark space. Lydima knelt down in front of them.

"We are going into a cave. It is perfectly safe. There is nothing living here except for a few small salamanders and crickets. Inside, there are some beautiful crystals. It is something amazing to see, but we do not have to go if you do not want to."

"I want to see it," said Katya bravely.

Dzhon jumped up and down. "Me too!"

"Saley, do you want to see it, or would you rather not?"

Saley held Lydima's hand tightly, but she stepped forward.

"All right, here we go." Lydima nodded Kyel forward.

The lantern illuminated a short, narrow tunnel, and they walked through it into a vast, empty space. Kyel lifted the lantern, and thousands of crystals winked and sparkled at them from every corner of the cavern.

"Oooh!" exclaimed Katya. "It is beautiful! Are they diamonds?"

"No, these are just crystals. They are not worth much, but they are very pretty, and there are a lot of them."

They stopped as Kyel picked up a sample for them to study. The children leaned in closely and gazed at the crystals embedded in the volcanic rock.

"Can I keep it?" asked Dzhon.

"These belong to my cousin, Lady Eemya, so we have to leave them here for now. I will write her a letter and see if you can have one." Dzhon nodded and handed it back.

They hiked carefully around the cave until Dzhon yawned, and Lydima asked Kyel to take them back. Kyel inserted a hook into a sunken slot in the door and pulled it back in place, then removed the hook.

Lydima, who knew what it was like to have nothing, checked their pockets briefly when they were back in the castle. She found a small crystal in Dzhon's pocket.

"Dzhon, you were not supposed to bring any out."

"But dis is a diffwen one."

Lydima sighed. "I will have to save it for you until Lady Eemya gives you permission to keep it."

"Awww."

He was the only one who had anything, but Lydima noticed a sly look in Saley's eyes. When she had put Dzhon down for his nap, and Katya went with Aylria for her sewing lesson, she took some time to talk to Saley alone. They went and sat in Saley's bedroom.

"Saley, I wish that those were diamonds in the cave. It would make it easy to get your siblings back. But, I want you to know that I am working on how to rescue them, as well as how to keep you safe. I know Lord Yoused, who is the ruler over that area, and I am sure that I can persuade him to help. I will not let you be taken back to that terrible place. If I could, I would make sure no one went there ever again."

The girl didn't respond, and Lydima didn't expect her to. Lydima leaned back on the bed and just rested, letting the child think about whatever she needed to think about. Saley took a slice of bread out of her pocket and handed it to Lydima. She wasn't sure what the girl meant by the gesture, but she broke the bread in half, took a bite of one, and gave the other piece back to Saley. Saley leaned back onto a pillow and chewed on her own slice. Somehow, the small act of sharing the bread seemed to bring them together.

In order to keep from falling asleep, because she still did not want to leave Saley unsupervised, she started telling Saley about herself. She told her how she had been orphaned, about her life with her aunt, and how she went to live with another aunt and uncle when the first aunt died.

When she told her what her uncle had done, she felt the girl stiffen next to her.

"I hated him then. I hated myself. Even now, it makes me sick to think about him. I thought I must have done something wrong, for that to happen to me, but now I know it was not my fault. He was a bad man.

"One day, a kind neighbor lady gave me an apple and smiled at me, and somehow, that action gave me the courage to run away. Somewhere, there had to be a place for me where people would be nicer. It took me a long time to find it. I am still finding it." Lydima was thinking out loud as much as she was talking to Saley. "Actually, I am making it. I want to make it for you."

Saley reached over and squeezed Lydima's hand.

∞∞∞

The next few days passed by without incident. After several hair-washings, Saley's head seemed to be louse free. Lydima was comfortable enough with Saley's behavior that she left all the children under Maygla's care one afternoon to conference with

Jayred and Byden.

"Have you heard anything from the scouts?"

"No one has noticed anything beyond the normal traffic on the road."

"It may take a while for news of her whereabouts to reach the port. We must stay vigilant. What about Lord Yoused?"

"Palyn reports that he is still at sea searching for news of Lord Stelan. He will stay at the port until Yoused returns. According to his information, Valryn, the keeper of the White Lily Inn, was still in residence two days ago."

"Good."

She could not imagine the man had given up, or was indifferent. In his line of business, he had to care. If one girl could get away, that would give hope to all the rest. Perhaps, like her, he was waiting to appeal to Yoused when he returned. Lydima couldn't believe that Yoused would take the man's side. It seemed more of a risk to appeal than to seek the girl out himself.

Whatever the reason, Lydima was glad of the delay. If she could get to Yoused first, then maybe a confrontation could be avoided.

When she returned to her room, Katya ran up to her with a drawing. "Look! I drew a picture of Saley! She let me draw her."

Katya and Dzhon had adapted easily to Saley's silence. They didn't seem to find it unusual at all. It was almost like a game to try and figure out what she was trying to say.

"That is very nice! Your observation skills are improving. I see a lot of detail in your drawing. Even eyelashes."

"Here is Saley's drawing. She drew a goat."

Lydima looked at the drawing. She had drawn a

111

Billy goat with horns and a long goatee. It seemed like the goat had an evil expression, and Lydima felt goosebumps rise on her arms. She glanced at Saley, who was looking in another direction.

"You have a good memory, Saley, to draw something without looking at it. I have to look at something to make a really good representation of it."

"You drew my mother, and you were not looking at her," reminded Katya.

"But I was looking at you. I could see your mother in your face."

"Really?"

"Of course. Children generally look like their parents. I just made you look older."

"So I will look like my mother when I grow up?"

"Most likely."

Saley had been listening closely to the conversation and pointed to herself and then to the drawing of Katya's mother.

"You want me to make a drawing of your mother?"

Saley nodded.

Lydima took the pencil and a fresh paper and sat down at the table. "Do you look like your mother?"

Saley shrugged.

"Have you ever seen yourself in a mirror?"

The girl shook her head.

Lydima got up and went to fetch a small, polished piece of steel and handed it to her. Saley peered into it, looking one way and then the other with wide eyes.

When she set it down, Lydima asked, "How did she arrange her hair?"

Saley pointed to Lydima's own hair.

"Piled on top, with curls?"

Saley's hair was much darker than Lydima's, so she drew a face with features like Saley's, but older, with dark hair. She took her time and worked carefully.

"What about her eyes? Were they blue like yours?"

The girl nodded. Light eyes.

The face that stared back at her when she was finished was one she recognized. It was the woman who had met her outside of Sonefast, the woman who had told her there was a place where she could have regular meals and a roof over her head.

When Lydima showed her the drawing, Saley took it and nodded, but then took up the pencil and made some adjustments on her own. Lydima watched as she mimicked her technique to darken the lips and smear some color on the cheeks. The girl had only seen her mother with color painted on her face.

Saley set the drawing on the table, leaned it against the wall and stared at it. Lydima had a feeling this might not be healthy for her, so she organized the children into a game, and they played until it was time for dinner.

All of them were eating in the hall now, except Lylie. Saley still put extra food in her pockets for later, but Lydima did not chastise her. If it made her feel better, she could carry around as much food as she wanted. The ladies still kept watch over her at night. Lydima expected to continue this at least until the issue of her siblings was resolved.

After naptime the following afternoon was the first opportunity the children had to visit the goats in nearly a week. The rain had stopped two days before, but the barnyard was so muddy that Lydima hadn't wanted to deal with the inevitable mess that would result from the trek.

Dzhon was nearly jumping out of his skin with anticipation. A new kid had been born, and he was excited to see it.

113

The barnyard still had a couple of puddles, but it was mostly dry. The goats had clumps of dirt stuck to their legs. Lydima expected that the children would have to change their clothes anyway.

Dzhon ran up to the stable hand and asked him about the new kid. The older boy went into the pen where the nanny and her new offspring were resting and brought out the new baby. He held it out so all the children could pet it. Dzhon was enthralled and could not stop touching it.

"Let the girls have a turn, Dzhon."

Obediently he stepped back so the others could stroke the animal's fuzzy hair. Katya took a turn, and then she motioned Saley over.

Saley reached her hand out slowly and touched the kid timidly. She stared at the animal with wonder on her face. As she ran her fingers over it she whispered, "Soft."

Katya turned excitedly to Lydima, "She talked! She said 'soft!' Saley talked!"

Lydima grinned, and Saley smiled shyly.

They played with the goats until Lydima judged it was nearly time for dinner. As they walked back to the castle, she felt happy and content. The children were making progress. She was making a difference in their lives. For the first time, she felt like she was accomplishing something worthwhile.

A couple of guards had accompanied them, at Lydima's request. Inside the courtyard, Byden came up to her.

"A cart just crested the hill, my lady. The men on watch say they do not recognize the occupants." Byden's own vision wasn't good enough to distinguish faces at that distance.

"I will take the children to have dinner in my room instead of the hall." She hurried them inside, trying not to worry them.

"Shall I shut the gate?"

"No, we will have to talk to them one way or another. Let them into the courtyard, but no farther. Summon all the men." She took the children into her room and called a couple of ladies to stay with them. "Do not come out until I come back," she instructed, then returned to the courtyard.

By the time she arrived, the cart was just coming through the gate. Jayred came and stood next to her. Every castle guard was assembled in the yard or on the surrounding wall. Two men sat on the seat of the cart. One had a wide-brimmed hat pulled down over his forehead. The driver got out and walked over to Lydima. She stared at him and had to make an effort not to gawk. His face looked just like the drawing of the goat Saley had made. Even the beard was the same. She could almost see the horns sprouting from his head.

"I see that I am expected," he announced. Lydima arched her eyebrow. "So you do not deny that you have my daughter here?"

Lydima knew how this kind of man worked. They tried to get you to believe that you were the one in the wrong, not them. "On the contrary, I most vehemently deny that."

The man was thrown off by her response and she could see his mind working on what to say next.

"Did you not take in a young girl delivered by a tinker almost a week ago?"

"Yes."

"That was my daughter. She ran away, and I have come to fetch her."

"I am afraid I am going to have to require some proof of that assertion."

"Since when does a man have to prove his child

belongs to him? My word should be enough."

Lydima looked at the goat-man's eyes. They were a dark brown, almost black. She realized now what had bothered her about Saley's drawing. The goat's eyes were human eyes.

"You cannot possibly be her father."

"You know nothing about it."

"I know her mother's eyes were blue."

Valryn narrowed his eyes at her. "She belongs with me. She will never fit in anywhere else. Nothing you can do will change what she is."

"You are wrong."

"You, of all people, should know I am right."

Don't let it get personal, Lydima told herself. That shifts the balance of power. With great effort, she forced herself to assert control. "You will not take that child. You are not welcome in these lands. Take your cart and go. My men will escort you back where you came from."

"Before I leave, I have someone who wants to renew an old acquaintance."

The man with the hat looked up and climbed down from the cart with some effort.

"Maybe he can talk some sense into you."

Lydima glanced at the second man and froze. She couldn't breathe. Her hand gripped Jayred's arm like a vise. Fear clawed at her heart and seized it with its sharp talons. She wanted to scream and run, but she could not. It was her uncle.

"Well, well," he lumbered over to her.

He still reeked of stale beer, but he looked much older than she remembered.

"Look at little Lyddie, all grown up," he leered at her. "Still as pretty as ever, but worthless for anything else. What makes you think you can take care of a child? You cannot even take care of yourself."

Lydima shrank behind Jayred, and he took matters into his own hands.

"The lady has told you to get out. Both of you." He motioned to the guards, who began to close in.

Valryn put his hands up. "We are leaving," he said with a sneer, "but this is not over."

Lydima's uncle started to walk away, but looked over his shoulder to throw a last insult. "I remember—" was all he got out before he felt Jayred's boot meet his tailbone. He sprawled ignominiously in the dirt. When he picked himself up, he hurried into the cart without saying anything else. Six guards mounted up to follow them to the border of Youseed's lands.

Jayred took Lydima's arm and led her back inside. She was shaking from the encounter. He guided her into the privacy of the study and poured her a glass of wine. She had to use two hands to keep from spilling it.

"You did very well, my lady. Lady Eemya would be proud."

"Oh Jayred, I could not even speak. Thank you for standing up for me."

Jayred smiled. "Happy to oblige. The man deserved a kick in the pants, and more. But you stood up to Valryn magnificently. He will not be back."

"He said it was not over." What other diabolical schemes would the man come up with? How had he managed to track down her uncle? That type of man knew exactly how to exploit someone's weaknesses to make them feel worthless and sordid.

"What can he do? He has no army. His only recourse is Lord Youseed, and we have the right on our side."

"I hope so."

117

The man had already shown himself to be creative and resourceful. This could just be a fraction of what he was capable. While she was worried about Stelan, she wished Yoused would return soon!

CHAPTER TEN

Stelan listened silently as Talia explained her mission. His expression grew serious, and he frowned as he realized the implications of his rescue on the success of her endeavor. Not following through with her original plan had put the entire operation in jeopardy.

"You must go on without me. The information must get through as soon as possible. I can find my own way back as soon as I am well enough."

Talia shook her head. "You do not even speak the language. How could you find a way out?"

Stelan opened his mouth to argue, but she held up a hand.

"No, I will not leave you except as a last resort. It will take me a couple of days to come up with a new plan anyway. I may have to do some scouting around. If I cannot find a way to get us both safely away, then I will go alone."

"Alright," agreed Stelan reluctantly. Then he took the opportunity to seek answers to other burning questions. "However did you manage to infiltrate the Cerecian army?"

"In the mountains on the border there lives an old Cerecian warrior. He is greatly revered for his skill in battle. When he retired, he married a Berushese woman and hid himself away in the hills. He has outlived all his family except a granddaughter. Because of tensions between our countries, and even more, because he fears the effect King Chysh's policies will have on Cerecia, he is concerned about her future.

"In exchange for providing a safe haven for him and his granddaughter in Berush, I was allowed to take her name. It was easy to gain a commission in the army on his recommendation, especially after their ranks had been so greatly depleted. Although, females soldiers are less common here than in Berush."

"Then you told them you had learned Berushese from your grandmother and could be useful as a spy?"

"Yes. I was to give them information, some true, some false, about the defensive capabilities of the island in hopes of gaining their trust and getting closer access to General Riash. The night we arrived, I was able to enter his study and forge a document granting permission for me to view the production warehouses."

"Is your real name Talia?"

"Yes. I used my real name while in Artylia pretending to spy for Cerecia. It was less complicated that way. Here, I am known as Dachia, granddaughter of Dachede."

An uncomfortable silence followed, and Stelan deliberated how to respond to Talia's revelation. There was so much he wanted to say to her.

"I do not hate you," he said softly. "None of what happened to me was your fault. You have saved my life more than once. I think you are incredible: an amazing warrior, and a beautiful woman."

Talia's lip quivered, and she looked ready to cry. Taking a deep breath, she blurted out, "I plan on remaining a soldier."

Stelan blinked, and tried to fathom what she was intimating. "Why would you not?"

Talia blushed slightly. "If I am to remain a soldier, I cannot have any intimate relationships."

"Oh," said Stelan, as her meaning dawned on him.

"I am sorry if I led you to believe otherwise."

"Even if you had not kissed me, I would have wanted to kiss you at the first opportunity. This conversation would have been necessary sooner or later." He smiled wistfully. "I am still not sorry."

"We had better eat again and get some more rest," Talia said brusquely as she brushed at her eyes. "I have a lot to do in the morning."

∞∞∞

The next day Janis and Talia agreed that the healer would do some reconnaissance and see what chatter there was in the streets about the fugitives. At the same time, she would look for the items on Talia's list and visit some patients. In exchange, Talia would fix the meals and look after Stelan for the day. Talia had some reservations about trusting Janis so completely, but they had no other choice.

Janis seemed to read her mind, and on the way out she reassured, "I may be old and crusty, but I have no love for the Cerecian army and how they operate. I do not need their blood money. I will not betray you."

With a small soup bone that Janis had left, Talia made a savory vegetable stew. The vegetables were not the freshest, but the wide variety of spices the healer had available made it quite tasty. Even warriors had to eat, and Talia was good at making do with whatever was on hand. She even cobbled up some biscuits to go with it.

Once the meal was ready, she brought some out for Stelan to eat. Sitting up was still painful for him. Any movement hurt, worse now that the healing process had begun. Because he had been chained with his back against the wall, his injuries were all on the front half of his body, so he was at least able to lie down or sit propped up without causing further damage.

After he had eaten, Talia followed Janis' instructions to redress the wounds. The healer had set out the necessary ointments, with labels, so there was no way she could mix them up. Having helped with the previous treatments, she knew what to do, but without Janis there, it seemed less clinical and more personal. In order to apply the salves, she had to lean over him closely and touch his bare arms and chest.

Stelan watched her without speaking as she worked. Her fingers shook slightly, and she dropped a bandage and knelt down to pick it up. When she sat up, Stelan leaned forward and caught her wrist gently. His head was very close to hers, and he spoke softly in her ear as he removed the bandage from her hand.

"Here, let me."

With a grunt, he sat up farther and deftly wrapped the strip of material around his forearm with one hand. Then, he reached for the pot of ointment and treated his legs himself. The exertion tired him, and he leaned back and closed his eyes when he was finished.

Talia was deeply moved by his effort to spare her

feelings. He understood, and he was not judging her or trying to change her mind. It was a whole different world of torture to want something so badly, something that was within reach, but that you could not have. At least, couldn't have without giving up something equally desirable.

If she was ever to fall in love, Lord Stelan would be the type of man she would want. He was compassionate, discerning, patient, and controlled, but strong, resilient, and the most handsome man she had ever seen. But she could not allow herself to think this way.

To take her mind away from temptation, Talia retreated into the kitchen and cleaned the dishes. Setting aside a bowl for Janis, she put everything else away and scrubbed all the surfaces. When the kitchen was clean, she returned to the front room and emptied Stelan's chamber pot. She peered cautiously out the crack in the door to make sure no one was passing, so she would not be seen before pouring it into the community cesspit. Then, she replaced it noiselessly so she would not wake him.

For at least another hour, Talia sat and tried unsuccessfully to concentrate on a plan to return to Berush. Finally, Janis returned with several items from the list and a good deal of pertinent information. Stelan stirred and sat up as she entered.

"In the tanning district, boots are easy to come by," she announced. Having measured Stelan's feet before she left, she knew what size to get. She held the soles up to the bottoms of his feet and nodded to herself. "So are leather flasks." She laid two large specimens on the table. "And information." Her eyes twinkled.

"What did you find out?" prompted Talia.

"General Riash is apoplectic. Evidently someone

stole a prisoner right out from under his nose. Then they got away with some sort of military secrets. The words 'traitor' and 'spy' were bandied about. The skill and audacity of the perpetrators is being touted as akin to magical powers. They seem to have disappeared completely in spite of the increased patrols. This I learned at the general bazaar in the city center. I also heard some quickly hushed references to the Chief."

"The Chief? Who is that?"

"Only a name people throw around when something goes missing, or something unexplainable happens. 'The Chief' was behind it. There is talk of a smuggler who goes by that name. I do not know if he is real or not, but there were a few who joked that the Chief would like to get ahold of you before Riash does. If he is real, I have no idea how you would contact him."

While Talia considered this information, Janis went to a shelf and brought down a pen, inkwell and some paper.

"The map was a little more difficult. I could not just go into a cartographer's and buy one. They are expensive, but more importantly, our beloved general is very crafty. I would not put it past him to set a watch on any place that might have information to aid someone in leaving the country.

"Instead, I went to the library. I gave the scribe on duty a story about looking into my family history, and he guided me into the genealogical room which was adjacent to the map room. When he left, I just ran around to the next room. I studied the maps intently, and I think I can replicate them with relative accuracy." Accordingly, Janis began to draw studiously on the paper.

Talia watched over her shoulder. "That is amazing,

Janis."

She gave Stelan a brief summary of what the healer had reported. This data would be pivotal to planning their route to Berush or Artylia, whichever lent itself best to a swift escape. Janis explained her map to Talia and added as much personal knowledge as she could. Talia poured over it the rest of the evening.

"Can I help?" asked Stelan.

Talia sighed. "Money is the real problem. It takes money to hire a boat or to buy horses. Stealing either one would draw too much attention. I am not a sailor, and neither are you, so stealing a boat would do no good anyway. That leaves us with traveling overland on foot, or in a cart if we could hitch a ride with someone. There are too many places along the way where we could encounter suspicion. I may need to go and see Ashur and find out if he knows any merchants we could travel with."

"That does not involve too much risk?"

"It does involve some risk, especially for Ashur, but I do not see any other options."

"Who else travels besides merchants?"

"Hmm. Soldiers. Harvesters, sometimes. Players. Do you juggle?"

"No, sorry."

"I will think on it. Maybe an inspiration will come to me as I sleep."

"If you are going to be gone most of tomorrow, can you ask Janis if she can teach me some Cerecian?"

Talia went into the kitchen to ask. She soon returned with an affirmative. "She will also dye your hair tomorrow to make you less noticeable."

Stelan nodded his acquiescence. There were not many blondes in Cerecia.

Early the next morning, before the first light of dawn, Talia left the healer's house. She was armed only with her dagger, and dressed as a rag-and-bone dealer, thanks to Janis. She had an unusual variety of female clothing styles and sizes. It was a perfect disguise. A person of such poverty was often passed over. Because of her above-average height, she also affected a stoop in order to be less noticeable.

Her plan was merely to roam the city and see what opportunities might arise. If nothing fortuitous occurred, and she found no means of transport, then she would seek out Ashur before returning to the house. There had to be some way she could get them both out. Sometimes it was just a matter of being in the right place at the right time. Perhaps she would hear something about this 'Chief.'

All she had to do was avoid the patrols, but that was easier said than done. Riash would have the city sealed up tightly. If they continued to elude him, he would start breaking down doors and searching house by house. She needed to find high ground, a vantage point from which she could analyze the patrol patterns and maybe find a weakness in the defenses they could exploit.

Other than the military watchtowers, the only tall structures were the lighthouses and the bell tower in the city center. The bell tower was surrounded by the central bazaar, and was crowded with people trying to buy what little food was available. The new lighthouse was manned constantly, so that was out. That left the original lighthouse.

When a more efficient fuel was discovered, rather than refit the old lighthouse, a second one was constructed. The new lighthouse was farther from the city at a more strategic point for guiding ships. It had a large, concave mirror inside and used oil lamps as a light source.

The old one was on a higher point, but further east. When active, it had used outrageous amounts of coal and wood to keep it going. It would afford the best view of the city and was most likely to be unoccupied. Unless General Riash had the same thoughts. Any good soldier would search out the high ground.

She climbed the hill on which the lighthouse stood and approached the ruin circumspectly. There were no other buildings nearby, and the area seemed deserted. No horses or men hid among the rocks. If it was a trap, it would only be sprung from inside.

Cautiously, she entered the hole where the door used to be and listened. Nothing. Talia took off her pack of rags, set it on the floor, and stretched. Her back was sore from stooping. Dead, brown leaves and the rotting remains of the door littered the floor inside the entrance.

A narrow stone staircase protruded from the circular wall. There was no railing, so she hugged the cold, stone walls as she climbed up the steps with trepidation. After several stories of going in circles, it was hard not to get dizzy. When she finally reached the top, Talia drew her dagger and walked around the large, raised fire pit to make sure no one was hiding behind it. She scattered a few dried leaves on the last several steps, to make it difficult for anyone to sneak up behind her. Then she turned her attention to the large windows and looked out over the city.

Herida was a huge, sprawling urban center that included the port, the garrison, the warehouse district, tannery, library, bazaars and many other important cultural landmarks. From what she had heard and read, it used to be a beautiful city with an educated populace. Now, everything was falling apart. Decay and filth were everywhere. The recent battle with the Artylian navy had greatly depleted their army and one of their main sources of livelihood by decimating their fleet of warships and commercial fishing vessels.

The city was located on a wide, triangular peninsula that protected the harbor and provided shelter for the ships. Separating the peninsula from the mainland were two sheer cliff faces with a canyon between them. Herida had no need for walls. All they had to do was guard the entrance to the wide ravine. Other than the sea, that was the only way in and out.

From the wide windows on the top of the lighthouse, Talia could see a maze of streets and buildings leading from the port all the way to the fortress that housed the garrison. She studied the landscape before her and analyzed the movements of the patrols. No means of escape was readily obvious. Did Ashur know anything about the Chief? It looked like her only option was still to get back in contact with him.

As she considered this, she felt the hairs rise on the back of her neck. It felt like she was being watched. Turning from the window, she listened carefully. She had seen no one approach the lighthouse and heard no one come up the steps. Barely breathing, looked around one more time.

"This old lighthouse does not usually get many visitors. It is nice to have some company."

Talia jumped. Backing against the wall with dagger unsheathed, she turned toward the direction she had heard the voice. In the darkness of the rafters under the pinnacle of the roof, a small figure lurked. She had failed to look upward, thinking no one would be able to climb up there. It could prove to be a fatal mistake.

"I have no weapon." The figure held its hands into the light. The voice sounded very young. "I am coming down."

With extreme agility, the lithe figure swung down from the rafters and executed a flip, landing on the floor on the opposite side of the pit from Talia. Clothed in rags, with a dirty face and stringy hair, a girl of maybe thirteen years stood with arms on her hips sporting a wide grin.

"Who are you?"

"Me? I am nobody. You are the one everyone is interested in, I would bet my boots."

"What do you mean?"

"You are good with disguises, but now you stand like a soldier. You are looking for a way out of the city, which means you are wanted. The general is looking for a couple of spies. I say you are one of them."

"If that were true, you would have been better off remaining silent or attacking me as I passed beneath you rather than speaking to me. What do you want?"

"I would like to take you to see my father. I think it would be a mutually beneficial meeting."

"Who is your father?"

"The Chief."

∞∞∞

When Stelan woke that morning, Talia was already gone. His heart clenched as he thought of the risk she was taking by exposing herself on the streets. He knew if anyone could handle it, she could, but he was still worried. Most of all, he was filled with an excruciating pain in his chest that was completely unrelated to his physical wounds. The fact that there could be no future for him and Talia was difficult to accept.

Except for a young kitchen maid who given him a quick peck on the cheek when he was twelve, he had never even kissed anyone before. Having grown up with Lady Eemya as a mentor, his ideals were high, and no woman had ever piqued his interest.

Talia, with all her amazing qualities, did not seem like a woman who would easily change her mind. He knew if he really cared about her, he should respect her wishes. It was going to take all his self-control to keep his distance, physically and emotionally.

Stelan couldn't blame her for wanting to remain a soldier. Anyone with her level of skill would want to put it to use. He would not try and talk her out of it, but he regretted that they would never have the chance to find out if their attraction could turn into something deeper.

Janis brought him breakfast and checked on his progress. All the while, she spoke to him with simple words and phrases in Cerecian. When she was finished looking him over, she brought in a large basin and some smelly indigo and henna pastes. She set a chair by the bed and set the basin on it. Then she helped him to sit up, had him lean over the basin, and she washed his hair.

Into the wet hair, she worked the pungent paste, still talking in Cerecian. She also dyed the short beard that had begun to grow. Usually he kept himself clean-shaven, since his beard hadn't completely come in, but that might not be possible once they escaped from Herida and began their journey home.

While the dye set, she began giving him a lesson in earnest. Starting with simple phrases like "My name is Janis," her face soon showed how impressed she was at how quickly he picked it up and how good his accent was. "Good," she said whenever he was doing particularly well, and nodded to express her meaning was affirmative. The lesson was interrupted briefly when it was time to rinse his hair, then they continued.

Some of the more abstract concepts, like state of being verbs, she explained by teaching nouns and adjectives and putting them together in a sentence. Taking an orange, she held it out and said "orange." Stelan repeated the Cerecian word for orange. Then she ran her hand around the surface and said "round." Next she said, "orange [an unknown word] round." Stelan correctly understood this as a complete sentence, "The orange is round."

In this way, he learned 'is,' and he gathered that articles in Cerecian were implied rather than explicit. They repeated this formula to associate a number of other words, objects and their attributes.

The healer was such an excellent teacher that Stelan guessed she must have had prior experience teaching language. He tried to ask a question, but didn't have a big enough vocabulary and had to make up for it with a lot of hand gestures. Janis merely looked at him with a puzzled expression. He gave up for the time being and let her resume her own prescription for imparting the words. After a suitable amount of time, she quizzed him on what they had covered so far, and he was nearly perfect in his recall. Then she indicated to him that he should rest for a while.

He closed his eyes, but all he had done the last couple of days was rest. His body needed it, but his mind wanted occupation. To try and divert his thoughts from Talia, he reviewed the words he had learned that morning over and over until he nearly drove himself insane. He didn't think he could stand another week of this, let alone two.

∞∞∞

Talia resumed her role as a stooped rag-and-bone dealer and followed the Chief's daughter in a slow, zig-zagging pattern toward the east side of the city. Their path avoided most of the general's patrols. The cheeky urchin reminded her of herself at that age: self-confident, enthusiastic and boyish. She wondered if this girl had a brother, like she did. Talia had refused to be left behind when Tomus got to do anything she considered more fun than what she and her younger sisters were supposed to do.

When she'd headed out this morning, she'd had no idea what she would find, but knew she wouldn't find anything if she stayed indoors. An opportunity had presented itself, but she did not yet know if it would be to her advantage. The girl seemed to think it would be. The Berushese spy network had only recently begun to infiltrate Herida, but it was still strange they had heard nothing of this 'Chief.'

They passed through a section of town where all the craftsmen lodged. Weavers, tailors, potters and other artisans produced and sold wares in shops along their path. They were less busy than normal, as most citizens had to spend all their money on food, for which the price had more than doubled.

A couple of times, they couldn't avoid passing a patrol, and, along with everyone else, they gave them a wide berth. No one looked twice at the ragged pair of females, one burdened beyond her years, the other nothing more than a beggar. With their dark hair and eyes, they could have been sisters.

After walking for nearly an hour, the girl finally

led her to a complex of houses built around a central courtyard. Dozens of rugs hung from racks set up all over the open area. Some of them looked like Berushese goat hair, but Berush hadn't traded openly with Cerecia for generations.

Her guide led her through an archway in the back where a sentry challenged them.

"Who is this, Zariana?"

"It is her. I have found her!"

"You mean the spy who got away from Riash?" He peered at Talia. She put down her pack and stood up to her full height.

"Yes!" asserted the urchin.

"Wait here." The man disappeared down a dark passage.

Zariana leaned against the wall, nonchalantly picking at her nails while they waited for a summons from the Chief. They didn't have to wait long before the sentry returned and beckoned them forward. He led them into one of the surrounding houses and brought them to a well-furnished salon.

A middle-aged man with a long braid of gray hair, which had been a fashion for men of nobility in Cerecia for many years, and clothing of fine, embroidered linen reclined on a settee. Several scrolls and stacks of papers were strewn around the floor. The man looked up as they entered. Everything about him declared him to be a successful merchant. He was nothing like she had expected.

A beautiful woman, several years younger than the man, lounged nearby. Two young children played next to her. If this was Zariana's family, then her poor clothing and dirty face were merely a disguise, not her normal attire.

"So, you are the one who has Riash in a fit of rage."

It was a statement, not a question. Talia wondered

how he could be so sure at first sight that it was she. Because he had asked her nothing directly, she decided not to respond. There was no reason to give out information without getting anything in return.

"My own men have not yet been successful in infiltrating the fortress. How did you do it?"

"Your daughter assures me that I will have something to gain from this interview."

"Since you linger in the city, you either have unfinished business, or your plan of escape is no longer viable. I assume you had a plan, as you do not appear to be a reckless sort of person." He glanced at his daughter, who gave him some sort of sign that she suspected the latter reason. "I can offer you a way out."

"And what do you require as payment?"

"I would like two things. First, a detailed description of the layout of the fortress and the disposition of the garrison. Second, an exclusive trade agreement with Berush and Artylia for grain. Food is scarce right now. It would make me a fortune."

"I can give you the first easily, but I have no authority to give you the second."

"I am a smuggler. I do not need an official agreement, just a contact willing to supply me."

"I can make no promises, but I know that for the right price, you can find someone to do anything."

"Indeed. I will accept your word that you will do your best to find a supplier for me. So we have an agreement?"

"I need passage for myself and one other. We will not be ready to leave for at least a week. If you can accommodate us, then I agree to your terms."

The Chief rubbed his hands together gleefully and motioned for her to take a seat. He provided her with paper and ink, and she drew out a map of the fortress, made notes about security and watch shifts, and listed all the points of entry and their vulnerabilities. With open admiration, the Chief listened as she explained about Dachede and how she had gained entry into the Cerecian army. She told him more than she had told Stelan: that she had had to prove her supposed ancestry with several skill tests, including sword fighting.

When she had finished her story, he said, "Now, I am trusting you with my identity and location. Zariana will follow you back to where you are staying, so you must trust me also. We will communicate with you when it is time to leave. There is a festival here in a week's time. It will last three days. When everyone departs to return home, it will be the best time to leave. That should give your companion enough time to recover."

Talia raised her eyebrow.

"Oh yes, there is not much that goes on in this city that I do not know. The fortress is my one blind spot." Chuckling, he gestured to one of his servants who ducked into an adjoining room. "As a gesture of good faith, let me return something to you."

The servant reappeared with Talia's bow and quiver. She could barely keep from exclaiming in surprise.

"We have been keeping an eye on your man, Ashur, for some time, but I only had one tail on him, and he could not follow all of you. He kept to his assignment but brought me this as evidence.

"I assume you will not want to draw attention to yourself by carrying it now, so I will hold it for you until it is time for you to leave. If you are feeling particularly generous, a letter of introduction to your spy might be useful in the future."

"I will consider it. How is it I have not heard of you

before this?"

The Chief laughed. "You cannot hunt someone you do not know exists."

There were many other questions Talia wanted to ask the smuggler, but he nodded to his daughter, and she indicated that it was time to leave. On the way out, Zariana stopped by the kitchen and got them both something to eat.

"I am father's best reconnaissance agent," she stated matter-of-factly. It was not bragging if it was the truth. "But I cannot do it on an empty stomach."

The cook gave them a plate of cold meat with some dry bread and broth to dip it in.

"Well, you did find me," conceded Talia. "Even General Riash failed to consider the lighthouse as a good place to wait."

Zariana grinned.

When they finished eating, they took another circuitous route back to the tanning district. It was late afternoon by the time they arrived back in Janis' street.

"Here is where we are staying."

"Ah, the healer's house. I know of her."

"What do you know?"

Too late. The girl was already heading back down the street. Talia sighed and knocked on the door. After checking to see who it was, Janis unbarred the door and let her in. When Talia saw Stelan, she couldn't help pursing her lips and making a face.

"What is it?"

"You look very different with dark hair."

"Good or bad?"

"Just different. How were the language lessons?"

"Oh, excellent! I have a feeling Janis has done it before. Can you ask her? I was trying to ask, but did not know the right words."

Talia asked, and Janis replied in the affirmative, but didn't elaborate. Then Talia told Stelan about meeting the Chief.

"I will be more than ready to get out of here in ten days."

"Waiting around does not suit me either."

"You really should go without me. The sooner you get the information back, the better."

"The Chief assures me that the days after the festival will be the easiest to get away unnoticed. We will just have to wait."

CHAPTER ELEVEN

Lydima did not tell Saley about Valryn's visit. There was no reason to worry the child unnecessarily. She made sure the girl was never left alone, but always accompanied by one of the ladies. They continued to visit the goats, but always with at least two guards. Lydima herself was nervous and had trouble sleeping. Valryn was sure to have some scheme in mind to get the girl back.

Katya was excelling in her sewing lessons. The little alphabet book was almost finished. Lydima gave both the girls drawing lessons, as well as reading and spelling lessons. Rather than require Saley to read aloud, Lydima read words to her and asked her to spell them out on a piece of slate. Katya was beginning to sound out words on her own. One of the other ladies would eventually have to start teaching them sums. That was beyond Lydima's capabilities.

Dzhon still occasionally threw fits when he didn't get his way, but they didn't last as long once he figured out no one was going to give in to him. Often, Lydima ignored him altogether when he was throwing a fit, making sure to praise him when he was doing well. He now had the job of helping Maygla clean up after meals and carry trays and empty jugs back down to the kitchen. He fulfilled his duties proudly.

The news from around the holding was good. There were fewer and fewer new cases of the fever. The castle infirmary was empty, and Yula made home visits to those who were still ill. Most of the new cases were among those who had been nursing the sick and were exposed to the illness that way.

A wet nurse had been found for Lylie. A young widow who had lost her child to the fever had come to the castle looking for work. At first, Lylie would not latch on to her new food source, and Lydima and the nurse, Puriya, had to work together to coax her to drink.

After a few awkward sessions, Lylie finally would feed without Lydima being present. This made life much easier for all concerned. The nurse was installed in the room next to Lydima's, and when Lylie woke in the middle of the night, Lydima would take her next door for her feeding. The infant would fall asleep afterward and stay with Puriya the rest of the night.

In the midst of all of this, Lydima felt like she was finally being respected as a leader. Eemya's ladies, in particular, no longer snubbed her and were happy to talk with her about the children. If she could just get the matter of Saley settled, she would be perfectly happy.

∞∞∞

Lord Youseds's yacht sailed slowly back into the harbor with a light, southern wind. At sea for over a week, there had been no news of Stelan. They had sailed all over the eastern sea, even venturing into the hostile waters off the coast of Cerecia. Sightings of an Artylian warship sailing south were reported, and a couple of fishing boats were missing and assumed lost. That was all they had been able to learn. If there was no demand for ransom awaiting him when he returned, then he would have to believe the worst.

As the boat docked, Yoused's oldest son, Warryn, and two other men were waiting for him. One of the men he recognized as a soldier from Freosyd, and the other was a man he had no desire to speak to whatsoever.

"Any news of Stelan, father?"

Yoused shook his head. "Nothing conclusive. An Artylian warship was sighted sailing south. It could have been one of the missing ships that has turned pirate or defected to Cerecia. We did not see it."

"There is another pressing matter that needs attention, and I am unsure how to proceed."

Yoused sighed. He was tired, and didn't want to deal with anything at the moment. "Let me go to the manor and take my dinner. They can speak to me afterward."

"My lord," Valryn showed impropriety in putting himself forward.

Yoused was in no mood to accommodate him. "You will speak when spoken to, or find yourself in a cell," he threatened, and stalked off toward the manor.

His guards gave him some space, and the exercise helped to calm him. It was an uphill climb, and he was quite ready to eat by the time he arrived. After a hot meal and a glass of wine, he felt relaxed and signaled his son to call the men in to present their complaints.

The soldier from Freosyd deferred to Valryn, so Yoused turned to him first.

"Speak."

"Your lordship, the Lady Lydima is harboring a runaway from my establishment and refuses to give her up. I humbly request that my lord exert his influence to require that she be returned."

"Do you have a proper contract of servitude?"

"I do." He reached into his pouch, pulled out a sheet of folded parchment and handed it to Yoused.

Yoused took the document and looked at it carefully. Artylian law forbid outright slavery, but a person could be indentured as a servant to pay a debt. In such cases, a contract was required, and it could extend no longer than seven years.

The girl referred to in the document was very young. Her 'debt' was the room and board she had been provided until old enough to do chores. He hoped she had not been put to work with the other ladies that young. The thought was sickening. He looked down his nose at Valryn. "The paper is old, but the ink is new. It cannot have been written three years ago, as stated."

"The original document was damaged and had to be copied."

"Where is the girl's mother? I would like to speak to her."

"She is dead."

"How convenient. I assume she died after affixing her signature to this paper, not before," he said sarcastically. "How many employees do you have under contract currently?"

"All my other ladies work voluntarily. They enjoy the security," he grinned lasciviously.

"There are no other children in your establishment?"

"What age does your lordship consider to be a child?"

There was no set age of consent in Artylia. Rites of passage were generally determined by one's parents.

"Any others under fifteen?"

"No, my lord."

His answer came too quickly and made Youdsed suspicious. "There must have been other children. What happens to them?"

Valryn waved his hand deprecatingly. "There are always childless couples looking to adopt. I keep a child now and then, but I cannot support them all."

Youdsed was starting to have an unsettled feeling in the pit of his stomach. There was no way he was going to give this man satisfaction if he could avoid it, but the law was tricky. He would have to write to Tomus about proposing a change at the next Council of Lords. In the meantime, he needed a chance to think. "I will look into this matter and get back to you."

Valryn looked like he wanted to press the issue, but he held himself back. "Thank you, my lord." He bowed and left the room.

Palyn, the man from Freosyd, was summoned next. He had stood quietly, shifting his weight back and forth while the other man spoke.

"Well," opened Youdsed, "you have heard what the previous plaintiff has stated. Does your message pertain to this issue, or something else?"

"To this issue, my lord. I am merely to state that Lady Lydima's opinion on the matter differs, and she would like to speak to you personally, as soon as possible."

"I am sure." This time he spoke with amusement rather than sarcasm. At least one good thing would come of this. He would have an excuse to see Lydima

143

again.

Lydima received word the next morning to expect Lord Yoused that evening. Palyn had ridden through the night to bring her the news. She made a mental note to commend Eemya on the enthusiasm of her people in their assignments. After sending Jayred to the cook to arrange a more elaborate dinner, she went about her routine with more than normal exuberance.

Katya noticed she was behaving differently than usual. "You are humming today. You do not usually hum."

"Am I? I had not noticed."

"Yes, you are."

"Humming! Hum, hum, hum," parroted Dzhon while galloping around the room on a stick horse Udmyla had made for him.

"All right children," she clapped her hands, "let us begin our lessons."

Dzhon went off to 'help' Maygla, and the girls sat down to study. Saley did particularly well with her spelling lesson, and she smiled shyly when Lydima praised her.

In one of the spare rooms, Lydima had found a small guitar. While she didn't know how to play herself, she gave it to Saley to play with and hoped the girl would use the instrument since she was not expressing herself otherwise.

Saley tentatively plucked at the strings, and Katya instantly began singing a nonsense song to the random notes. The girls had picked up Lydima's happy mood, and even Saley giggled as she played and watched Katya. Lylie was starting to laugh and

144

gurgle, and she waved and kicked along with their music. She could hold her head up now, so Lydima let the other girls take turns holding her and dressing her.

The day passed by quickly and pleasantly. In the late afternoon, Jayred found Lydima and announced that Lord Yoused had arrived. She left the children with Aylria and went to meet him. There were butterflies in her stomach, but she didn't know why. She attributed them to concern about Saley and tried to calm herself as she entered the study.

"Lord Yoused," she held out her hand to him. "Thank you for coming to see me."

He bent and kissed her hand and held it as he replied, "I am happy to be of service. It is, unfortunately, a very serious matter we have to discuss."

Lydima felt a hint of worry, and hoped she wouldn't have difficulty persuading him to see it her way. "First, tell me if you have any news of Stelan."

She took a seat and indicated that he should do the same. He repeated to her what he had told Warryn.

"I am very sorry to hear that, my lord."

Yoused canted his head in acknowledgement. "Now, about this other business. You do have the girl?"

"Yes. You know about it?"

"Valryn met me at the pier."

Lydima's eyes flashed. "That monster cannot have her back!"

Yoused held up his hands. "It is my sincere hope to prevent that from happening, but he does have a contract of servitude with four years left."

"Really? He told me he was her father and said nothing of a contract."

"Indeed? Well, I had already suspected the

document was a forgery, but there is no way to prove it if the mother is dead, as he states."

"Saley, that is what I am calling the girl since she will not speak, confirmed that her mother is dead. However, she has two siblings who are still there, and she is worried about them."

Yoused frowned. "He told me he had no other children presently."

"Maybe he has hidden them elsewhere, but he still has them. He will hold their safety over Saley's head to try and entice her back."

"Do you think it is possible that he is her father?"

"I have not asked her, but I do not think it is possible. Both Saley and her mother had blue eyes. Valryn's eyes are as black as his heart."

"How do you know her mother had blue eyes?"

"I met her once. It was five years ago on the road outside of Sonefast. She tried to convince me to come and work at The White Lily. Of course, I declined."

Yoused's face blanched as he took in what she had said. "How do you know it was her mother?" He asked hoarsely.

Lydima explained how she had drawn the picture and come to that conclusion. Yoused appeared to be struggling with what to say next. Lydima observed his discomfort and waited for him to speak, curious to know what he was thinking.

"I am sorry," he said finally.

"For what?"

"I am sorry that I put you in that position. If I had it to do over again, I would have handled it differently."

"How so?"

"I would have made sure you had a safe place to go. Please forgive me."

Lydima nodded. "Thank you. I accept your

apology. However, it is unnecessary. You had no obligation to me. You owed me nothing."

"I had an obligation to do what is right. I failed. I have failed many times, I am afraid."

"But at least you try! If you fail, you make amends. That is more than most men. I admire that."

Youssed gave a melancholy smile. "Do you?"

If she had been trying to flirt with him, as she was in the habit of doing with any man of stature, she would have squeezed his hand and given him a dazzling smile. This would not work with Youssed, she knew, and she had no desire to flirt with him or anyone else ever again. Now she had a much more important purpose.

"So what can be done about this girl?"

"Well," Youssed put his fingers together and reflected, "there are several things. I might try to catch him in one of these lies. I will search the inn for these other children you speak of. If they are not there, I will put a watch on him and he may lead us to them. Does the girl have any scars?"

"I do not think so. She had some bruises and welts, but I doubt they will scar. Why?"

"Under Artylian law, an indentured person's body does not belong to themselves, so technically, the holder of their contract can do whatever they like. But, when the contract is over, the person should be released in the same condition in which they entered the contract. If not, then they are owed compensation. It is possible to get out of a contract early if permanent injuries are sustained so the other party can avoid paying a penalty."

"I will check again and see if there is anything. Oh, she does have a tattoo of a lily on her neck. Does that count?"

"I do not know. That might not be considered an

injury, though it is not reversible."

Lydima thought for a moment. "What if she was an innocent when the contract began, but not when it finished? That can hardly be said to be the same condition."

Yoused's eyes flickered and his jaw hardened. "Yes, I would agree with that. It might be hard to prove, and there is no precedent for this interpretation of the law, but I hardly think Valryn would take this matter to the Artylian council if he disagreed with my ruling. If he does, I will push for new laws banning children from being indentured in this · way. I plan to do that anyway. According to Valryn's contract, the girl's real name is Kandys, by the way."

"If he used her real name in this so-called contract."

"Yes."

Jayred appeared at the door and announced that dinner was ready. Yoused gave Lydima his arm to lead her in. She had been led to dinner many times before, by a wide variety of men, but this felt strangely different. This must be what her cousin felt like every day of her life, having a legitimate position and the respect that went with it. No one expecting compensation for their chivalry, but giving it because it was your due.

The children were already squirming in their seats under the watchful eye of Aylria.

"I am hungwy!" protested Dzhon. "Can I eat?"

"As soon as Lady Lydima sits. Then you may eat," instructed Aylria.

"Wydima, sit!" Dzhon called loudly, and banged his spoon.

Several of the diners chuckled, and Lydima smiled. She made a dramatic show of sitting and bowed to

Dzhon. "You may begin."

He quickly gobbled up a piece of meat.

On her other side, Yoused asked quietly, "Is the older girl the one in question?"

"Yes," Lydima answered softly.

Saley was dressed in a simple dress and apron, with her shiny, clean hair combed and braided tightly. Her wide blue eyes and clear forehead gave her a particularly innocent and vulnerable look. Lydima gave Aylria credit for strategically dressing the children for dinner. They all were looking their best. She would have to remember to thank her later.

Yoused looked at Saley and his lips formed a hard, thin line. "She will not go back there, I promise you," he vowed firmly.

"Thank you!" Lydima's eyes shone, and this time she did cover his hand with hers, but out of true gratitude, not flirtatiousness.

Yoused caught his breath, and confusion appeared on his face. Lydima looked at him with concern. Afraid she may have communicated something other than she intended, she withdrew her hand.

Yoused asked after the baby.

"Lylie is doing very well, in spite of me," she laughed. "You must see her later. She has grown since you rescued me with your knowledge of babies."

He nodded, but grew silent.

The children absorbed her attention for a while, but they soon finished eating and were anxious to be dismissed. Nyla rose to take her shift with Saley and followed the children upstairs.

∞∞∞

Yoused observed Lydima closely as she interacted with her young charges. Her expression was open

149

and unguarded, and she showed genuine concern and affection for the youngsters.

She seemed a completely different woman than when he had first met her. Her outward persona at that time had felt like a mask. He had wanted to rip it off, to see the woman underneath, but did not know how, so he had sent her away rather than become entangled with her for the wrong motives. The young orphans she was caring for had done what he could not.

Now, he had to consider his next steps very carefully. The more immediate concern of what to do with the girl, Saley, and The White Lily must be dealt with first. Once that issue was taken care of satisfactorily, what did he want to do about the enigma sitting next to him?

He knew what part of him wanted to do, of course. As did every other man, he had always found her extremely attractive. However, he was an all-or-nothing type of lover, and he would want her heart as well as her body. That was what held him back, then and now. Could she ever be interested in him for himself, not just his wealth and position? With their age difference, it didn't seem possible.

Her previous experiences with men would be an inhibiting factor also. She had known too many men like Valryn and his clientele to let her guard down completely. The mask could easily be picked up again. Could he make her believe that he valued her for more than her appearance? Did he care enough to leave himself open to rejection again? Or worse, could he expose himself to the possibility that she would accept him, but for the wrong reasons?

Lydima turned her attention back to her guest now that the children had been excused. They conversed pleasantly about various subjects until the meal was over. When they rose to say goodnight, she gave him what he was sure was a warm, genuine smile, and his heart did a flip.

As he watched her leave, he longed to run after her and take her in his arms, to make her accept him as her protector, her shield from the harsh world she had had to face alone all these years. To be to her what she was trying to be for those children. Oh yes, he cared enough. Absolutely, he cared enough. When the time was right, he would take the risk, but he must prove himself first.

CHAPTER TWELVE

Three days after Talia's meeting with the Chief, Zariana knocked on the healer's door. Talia was grateful for the distraction. Janis and Stelan had continued their language lessons, and Talia had interpreted occasionally when they were discussing a more complicated concept. The atmosphere was a little strained. Both she and Stelan were trying too hard to behave as if there was nothing between them.

After a nod from Talia, Janis opened the door and the Chief's daughter, still dressed in her street urchin garb, entered the room. She addressed herself to the Berushese warrior.

"General Riash and his men are systematically searching the city, one house at a time. We believe they will be here today. I have come to move you to a safer location."

"The man is not yet able to be moved. His wounds still need constant care," interjected Janis. She knew Stelan's name by now, but wasn't sure if Zariana did.

"If the soldiers find him, they will move him, ready or not."

"They will not," grinned Janis. "I am not without my own resources. The man will be safe with me. They are looking for two, not one. Take the lady, and I will look after him," she inclined her head toward Stelan's cot.

Zariana looked to Talia for her opinion. "We have a cart for him to ride in," Zariana argued, "But it will attract attention if it waits too long. It is up to you."

Stelan was healing well, but moving around too soon might reopen his injuries. The risk of discovery by a patrol while driving around in a cart seemed almost as great as remaining in Janis' house.

"He will stay here. I will come with you." She picked up her rag-and-bone pack and stuck her dagger in her boot.

Zariana appeared skeptical, but didn't question the decision. She merely shrugged and turned toward the door.

"Stop by the last house on the left, with the blue door, and tell the woman who answers that I need to borrow Gashpar again," Janis instructed Talia, who acknowledged the request with a dip of the head.

"I will be back," she threw at Stelan in Berushese, and they were gone.

∞∞∞

As soon as Talia left, Janis went quickly to work. She brought Stelan a loose shirt and trousers to cover up his wounds. He was healed enough that he could wear clothes over the scabs and remaining bandages. She set another chamber pot by Talia's pallet on the floor. Then she brought Stelan a leather flask filled with hot liquid, which she placed behind his back. Next, she wrapped a hot stone from the stove in a towel and stuck it between his feet.

154

Stelan became warm very quickly, and began to perspire. He didn't complain, since he knew she must have a reason for what she was doing, but he was extremely uncomfortable.

A light rap sounded at the door. "It is me, Gashpar," said a youngish voice.

Stelan was able to understand this simple sentence thanks to Janis' lessons.

She opened the door and a young boy of eight or nine entered the room. He went right over to Stelan's chamber pot and to the lord's great surprise, stuck his fingers in his throat and vomited into it. The boy then skipped over to the pallet where Janis had another hot flask and stone ready for him. She gave him some food and drink, which he gobbled down enthusiastically, then laid down under the blankets. Stelan gathered that they had enacted this little routine before.

Janis gave Stelan instructions that he was to pretend to sleep when anyone came to the door. "If they try to wake you, pretend to be delirious and keep your eyes closed." She mimed what she wanted him to do so he would understand.

Throughout the day, she reheated the stones and flasks, and with the added stench from the boy's vomit, Stelan began to feel that he really would become sick. By late afternoon, he was drenched with sweat and becoming nauseous. Janis brought him some water and he gulped it down.

Finally, in the early evening, they started hearing commotion down the street. There was the sound of fists pounding on doors and residents protesting the intrusion. Janis had assured them that the tanning community would close ranks against the heavy-handed tactics of the Cerecian authorities, but he was still nervous that someone might say something that would give them away. The healer's door protested with loud creaks as someone hammered on it insistently. Stelan closed his eyes.

"Coming!" Janis called. "You do not have to splinter the wood." She opened the sliding peep hole.

"Open up," demanded a soldier at the door. "We are searching for two fugitives from the fortress."

Janis threw open the door and waved him in. "Look all you want. All I have currently are fever patients."

The soldier stepped over the threshold and made a noise of disgust at the rancid smell. The fumes from the tannery were bad enough, but inside the warm, closed room it was almost unbearable. On cue, Stelan heard Gashpar lean over pitifully and throw up into the pot next to his pallet.

The soldier's footsteps never approached the boy, but turned toward the cot where Stelan was resting. After a tense moment of silent scrutiny, he quickly searched the rest of the house and practically ran out the door.

Once the door was securely barred again, Janis chuckled and removed the hot flasks and stones. Then she brought her 'fever patients' some dinner, changed their drenched bedclothes, and emptied the bedpans.

Gashpar would spend the night, just in case any soldiers were still around. His mother would be repaid for his charade with a pot of liniment for her back pain. Gashpar seemed to heartily enjoy the whole episode, and being encouraged to put his dubious skills to use was payment enough.

Now that the immediate danger was past, Stelan relaxed. Janis told Gashpar stories until he fell asleep, and Stelan listened to as much of it as he could understand. He was worried about Talia, but he knew she could take care of herself, and he tried to put her out of his mind. Eventually, he fell into a restless sleep.

∞∞∞

Zariana dismissed the cart, and once again the two females wove their way sporadically across Herida. This time, the girl led the fugitive to a wealthy part of the city where a fortunate few still had the money to buy whatever they wanted to eat. Most of the residents of this area were close friends and confidants of King Chysh. Zariana pointed out the small palace where the king stayed when he came to the city.

They turned into an opulent courtyard decorated with exotic plants in the finest urns and pots. The entire yard was covered in beautiful tiles forming an elaborate mosaic. Talia was impressed. The Chief did indeed have eyes in almost every section of Herida.

"This house belongs to the widow of a lord who opposed Chysh's rise to the throne. He led an unsuccessful revolt against him, and the king had him beheaded. Lady Parisha was allowed to keep most of her property only because she is the king's cousin."

Talia was unable to reply as a servant came out to meet them and ushered them into a small receiving room. An elegant, stately woman rose from behind a desk. She was swathed in rich fabrics draped stunningly over soft skin and supple arms. Her black hair was elaborately dressed, and glints of gold and gemstones sparkled between the curls and braids. Gold bracelets tinkled against each other as she moved. She was a handsome woman, as tall as Talia, and she walked around her in a circle appraisingly.

"Yes," she spoke mostly to herself. "Yes, you will

do." She scrutinized Talia's face carefully. "We can work with this." She waved at Zariana in a dismissive motion.

The Chief's daughter made a dramatic, sweeping bow and backed out of the room. Talia began to have even more admiration for Stelan's patience during his captivity. She had less than he, and did not like being ignorant of what was going on.

"What will I do exactly?"

Lady Parisha smiled. "It is my understanding that you are here to learn as much as you can about the situation in Cerecia, and you need to keep out of the way of the patrols. I could hide you in a closet all day, but I assume you would prefer to do something more productive." She indicated that Talia should follow her as she continued, "I am entertaining a few important officials this evening, and you will help serve at the dinner. You may be able to learn something useful."

"I am known by General Riash and most of the members of the garrison." Talia frowned.

"He is not on the guest list, but even if he were, he would not recognize you when I am through with you." The lady led her into a room where several other ladies were dressing. She called to one of them, and the woman came over and scrutinized the newcomer. "This is the one I told you about, Enida. Get her prepared for this evening."

"She will need a bath first," the woman looked at Talia like she was a dog dragged in off the street, though her ear showed the piercings that marked a Cerecian slave. Evidently, she was highly regarded.

"Everything. She must look like a new person."

Enida grimaced and got to work. Talia was taken to a large washroom and given a warm bath in the largest tub she had ever seen. When the bath was finished, scented oils were rubbed all over her hair and body. This was not normally something she indulged in, but she tried to relax and enjoy the pampering.

Enida tsked at the scars on her upper arms. "We will have to cover those up." The costumes worn by Cerecian women for formal occasions often displayed bare arms.

Two other ladies came in to help with her long hair. One of the women twisted some thread and used it to shape her eyebrows by pulling out excess hairs. Talia had a high tolerance for pain, and didn't flinch, but she wondered that women would regularly submit to this type of torture for the sake of beauty. She hadn't put this much work into her appearance for her own brother's marriage feast.

A long, white robe was pulled over her head, and shimmering blue fabric was artistically pinned on top of it. The corners were brought up and tied in loose knots around her elbows, and gold clasps expertly held the material together over her scars. Then a gold-colored sash was tied around her waist. Lastly, her face was painted, eyes lined and lips colored. When they stood her in front of a long mirror, she did not know herself.

Lady Parisha returned and smiled approvingly as she beheld Talia's transformation. Then she took Talia for a walk on the rooftop garden and gave her a brief summary of all the guests and their backgrounds.

"The one you will want to stick close to is Lord Tharch. He is very close to King Chysh, and does a lot of his dirty work."

"Why are you helping me?" Talia usually tried to keep to her own business, but she couldn't help asking.

Parisha studied Talia for a moment and seemed to come to a decision.

"I am for anything that will cause problems for my cousin. To see him dethroned is my ultimate goal." There was a smoldering fire in her eyes as she spoke. "He is a ruthless, power-hungry despot. I am not helping you as much as I am trying to undermine him. Unchecked, he will ride this country into the ground."

"That is why you are working with the Chief?"

Parisha glanced around furtively. "Hush now, we must speak no more of this. Not all of my servants can be trusted. I am sure Chysh has ears among them."

Talia was shown into the hall, and she and several other similarly dressed ladies were given instructions from the steward on serving the dinner. Fortunately, Talia had some prior knowledge about Cerecian banquet etiquette, so the concepts were not completely foreign. In the middle of the preparations, a manservant rushed in and whispered something to the steward. He widened his eyes slightly and then ordered another place at the table next to Lord Tharch. Then he had a couple of candelabras moved to different positions.

"You there," he beckoned to Talia. "My lady has instructed that you are to be serving Lord Tharch. He has just sent word that Princess Bashalis is in his company. Have you been in her presence before?"

"No, I have not."

"You must be careful not to take any notice of her appearance or give the impression that there is anything unusual about her." The steward looked at her sharply. "Do you understand?"

"Yes, I understand," Talia bowed her acknowledgement.

She had heard rumors that there was something

different about the princess, but nothing specific. Soon everything was ready for the party, and guests began to arrive. Everyone was dressed lavishly with what Talia viewed as a ridiculous display of wealth. In Berush, the wealthy, and even the royalty, dressed with practical simplicity.

Lord Tharch and the princess were the last to arrive. Talia's training did not fail her, and she showed no change in expression as she took in the girl's unusual coloring. Though she looked to be in her late teens, Bashalis' hair was pure white, her skin was a very pale pink, and her light blue eyes were so clear that they had a reddish tint to them. Lord Tharch led the princess to her seat, and Talia poured wine for them as soon as they were seated.

As the meal progressed, Talia served the meal flawlessly, mimicking the movements of the other servers. In contrast to her normal bearing, she tried to be more fluid and graceful. She listened intently to the conversation, but other than complaints at the price of goods, the talk was somewhat stilted.

"My lord, what plans does our king have for getting back at the Artylians for what they did to us in the channel?" Talia's ears perked up.

Tharch laughed. "Just you wait. Our army is testing some new weapons that have the potential to decimate the enemy in battle. Next time we meet them, the outcome will be different I assure you."

This declaration was met with cheers.

"Though you know," Tharch continued. "The real threat is Berush. It was King Cyrus who was behind our defeat."

"Those barbarians!" snorted another guest derisively.

Talia thought this rather hypocritical, since Cerecia was the aggressor in every incident for the last hundred years, and their tactics were more barbaric than those of Berush. At least Berushese law was straightforward and fair. Cerecian law was enforced almost arbitrarily, based on the whim of whoever had the biggest stick.

"Is it not barbaric to attempt to take by force something that does not belong to you?"

Princess Bashalis' timid voice was heard for the first time, but her tone held a hint of irony. Talia suspected there were hidden depths there.

"You do not know of what you speak," reproved Tharch harshly. "Take care, or you will be suspected of sympathizing with the opposition."

"Speaking of opposition," broke in Parisha, "What is the latest news on the spies who escaped from the fortress?"

"I expect General Riash at any moment to give me his report. That is part of the reason for my visit, to look into this debacle. Chysh will have Riash's head if he does not find them."

Talia shifted her feet nervously, and hoped that her appearance was enough altered that she wouldn't be recognized. Since the candles had been moved, the light was dimmest near the princess, which would be beneficial in obscuring her identity.

At that moment, a servant entered and announced the general. Riash strode into the room in full armor, and the candlelight reflected off the polished metal of his breastplate. Bashalis had to bring her hand to her sensitive eyes to shield them from the light. The general bowed to the assembly, and Lord Tharch rose from his seat.

"Lady Parisha, is there somewhere the general and I may speak privately?"

"Certainly, my steward will show you to the study." The men followed the steward out of the room. Riash didn't even glance Talia's way.

Talia was wishing she could contrive an excuse to follow them when Bashalis spoke again.

"Parisha, my eyes are tired and could do with a walk in the starlight on the roof, if you will excuse me?"

"Of course. Would you like me to accompany you?"

"No, thank you. I want to be alone for a while."

"At least take one of the servants to be within call in case you need something."

"Very well."

Parisha signaled to Talia to follow the princess. This was quick thinking on Parisha's part. When they arrived on the roof, Talia could position herself above the study and perhaps hear something through the window.

Bashalis had obviously been to Lady Parisha's house before, and she found her way unerringly to the rooftop. She sighed and stood leaning on the wall looking out at the city.

Talia stood silently nearby, straining her ears to hear the men's conversation. She didn't have to work hard to hear them. Lord Tharch was yelling at Riash, and she could clearly hear them from the wall over the room.

"You were completely taken in! How could you let a spy into your ranks?"

Riash's reply was muffled, but he rehearsed the credentials he had been given.

"You did not think to verify her claims?"

Again, the general's reply was muffled.

"She is *not* Dachede's granddaughter. He and his people have cleared out. We suspect they have escaped to Berush."

The general's curse was clear enough to hear. "The spies will not escape! We will find them."

"If they are not already gone."

Talia tried to catch the rest of the conversation. The men were saying something about the roads being watched. The princess' voice at her elbow startled her.

"My betrothed is very forceful is he not?"

Talia did not believe Bashalis really wanted an answer, so she remained silent. She felt sorry for Bashalis if she had to marry this man. Perhaps this was the real meaning behind her comment about taking things by force. The union was not her choice.

"I must marry him to please my brother."

Her words confirmed Talia's surmise, as if she had read her thoughts.

"They are very alike. All they really care about is destroying everything beautiful." She gazed up at the stars as she spoke. "On the way here, we stopped to see the new weapons tested that he spoke of. It was terrible. They blew up a herd of cattle. Blood splattered everywhere. Not all of them died. Some of them were badly hurt and lowed so mournfully I could not bear it. Chysh and Tharch just laughed. They thought it was great sport."

Talia was so shocked that she forgot herself. "Blew up?" she queried, "What does this mean?"

Bashalis didn't seem to mind that Talia asked a question. "They put some of their fire potion into sealed containers and lit them from a distance with a special cord of some kind." The princess' voice had a far-away, dreamlike quality to it. Her deep sadness was so palatable that Talia began to feel affected herself. "When the fire reached the container, it burst into countless pieces and flew outward, hitting the cattle."

Talia wanted to ask more questions. How far did the debris travel? How many cattle were there? How big was the container? What was the cord made of? But she dared not draw attention to herself by being too inquisitive. Already she had learned more than she ever dreamed she would, and from a completely unexpected source. She followed the princess' example and stared out over the wall.

"I am tired. I will go and wait for Tharch to be ready to leave." Bashalis turned and walked away, and Talia followed.

∞∞∞

The next morning, Talia scrubbed the paint from her face and took out all of her braids. When she left the house, she must be able to blend back into the crowded streets. Parisha had made sure that her own clothes were ready for her to put on again. Her eyebrows were the only thing that could not be returned to normal.

Zariana arrived very early in the morning, and Talia didn't get a chance to say goodbye to Parisha. "Thank her for me, when you see her again," she instructed the Chief's daughter when they returned to the healer's house.

Zariana told Talia to stay back while she knocked on the door.

Janis opened it when she saw who was there. "All is well," she assured the girl who beckoned to Talia.

"My father would like to retain your services against future need," Zariana told the healer, and she held out a small bag of coins. "He is impressed with your resourcefulness and reliability."

Janis looked at the bag and considered for a moment before accepting it. "I will do what I may. I am getting old, you know."

Zariana nodded and took her leave.

Talia was more relieved than she could say to see that Stelan had not been dragged off by the general's soldiers. He made her laugh with the story of Gashpar and his vomit.

"Is the boy often employed in this manner?" she asked Janis.

"Once in a while a tanner gets in trouble and has to lay low until things blow over. Like I said, we stick together around here."

When Janis was called away to assist in a birthing, Talia told Stelan what she had learned at Lady Parisha's. His face was grim. He didn't pressure her again to leave without him, but she knew he was thinking it. There was no way around it, what they were doing was dangerous. Every option they had involved some element of risk. She was following the plan she felt had the best chance of success.

"In case we are separated, or something happens, you must be able to report what we have learned." Over his protests, she made him memorize the process for creating 'magic fire' and repeat it back to her. Then she made sure he could repeat what the princess had said about the new weapon.

When he was able to recite everything to Talia's satisfaction, she and Stelan sat and stared at the wall. Her thoughts began to turn morbid. She wondered if they would even make it home alive. If not, all her effort to resist Stelan would be sand in the wind.

She got up and walked over to study Janis' map and tried to deduce the likely location of the weapon testing site. After she had exhausted this resource, she turned and leaned against the table, deep in thought.

"What have you done to your eyebrows?" Stelan asked.

Talia laughed.

CHAPTER THIRTEEN

Yoused left Freosyd the next morning and returned to his own holding. Without letting anyone know what he was planning, he arranged to take an armed escort of his most trusted soldiers to the port to raid The White Lily. They rode through the night and arrived at the door of the inn with the first light of dawn. He signaled his captain to knock on the door, while four of the soldiers went around the back to guard the rear exit.

After what seemed like an excessively long wait, a woman finally opened the door.

"It is a little early for business, my lord, but I am sure we can accommodate you," she said seductively. She stuck a leg out from under the folds of her silken robe to show she had nothing on underneath.

"Our business is with the proprietor, Valryn. Where is he?"

The woman gaped at him. "He is still abed."

"Well then, we shall wake him up." Turning to his captain, Yoused commanded, "Search the house for evidence of anyone held against their will or any young children."

The captain pushed past the woman, and Yoused followed with the rest of his soldiers. Valryn employed one male servant, a large, burly muscle-man with little intellectual ability. He tried to prevent the soldiers from entering and got several good punches in before he was subdued.

Yoused and his men looked in every corner, every closet, every cupboard and wardrobe. They surprised several of Valryn's working women, in various stages of undress. Every bed was upended, and other than a few lingering customers, all appeared as one might expect in such an establishment.

"What do you think you are doing?"

Yoused heard Valryn's bluster down the second floor passage and went out to meet him.

"You will ruin my business! No one will come here if they do not believe their visits will be kept confidential!"

"We are not after your clientele." Yoused's disdain was evident. "I am here to verify your statements while investigating your claim."

"I am not sure what you mean."

"According to your contract, the girl, Kandys, has been working for you for three years. What kind of work has she been doing?"

"Helping in the kitchen, cleaning, that sort of thing," he shrugged and smiled.

"She has not yet received clients?" Yoused could hardly get out the question.

"No."

"At what age do they normally begin?"

"It depends." Valryn grinned widely.

Yoused wanted to knock all his teeth out. He really didn't want to know any more, but he had to keep asking questions until he found a good reason to revoke Valryn's license or throw him in prison.

"Cease from trying my patience and answer the question."

"The first time is a special event. It commands a steep price."

"Let me be very clear about this. According to the law, an indentured servant must be released from their contract in the same condition in which they entered it. In my interpretation, this includes their state of innocence. If I find that you have not told me the truth, you will be the one paying the steep price."

Valryn's eyes narrowed. "The law has never been enforced that way in the past."

"It will be now."

"You cannot do this," the vile man protested through clenched teeth.

"I think you will find that I can. Do not push me."

"My lord!"

One of Yoused's men called to him from the ground floor. He turned on his heel and hurried down the stairs.

"The floorboards squeaked and I pulled back the rug to find a trapdoor to a second cellar." The root cellar had already been searched, and nothing suspicious was found.

Yoused grabbed a lamp from a table and cautiously descended the ladder into a dark space below. What he saw sickened him. Into the wooden joists holding up the walls of the small cellar were set several pairs of shackles, some of them very small. A few battered dishes lay scattered on the floor, and in one corner was a rag doll.

"Throw that fellow down here!"

Valryn scrambled quickly down the ladder before anyone could obey Yoused's order. Yoused grabbed him by the collar and shook him.

"Where are the children you have been keeping down here?"

"There are no children. Some men like to see the women down here."

Yoused was getting tired of this vermin's smirk. He shoved Valryn toward his captain, who had followed him below. "Chain him up to his own manacles while we finish the search." He ascended the ladder and stood in thought. "Take down the clients' names and let them go. Search the house again, this time for any documents you can find."

While his men searched, Yoused went over to a desk in a corner of the room. In one of the drawers was a ledger. Valryn seemed to be quite a skilled businessman. Not only could he read and write and draw up what could pass for legal documents, he also kept a very detailed list of transactions going back many years. It looked like this was just the most current volume. There must be more around somewhere.

Yoused flipped through the book. Each page had four columns. The first contained a date, the next two contained initials, and the fourth a number. He noticed that the initials in the third column occurred on a more frequent basis. It appeared that there were only ten unique sets of initials in that column. There were nine women in the inn that morning. That column must represent the woman involved in the transaction.

The numbers in the fourth column looked like payments. Occasionally there was a cryptic notation in place of a monetary amount. Yoused assumed there was an alternate method of payment in these instances.

He turned to the last page of the book and worked backward. He didn't have to go far. On the next to the last page was an entry with a new set of initials in the third column. The price in the fourth column was nearly a hundred times that of the other entries. The date coincided with the day that the girl had reportedly run away. He wished he had a way to figure out who the client's initials stood for.

One of his soldiers entered the room with a sheaf of papers. "Here, my lord. We found these in Valryn's room upstairs."

Yoused took the papers. Among them were several drafts of contracts of servitude. Two of them were for a boy and girl younger than Kandys. They weren't signed, but they were dated several months in the past. Now he had all the proof he needed.

"Drag him back up," he shouted to his captain. The innkeeper's head soon appeared in the opening and he climbed out of the hole hastened by the point of the captain's sword. "I will ask you again, where are the other two children, the ones you were forging these contracts for?"

Valryn knew he was caught now, but he refused to answer. He merely smirked.

"Tie him up and take him to the manor," directed Yoused with disgust. Two of his soldiers complied and escorted the man away.

Yoused then went to speak with each of the women personally. He intended to see them separately and try to find out the location of the missing children. If he spoke to them as a group, he was afraid none of them would want to talk.

"Your employer, Valryn, is gone and will not be back," he told the first woman.

Shock, concern, and fear played across her face.

"The inn will be closed, and its license revoked, but you are free to stay here as long as you need to. I will help you find employment in another line of work."

To himself, he thought he would need to seek Lydima's advice on how to approach this.

"What is your name?"

The woman stared at the floor and refused to answer.

"Where are the other children?"

There was no response other than fear and trembling. The succeeding interviews followed the same pattern.

A few of them sullenly told him their names, but none of them would say anything about the boy and girl mentioned in the documents. They all appeared scared. Valryn's influence would not be easily erased. As an afterthought, he asked his last interviewee about the tenth woman in the ledger.

"She left yesterday," the woman shrugged, then snapped her mouth shut.

"Where did she go?"

The woman looked away.

Yoused left her and stood in the passage lost in thought. He remembered how Kandys' mother had been sent to recruit Lydima on the road. Evidently Valryn had trusted some of his 'employees' to carry out certain tasks for him outside of the inn. Could Valryn have sent the tenth woman to do something for him? Was she watching the other children somewhere? He called his captain again.

"Set a watch on the inn. If anyone visits, or attempts to communicate with anyone inside, follow them. If any of the current residents leave, follow them. You will need to have several people watching. We must find these missing children."

∞∞∞

Reyla walked wearily toward Freosyd Castle in the early morning fog. The cook had let her go home to visit her parents for a few days, but she was due back. The kitchen work was tiring, but it paid well.

Her parents were too old to work, and the money she earned helped to take care of them. Her own needs were often set aside so they could eat. She could walk in boots that pinched her feet as long as she knew mother and father were all right.

The dense mist muffled the sound of her footsteps. Still, it almost sounded like they had an echo. She turned to look behind her, but it was too late.

A hand clamped over her mouth, and a knife silently slit her throat. Her body was dragged into the woods by the side of the road and covered with fallen leaves. The killer quickly changed from blood-spattered clothes to clean ones from a pack, then stuffed the soiled clothing under a bush. Once more, soft footsteps could be heard padding toward the castle.

∞∞∞

"Tell me again, how do you happen to be here, Mariya?" The cook still didn't understand why this strange woman had shown up in her kitchen.

"Reyla was unable to return today, and she asked me to work a few days for her."

"I suppose her parents took a turn for the worse?"

The new maid shrugged.

"Well, I need the help, either way. I suppose you know how to work in a kitchen?"

"A little. I can follow directions."

"Humph. That is a rare thing. All right then, you can start by washing and slicing these carrots."

The woman took the carrots and got to work. She

had to be shown a few things, like how thinly to slice the vegetables, but overall, her work was satisfactory. The cook could find no reason to complain. At least the new kitchen maid didn't chatter her ear off like all the younger girls did. Still, something about the situation bothered her, and she didn't know what.

∞∞∞

Later in the afternoon, Mariya carried a basket of peelings out to the pigpen. Byden saw her and frowned. He knew almost everyone within riding distance of the castle, and this woman was not one he recognized. His eyesight wasn't the best anymore, but even though the details were fuzzy, the woman's gait appeared unusually provocative from across the courtyard.

That in itself was not a major cause for concern. Many women walked that way. He had even seen Lady Lydima swing her hips that way in the past, but it was not behavior that Lady Eemya encouraged. He made a note to look into her identity when he was through with his watch.

∞∞∞

Mariya worked hard in the kitchen all day. When the evening meal was finally over, and all the pots were cleaned, she was dismissed to the servants' quarters. There, she listened to the other maids gossip and talk. Pretending to be asleep, to avoid being questioned herself, she was able to learn almost everything she needed to know. It was going to be too easy. 'Good' people were so gullible.

All she had to do was avoid the Lydima woman. She was the only one who might suspect her. Like would always recognize like. She would know what Mariya really was.

After a long day's work, it was easy for her to quit the pretense and truly fall asleep. She slept with a satisfied smile on her face.

∞∞∞

By the time Byden finished his shift and ate his own dinner, the kitchen staff had already retired. The servants in the hall kept later hours and cleaned up after the diners.

There was no rush. He could look into the new maid's origins tomorrow.

∞∞∞

Early the next morning, the soldiers watching The White Lily were finally rewarded by seeing one of the women sneak out the back of the building with a basket. Two of them followed her at a discrete distance, one after the other. They didn't have to follow her very far. The woman carried the basket down an alley to a shed behind an abandoned warehouse. She unbarred the door and opened it. The soldiers took that moment to apprehend her.

"Hold her while I look inside," ordered the senior guard. It took a moment for his eyes to adjust to the darkness, but he soon saw that he was not alone. Two small figures huddled in a corner. "Come on, we are here to help you," he said reassuringly.

When they didn't move, he held out the basket to them. He set it on the floor, and tiny hands reached timidly forward to empty it of the food. When they had finished eating, the guard held out his hand and tried again. He could always pick them up and carry them, but that would be a last resort. If he could avoid causing them additional trauma, he would.

"Come with me. You are safe now. We will take you to your sister."

That did the trick, and the frightened young children followed him out into the yellow light of dawn. Bedraggled and filthy, with stringy hair and grimy hands, what appeared to be two small girls emerged from the shack into a freedom that was as yet incomprehensible.

∞∞∞

Youset was overjoyed to hear the news that the children had been found. He thought of how happy Lydima would be that everything was resolved satisfactorily.

The guards had brought them up to the manor and handed them over to the housekeeper. She turned up her nose at their condition, but took them in hand and gave them a thorough scrubbing. Very quickly, she sought Youset out, frazzled and perturbed. It looked like the entire front of her dress had been splashed in water.

"The older one is a boy, my lord."

"Oh, is he?" He had seen them briefly when they had been brought in. Due to finding the contracts, he had expected a boy and a girl and had been surprised to see two girls instead. The boy's long hair had been braided like a girl's, and he had been wearing a dress. Short dresses were common for toddlers, but not boys of his age. Why would Valryn have dressed him like a girl?

"He put on the clothes we gave him, but we tried to cut his hair and he screamed and thrashed so that it was impossible."

"The boy has undoubtedly been through some terrible ordeals. We will leave it alone for now and give him some time to adjust."

"Yes, my lord." The housekeeper curtseyed and left.

Yoused wanted to pack the children up and take them to Freosyd immediately, but first he had to decide what to do about Valryn. There was no prison system on the island. Most offenses were taken care of by paying fines or providing restitution. Neither option would work for this situation.

Yoused felt guilty that he had let The White Lily exist this long. How did one justify allowing such a den of evil to continue? He could only tell himself he didn't know it was that bad. A man had a right to do what he wanted with his own time, and Yoused hadn't thought it his business to interfere, but he had never viewed it from the woman's perspective before. Indentured servitude, or a job that payed only your room and board, was just as bad as outright slavery. Everyone needed to have a choice.

The search of the premises had uncovered a large amount of opium as well. The women who worked there were already complaining to the guards that they needed their 'medicine.' By keeping them hooked to the drug, Valryn had made it even more impossible for any of them to leave, or want to leave, his employ. Without their daily dose, they were becoming ill, and Yoused had had to send a healer to help them through the transition.

He considered calling the island lords together to ask their opinions, but there were none among them whose judgment he respected more than his own. Berushese law was reputed to mete out harsher punishments than Artylian, and he was leaning toward sending Valryn to Tomus and the council for consideration. It would be a good opportunity to bring up the subject of indentureship and propose changes or clarifications to the law that would prevent the kind of abuses Valryn had perpetrated. In order to do that, he would have to go himself, and he was loath to leave with his feelings for Lady Lydima undeclared.

As he was ruminating over these things, he remembered that the tenth woman was still missing. The children had been left unguarded, locked up, but alone. She was not with them. Where was she? His brow furrowed as he racked his brain to figure out where she might have gone. Then it hit him. Valryn still wanted the other girl who he considered to be his property. He had failed in bullying Lydima to surrender her, so he might have sent one of his women to try and retrieve her. Freosyd had to be warned! Lydima needed to be warned! He must leave immediately.

Rather than subject Saley's siblings to a frenzied ride that would last into the night, he left instructions for the children to be brought by wagon the next day. So confident was he that his surmise was correct that he didn't even bother to task Valryn with it. The man would most likely refuse to answer anyway, and he would waste precious time trying to persuade him. Leaving the villain under heavy guard, he took several of his men and rode north as fast as his horse would gallop.

∞∞∞

Byden had been kept busy all morning and finally made his way to the kitchen after noon. The new maid was not in evidence, so he asked the cook about her and heard the story. Instead of waiting for the maid to return, he went in search of Palyn and asked him to ride over to Reyla's parents' house and verify the story. He was sure everything was fine, but it didn't hurt to check. The fact that he had never seen the woman before still worried him in the back of his mind.

∞∞∞

Mariya was being careful to avoid Lydima and Kandys until she found an opportunity to steal her away. She had learned that Saley, as they were calling her, was never alone. Luckily, she had come prepared for that. This evening, she would make her move. Valryn would be extremely pleased with her.

∞∞∞

That night, after Lydima had said goodnight to Saley, Aylria took a shift watching her. She was pleased to see that the girl had put on some weight, her skin had less pallor and her cheeks were a healthy pink. A knock sounded on the door, and she opened it to a maid she had not seen before.

"Good evening! I thought the girl might like some warm milk to help her sleep." She handed a mug to the girl who took it with wide eyes. "Here is some dandelion tea for you," and she held out a cup to Aylria, who took it gratefully.

"Thank you. That is very thoughtful. Are you new here?"

"I am just filling in for a few days."

Aylria nodded as the woman left the room and began to sip her tea. It had an unusual, but not unpleasant, flavor. Saley was staring at her rather disconcertingly, but she was a strange child who had been through a lot, and Aylria tried not to be offended.

As she continued to sip her tea, she began to feel sleepy. She tried to fight it off and stay awake, but darkness began to encroach on the edges of her vision. There was a very important reason why she wasn't supposed to sleep, but she just couldn't remember what it was. Eventually, her eyes closed and her head began to nod. She fell out of her chair onto the floor, breathing shallowly.

Not long after that, the door opened again. "Playing the mute, eh, Kandys? That is good. Then Valryn will not have to cut your tongue out. Come with me. Tye and Mya are waiting."

Silently and solemnly, Saley padded past the drugged Aylria and followed the woman into the passage.

∞∞∞

Close to midnight, Yoused rode up to the gates of Freosyd. The doors were closed for the night, but they were opened immediately for the acting governor. Upon inquiry, he was told that there was nothing amiss. Relieved, he asked to speak to Jayred and Byden. They were quickly rousted out of bed and met him in the hall.

"There is one of Valryn's women still unaccounted for. I suspect she will try to steal away the girl for him. Have you had any newcomers to the castle in the last two days?"

"Do you have a description?" asked Jayred, but Yoused's attention went to Byden who had suddenly become pale.

"What is it?" Yoused questioned with urgency in his voice.

"A new kitchen maid showed up yesterday. I inquired about her this afternoon and found out she had replaced Reyla temporarily. I then sent Palyn to verify this, but he has not yet returned."

"Go find this woman and bring her to me without delay." Byden set off to search for her, but as he reached the door, it opened to admit Palyn.

"My lord," he bowed, seeing Youlsed, but Byden bade him speak with an impatient bark. "When I arrived at Reyla's parents' house, I found that she was not there. She had left yesterday morning for the castle as planned. I took the liberty of forming a search party. The headman of her village has a hunting hound, and he easily traced her scent. We found her hidden in the forest halfway here with her throat cut."

The men received this news with grim expressions, but sprang instantly into action. "I will muster the men," said Byden. "We will search the castle from top to bottom starting with the maids' quarters. The girl, Saley, was with Lady Lydima when the gates closed, so the woman must still be here," he said as he left to implement his plan.

Jayred turned on his heel. "I will check on the girl and wake Lady Lydima. We will need to place Saley under heavier guard." Youlsed followed close behind him.

When they reached the second floor passage they could see that the girl's bedroom door was ajar. Rushing in, they found Aylria passed out on the floor, but alive. Saley was gone. Youlsed felt the bed where the girl had lain. It was cold. There was no telling how much of a head start they had.

Jayred checked to make sure Aylria was still breathing. "Fetch Yula," he instructed a servant who had followed them.

"I passed no one on the road. Where could they go?" Yoused inquired.

"They cannot have gone out the main gate. We have had guards posted at all the gates since Valryn's visit. They must still be in the castle. Lady Lydima must be informed." Jayred took a deep breath and headed down the hall.

∞∞∞

Since becoming a surrogate mother to an infant and three young children, Lydima had also become a light sleeper, and she answered Jayred's knock almost immediately with a robe already thrown around her shoulders. "What is it?"

Jayred told her.

"No!" She rushed past Yoused without even registering his presence and arrived in Saley's room right after Yula. The healer bent to tend the lady-in-waiting, and Lydima pulled up in front of the empty bed with a cry of anguish.

"We will find her, my lady. She cannot have gone far," assured the steward. "Fortunately, Lord Yoused brought us warning before much time had passed."

Lydima turned around and finally noticed him. "Lord Yoused. How did you know this would happen?"

"I did not know, but I feared an attempt might be made." He described to her the raid on The White Lily, the state of the women, and the finding of the young boy and girl.

"You found them?" Lydima clutched his arm.

"Yes, we found them." He patted her hand and smiled. "They will be here tomorrow."

"We must find Saley before they arrive!"

Yoused explained to her about the ledger and the

missing woman. "Byden went to organize a search of the castle. We can go and await news in the hall."

"First I will check the rooms of the children and my ladies myself to try and minimize any disturbance."

As she spoke a couple of soldiers reached the passage. Lydima instructed them to wait by the door of each room as she searched it in case she needed assistance.

Quietly she entered the chamber where the nurse and Lylie were sleeping. Once she was sure there was no one hiding in the room, she went on to the rest of the rooms in the passage and managed to avoid waking all but one of her ladies. Before going down to the hall, Lydima returned to her own room and quickly changed into a serviceable dress and boots. Her hair she left in its night braid.

On the way past Saley's room, she checked on Aylria who had been moved to Saley's bed. "How is she?"

"She is lucky. Whatever was given to her was extremely potent. Probably a large dose of opium. It could have killed her," replied Yula.

"Will she be alright?"

"Since she has not died yet, she will most likely live, but she will be very sick when she wakes. It will take her some time to recover. Do not worry. I will stay with her."

Lydima nodded and made her way downstairs.

∞∞∞

Yoused and Jayred were waiting for Lydima when she entered the hall. Not having slept much the last few days, Yoused would have given almost anything to crawl into bed, but he would not leave Lydima's side. His sympathy for her anxiety kept him wide awake. The responsibility for the situation rested on his shoulders, and he felt the weight of it. He had looked the other way too long, and now others were suffering for his laxness.

With every guard employed in the search, it was soon finished. Lydima stopped pacing when Byden entered, but it was clear from his expression that the search was unsuccessful.

"Neither Saley nor the new maid have been found, my lady. They did not leave through any gate. I do not know where they could be hiding. Palyn has gone back to Reyla's village to fetch the headmaster's hound. At this point, tracking their scent will be our best chance of finding them."

"Could they have used a rope to lower themselves over the wall?" Yoused suggested.

Byden shook his head. "They would have been seen by the guards. The girl's window overlooks the courtyard, so they could not escape that way."

"The cavern!" exclaimed Lydima. "Saley knows where the entrance is. Does it have another exit?"

Jayred frowned. "There are several smaller chambers and passages, but only one that leads to the surface. It is almost impossible to find unless you know where it is. Only a handful of people living know its location."

"I would not say anything would be impossible for Valryn to discover. He is in a position to leverage information from any man who would not want his visits to the inn exposed. Consider how quickly he found my uncle."

"I will have the cavern searched immediately." Byden turned on his heel and walked toward the door.

"I am coming with you!" Lydima hurried after him.

Yoused followed as well. He didn't want Lydima to face whatever they found alone.

∞∞∞

Byden sent soldiers to fan the woods near where the crawl exited the mountain, and left instructions to have Palyn meet them there with the dog. Then he called a few men to accompany him into the cave. Soon, a small party of searchers was assembled outside the door sealing the entrance to the cavern. Kyel pushed open the door, and the rush of air made the torches in the soldiers' hands flicker.

"Ah!" Lydima's lantern caught a flash of red on the floor in front of the passage. "This is one of Saley's ribbons! I tied it on myself. She must have dropped it here on purpose. It would not have come loose easily."

Lydima knew all it would take to persuade Saley to come quietly would be a threat of harm to her siblings. It lifted her spirits to think that the girl still hadn't given up hope of rescue and had thought to leave a clue.

They passed through the door and entered the cavern single file, following closely behind their guide. "I had no idea this was here," remarked Yoused as he gazed around in amazement.

"Exactly." Byden grumbled. "No one is supposed to know. It is a last place of retreat if the castle is taken, and a means of escape, if need be. After we find the girl, my next task will be to find out who leaked the secret about the exit." His expression implied that he didn't think Yoused should know it either.

Kyel paused at the head of the column of searchers and lifted his torch. "Someone has passed through here recently." He pointed to a fresh disturbance in the earth where little feet had slipped in the loose soil and rocks. "It looks like they headed straight toward the exit."

The searchers scrambled down the steep slope on the southern side of the cavern. Yoused held Lydima's elbow to steady her. At the bottom of the slope, a horizontal cleft in the wall was obscured by an overhang. The entrance was invisible from the main part of the cavern, and without directions, someone would have to search long and hard to find it.

They had to get down on their hands and knees and crawl through the damp darkness to reach the small cave at the end. All but one torch was put out, and it was carefully passed through the narrow space and used to relight the rest on the other side. Lydima guessed that Valryn's woman must have brought a lamp. Saley was reluctant to enter the cave the first time. How was she managing through all of this?

Several passages branched off from this one, and they entered one on the right side, but not before Byden had sent men into every other passage to make sure the fugitives were not lost or hiding in one of them.

"We are still on the right track." Kyel pointed to a freshly squashed cricket on the hard rock of the cave floor as they continued through the next opening. "The kidnapper was well informed."

At one point, the fissure through which they travelled narrowed enough that they had to turn sideways to get through it. Progress was slow, and water seeping through the cracks in the volcanic rock dampened their clothes. Eventually the crack opened into a wider cave again. From here, two small caves branched off, and once more they took the right-hand passage while a few men searched the other. Before continuing, they paused to drink a handful of water from a small pool that Kyel assured them was safe.

Most of the igneous rock they had seen so far did not contain enough calcium to form stalagmites or stalactites, but as they drew closer to the surface, the rock changed to basalt. A flowstone had formed on the side of this cave, and the floor was very slippery. Lydima's boots were not hobnailed like many of the men's and she nearly lost her footing.

Youssed grabbed her around the waist to keep her from falling. "Are you alright?"

"Yes, thank you," she replied breathlessly and continued forward.

They had nearly reached the end of the system of caves, and the last stretch of tunnel was a low crawl that required the searchers to stoop. All the torches were doused, and the only light was from Kyel's lamp at the front of the column. It was long and tiring, and Lydima began to feel some panic as the walls closed in. She could barely see where she was going. Most of the path in front of her was blocked by Byden's hunched figure.

Her heart beat fast, and she began to perspire. With effort, she forced herself to breathe evenly. Lydima's neck was becoming quite sore, and she wasn't sure how much longer she could proceed like this. Something squished under her fingers as they brushed along the wall of the tunnel, and she barely kept herself from screaming.

Just as she began to feel like she couldn't go another step, they finally reached the surface. A faint glow of light could be seen in the opening ahead. That meant that it was nearly dawn. The searchers tumbled gratefully out of the mountainside and into the dim, grey morning.

CHAPTER FOURTEEN

Two days before the festival was to begin, Zariana returned to Janis' home once more. She seemed very excited.

"Princess Bashalis has asked for you!" she told Talia. "She wants you to accompany her home to Gabrishia. Festivals are too taxing for her, and she wants to leave before it starts. Lord Tharch will remain with Riash for a few more days. My father says this is an excellent opportunity for you to escape Herida under Tharch's very nose!"

"Me? Why does she want me?"

"I do not know, but she does. Lady Parisha is waiting to transform you back to a lady in waiting."

"What about my friend?" Talia gestured to Stelan.

"My father has made other arrangements to smuggle him out of the city as soon as the festival is over. You will be reunited in the capital."

Talia considered this proposal. She was not completely comfortable with it. Too many variables were out of her control. However, the opportunity to learn more from the princess, and possibly from within the palace itself, was too good to pass up. "What about my sword and my armor? I hate to leave them."

"I can take them home in your rag-and-bone pack, and my father can find a way to get them to you. We are smugglers, after all."

Talia turned to Janis who was also in the room. "Have you had any luck procuring another sword for Stelan? If the chief sends mine ahead to the capital, he will need his own."

Janis nodded solemnly. "I have one already." She left the room and came back with a sword in a leather scabbard. Talia removed it from its sheath and examined it. The design was simple, but the steel was good quality, and it was well-balanced.

Talia gave Janis an intense look. "This is not a sword you purchased recently. To whom did it belong?"

"It was my son's." Janis' eyes were misty, and Talia sensed great sadness behind them.

"We cannot accept this," she said as she returned the sword to its scabbard. "It is too valuable. It should stay in your family." Janis shook her head, and her chin was set determinedly. "I have no family. My son died defending an islander, his wife, who he loved dearly. He would be happy to know it was being used to help another islander. It was she who I first taught Cerecian to."

"Your daughter-in-law was from Lyliana?"

"She was captured during a raid and brought back as a slave. It was the last successful raid before Artylia completed their fleet of warships." Janis took a deep breath and closed her eyes for a moment, remembering. "My son had been conscripted into the navy, but after one raid to the island, he saw the atrocities our men were committing against the

190

citizens there, he refused to participate in any more. He sought a station at the port, maintaining the ships. When he saw this young woman being dragged off of a returning ship, he loved her at first sight and spent everything we had to buy her freedom.

"She agreed to marry him, and they were very happy. However, the general sentiment in Herida at the time was that islanders should not be given privileges equal to citizenship. Even freed slaves were seen as lower class than the poorest Cerecians. Everywhere she went, she was slighted.

"One day, when she was heavy with child, some thugs began to tease and torment her as she shopped in the market. My son tried to stop them, and they beat him and threw him to the ground. His head struck a stone wall, and he died."

"Oh, Janis, I am so sorry."

The healer wiped at her eyes and continued her story without acknowledging Talia's condolence.

"I had a cousin who was a fisherman, and he agreed to sail my daughter-in-law secretly back to Lyliana. It was better for her to return to her own home. The child would have had a difficult time here, especially if it took after its mother."

Janis went over to her desk and took a miniature out of a drawer and showed it to Talia.

"She is beautiful."

Stelan, who had been gradually moving around more each day, got up from his cot to take a look. When he saw it he made an exclamation of surprise. It was a portrait of a woman with honey-colored hair and amber eyes.

"What was her name?" he asked excitedly in halting Cerecian.

"Lydelia."

"And how long ago was this?"

"Nearly thirty years. Why do you ask?"

"Because I know your son's daughter."

"You do?" gasped Janis.

"If I did not know who this was, I would think it was her."

Stelan's Cerecian grammar was still not the most concise. He switched to Berushese and had Talia interpret.

"My patron's cousin is the mirror image of this portrait, and she is the correct age. Her mother died in childbirth and she does not know her own history. It was rumored that her father was Cerecian. She will be gratified to hear who he was."

"Tell me about her!" begged Janis.

Stelan told her everything he could about Lydima's good qualities, glossing over what he knew of her unhappy childhood and subsequent occupation, which wasn't much, and ending with her current status as acting lady of Freosyd.

As she interpreted, Talia couldn't help feeling a little jealous at Stelan's description of the lovely woman from the island. Janis, with tears in her eyes, thanked Stelan for the news that her granddaughter had survived.

"You should return with us so you can meet her!"

Janis shook her head. "I am too old to undertake such an arduous journey. I cannot start my life over and be a burden to a woman I do not know. Remember me to her. That will be enough."

Much as she sorrowed for Janis' loss, Talia was relieved to hear her say that. It was going to be challenging enough to get the two of them out already.

"We should be on our way," urged Zariana. "The princess wants to leave first thing in the morning, and she requests for you to wait on her this evening."

"Wait for me outside. I will just be a moment."

Zariana glanced sideways at Stelan and gave a curt nod, then stepped out the door.

Talia turned to Janis. "Thank you for all you have done for us. What do I owe you for the remaining days Stelan will be with you?"

"I am more than repaid with news of my granddaughter. The money from the chief will last me for a long time. I want for nothing else."

Talia placed her hands on Janis' shoulders and gave her a look of gratitude and understanding.

"Take care of yourself," Janis admonished, and she left the room leaving Talia alone with Stelan.

He made no move toward her, and he did not speak. What was there to say? She had told him not to say anything. She looked into his earnest blue eyes and saw reflected in them her own intense desire.

"If I do not see you again . . ." she could not continue.

Stelan gazed back at her with understanding. "I know."

∞∞∞

"What does the princess want with me?" Talia repeated her question to Parisha while a couple of trusted ladies redressed her hair and put her through their rigorous beauty regime.

Zariana had been given permission to remain for a while, and she stood silently observing the process. She had begun to look up to Talia and didn't want to leave yet. Plus, she wanted to be able to give her father as detailed an update as possible. Parisha had told them it was safe to talk freely.

"Bashalis does not like people to fawn over her or treat her differently because of her unique condition.

Her subjects are obsequious enough because she is the sister of the king. She is in need of a new handmaid, and she appreciated your gift of silence."

"I can be silent," snorted Talia. "That will be easy." She reflected for a moment. "What happened to her previous handmaid?" She helped herself to some refreshment that had been provided and tried to chew while her hair was being pulled in all directions.

Parisha grimaced. "Women in the Cerecian court are not always treated well. I do not know the particulars in this case, but Chysh keeps a tight rein on his sister, and he likes to remind her of her dependence at every opportunity. If he wanted the woman for himself, or disapproved of her in any way, she would be removed from the princess' service. Bashalis wants to replace her before my cousin assigns someone of his own choosing to keep an eye on her."

"What have you told her about me? If she visits here often, she will know I have not been long in your service."

"One of the ships that survived the battle of the channel captured a few enemy soldiers and brought them back to Herida. Among them was a female soldier from Berush. I convinced General Riash to give her to me with the argument that another woman might coax more out of her than a man could.

"Unfortunately, she died of injuries sustained in the battle. We were unable to save her. The rest of the prisoners were interrogated by the general, and you know what his methods are. Tharch was there too, and he ordered them all killed when they got nothing out of them."

"I know the soldier of whom you speak. We thought she was lost when her ship went down."

Talia had gone pale. "You spared her from being tortured. She passed in peace. Berush owes you a debt for that. If there is anything we can do, you have only to ask."

Parisha shook her head. "You do what seems best for yourself. That is what I do. Your very presence in this country is enough to bring trouble to Chysh. I could not ask for more."

"You will not suffer if the story gets out that the Berushese soldier still lives?" Talia assumed that this was where Parisha was going with this story.

"Not many knew of it to begin with. I did not bring her to my house, so none of my servants were aware of the situation. An associate of the Chief took her in.

"If necessary, I will put out that you were oppressed in your home country and asked for refuge here once you recovered. That is what I told Bashalis. Since our countries have not had normal relations in over a century, people will not know better than to believe conditions are the same everywhere. You were a lowly foot soldier and could tell me nothing we did not already know."

"That is still a dangerous story, for me too."

Parisha shrugged. "The more truth in the lie, the stronger it is. Even though your Cerecian is good enough to pass for a native, this still seems the best course. You will not have to keep up the pretense of being a lady's maid in front of the princess." She smiled wryly. "I suspect you do not have enough of the required skills to maintain the deception for long."

"You are probably right. I know little about fashionable hair or clothing, especially in Cerecia." Talia frowned as the hairdresser tightly wove a braid together. "The princess still wanted to take me with that background?"

Parisha grinned. "I tried to talk her out of it, but the story made her even more determined to employ you. She has a bit of a rebellious streak. If you face any danger, it will not be her doing."

∞∞∞

As it turned out, Zariana didn't need to take Talia's sword and armor home. Parisha rolled them up in a rug, and had a servant ready to accompany Talia to the palace to carry it and some other luggage and gifts for the princess. She assured Talia that Bashalis would be delighted to preserve them for her.

Talia slipped her dagger inside of the fancy leather boots Parisha had supplied her with. There was barely room for it.

When she said goodbye to Zariana, she handed her a letter. "This is the introduction your father requested in case he wants to reveal himself to my contact." Talia had decided that the relationship with the Chief was one Berush would desire to maintain. It might come in handy again in the future.

The girl hugged her impulsively and then ran off without another word.

When she passed through the archway into the palace courtyard, Talia couldn't help being a little nervous. Rather than march in boldly, as she had at the fortress, she walked demurely and kept her eyes downcast. Fortunately, she didn't encounter Tharch, or anyone else who might find her suspicious. The name of the soldier whose identity she was assuming was Shania, and she gave that name to the steward who led her to the princess' chamber.

Bashalis was waiting for her with the same far away, waif-like expression she had had the night of the party, but there was a hint of interest in her unusual eyes. She directed Parisha's servant to take the 'gifts' to her room without comment, and the corner of her mouth turned up slightly in a satisfied smile. With unabashed curiosity, she reevaluated Talia and seemed pleased with what she saw. She dismissed the maid who had been temporarily assigned to her back to her normal duties.

"I had admired your bearing before I knew that you had been a soldier. Now it makes sense."

Talia bowed her head in reply.

"You may speak. It is the substance of most people's conversations that bores me, not conversation in general."

"What would you like me to say, your highness?"

"First of all, call me Bashalis, at least in private. I need no further reminders of my station. Tell me about Berush."

Talia told her as much as she could without either lying or contradicting Parisha's explanation for her presence. She described the shifting sands of the desert, the rough terrain of the mountains, the shimmering beauty of the lakes, the relief of coming on a fertile, green oasis after a long and tiring journey.

Bashalis appeared wistful as she envisioned the land Talia described. "Do you miss it?"

"Yes."

"Even though you were mistreated there?"

Talia shrugged. She hated giving the princess a bad impression of her country, but it was unavoidable. "It is home," she replied simply.

Bashalis nodded in acceptance of this explanation. "But you told Lady Parisha you wanted to remain here?"

"My current occupation has, so far, been less dangerous than my previous one."

"I also assume you had no other choice."

Talia gave her a wry smile.

"Well, I will appreciate your service as long as it is available. If you happen to disappear one day, I will not search for you."

"I am not trained as a lady's maid, but I will serve you as well as I can for as long as I am able," Talia promised sincerely. She knew it wouldn't be for very long.

"That is good enough." Bashalis sighed. "Unfortunately, I must dine with Lord Tharch once more before we leave. Just having you around makes me feel a little stronger somehow."

She rose, and Talia followed her into a small, private dining room. The table was set for two, and the lighting was dim, which was normal for Bashalis's domain, but Tharch's self-satisfied expression implied that he had other motives for the deliberately intimate setting. He was dressed in a short-sleeved silk shirt and vest typical of what upper-class Cerecians wore at home. Though Talia judged him to be in his late twenties, she believed no amount of fancy clothes could possibly make him look handsome. His large forehead, heavy, dark eyebrows and hard mouth were nothing compared to the evil and lust visible in his eyes.

His expression turned from satisfaction to annoyance as he observed Talia enter behind the princess. "Who is this?" He had not paid any attention to those serving him at Parisha's and didn't recognize her.

Bashalis had returned to her normal vacant, dreamy visage, successfully appearing as colorless on the inside as she was on the exterior. "Lady Parisha lent me one of her maids since I am currently without one." She waved her hand dismissively as Talia attempted to melt into the background like an inanimate piece of furniture.

"Well, send her away," he said impatiently, then attempted to sound courtlier as he continued, "I will wait on you this evening."

"How lovely," said Bashalis without emotion, "but I am extremely fatigued. I may need her assistance later on." She drooped delicately to emphasize her words.

Tharch opened his mouth to argue, but evidently decided that letting her have her way would be more likely to endear himself to her.

Throughout the dinner, Talia watched his unsuccessful attempts to woo the princess with the utmost amusement. Bashalis managed to accept Tharch's obeisance without acknowledging that she had any understanding of his intent whatsoever. The girl affected such a bland personality that the casual observer would conclude she had no emotions at all.

After an hour or so of gradual wilting, the princess' eyes began to droop. "Thank you for the dinner, my lord, but I believe I must retire."

Tharch stood and offered her his hand to help her up. "You know, we are to be wed in the spring, my dear," he reminded her.

"Yes, indeed," she said brightly.

"I would like to give you some idea of what you have to look forward to." He put his arm around her waist and pulled her to him. He bent forward and kissed her heatedly, but she hung in his arms like a limp rag. Disgust showed in his face as he let her go. Roughly, he took her chin in his hand and glared into her eyes, but she merely stared back at him blankly. "I hope you can muster more enthusiasm than this on our wedding night."

Bashalis contrived a slightly hurt expression, and

he waved her away as he sat down to help himself to more wine. Talia came forward without speaking and offered the sleepy princess her arm for support. Tharch was lucky she was not wearing her sword; otherwise she might have been tempted to challenge him to a duel. In addition to the pleasure it would give her to rid Bashalis of her unwanted suitor, it would be satisfying to avenge the deaths of her comrades at his orders.

Back in the princess' chambers, she helped the girl prepare for bed without any unsolicited comments on the evening's events. The first thing Bashalis did was to wipe off her mouth with a damp cloth and gargle with rosewater. She spit the water into a basin as if she was trying to spit the memory of his kiss from her mind.

"Vile man," was all she said as she threw the towel into a corner. She sat on a stool and held a comb out to Talia.

"I have never combed anyone else's hair before," stated Talia with some doubt.

"It is no different from combing your own hair," Bashalis explained confidently. "Easier, actually."

With trepidation, Talia loosened the princess' simple hairstyle and carefully combed it out. She was right. It wasn't hard. Talia encountered a few knots, but fortunately the princess didn't have a sensitive scalp. Talia found it odd that she trusted her enough to be in such a vulnerable position. How easy it would be to assassinate someone when you already had them by the hair. She shook herself. Maybe she had been a soldier too long if she was always thinking of ways to kill people.

Once she had completely untangled the princess' long, silky, white hair, she braided it and tied the end with a ribbon. She helped her unlace her dress, but

Bashalis changed into her nightgown unaided.

"It will be kind of nice to do some things for myself," she mused. "Most of the time I am treated like a doll that cannot even put on her own clothes. I let them think so. It is amusing to be so underestimated. Sometimes it comes in handy."

That was true, thought Talia. She had used that strategy effectively in the past. Bashalis climbed into her bed and closed her eyes. Talia wasn't exactly sure what she was expected to do now. She hadn't been officially dismissed.

"Is there anything else?"

The princess shook her head.

"Shall I retire to the servant's quarters, or should I make a pallet on the floor?"

"Would you?" Bashalis opened her eyes. "I would rather not be alone."

Talia nodded. She found some extra blankets in a wardrobe and spread them out on the floor at the foot of the bed. The room was a little chilly, so she started a fire in the small fireplace and closed the curtain in front of the windows. It had been an unusually warm autumn, but she sensed there might be an early winter.

Before she lay down, she saw that the princess was already breathing the slow, even breaths of slumber. For Talia, sleep was elusive. It was the first time in a week that she was not in the same room as Stelan, listening to *him* breathe. She had become used to his easy sense of humor, his optimism and unselfishness, his handsome face. She missed him already.

Even though they had been careful not to touch each other the last few days, she had been acutely aware of him. Maybe this was a good opportunity to forget him. She could make her own way home from the capital and leave him on his own as he suggested.

No, she admitted to herself, she could never leave him in this country alone without knowing what had happened to him or if he made it out. She would stay with Bashalis until the Chief contacted her. Her heart would not let her leave without the islander who held it.

CHAPTER FIFTEEN

"Here is Saley's other ribbon!" Lydima spied it lying on the ground when she exited the cave.

"The fugitives are no longer inside of the mountain," Byden told his men. "We will concentrate on the road between here and Sonefast's harbor."

Lydima was beginning to feel faint from hunger and fatigue, but she ignored the sensation and pressed on. They had left too quickly to bring food. A few of the soldiers carried flasks of water, but that was all.

Before they had gone far, Palyn caught up with them. The hound followed closely at his heels. There were not many dogs on the island. The few that existed were used for herding goats as there was little to hunt on the island, and no large predators to threaten the livestock. This particular hound was a gift from a relative on the mainland who trained dogs to hunt and track.

"Do you have anything with you that belonged to the girl?" Palyn asked, panting from the climb up from the road.

"I have these." Lydima held out the hair ribbons.

Palyn took them and offered them to the hound to sniff. The dog eagerly nosed the items.

"Find, boy, find," commanded Palyn.

After snuffling around for a few moments, the hound stiffened and bayed, then took off. Instead of heading south as they expected, the animal ran farther up the mountainside.

The men rushed after it, but Lydima found that she could not keep up. Her long skirts hindered her in pushing through the undergrowth, and she was barely holding herself together. She stopped to lean against a tree and catch her breath. The fall morning was chilly, and she shivered.

Yoused came up behind her and placed his hand comfortingly on her shoulder. "Lean on me. I will help you."

Lydima turned to him gratefully and put her arm in his. He unsheathed his sword and hacked through the thick brambles until they came across a goat-path. They followed the path upward as the baying of the hound floated toward them through the morning mist. The sound grew fainter as they lagged further behind the others, but suddenly they heard it become more frenzied.

"Does that mean they are found?" Lydima asked urgently.

"Probably," Yoused affirmed.

They lengthened their strides with renewed energy. Soon they caught up with Byden, who pointed to an outcropping of rock. The early morning shadows made it difficult to distinguish anything, but the outline of two figures could be seen in the shelter of the overhang. Palyn was giving the hound a treat and patting his head.

"Saley," cried Lydima desperately as she rushed

forward, but Byden barred her way.

"Wait. Keep her back," he directed Yoused who was right behind Lydima.

"Is she alright?"

Byden did not respond, but signaled to a couple of the men who had been scouring the mountain overnight. They carried bows, and disappeared in opposite directions into the woods.

"What is happening?" Lydima questioned insistently.

Byden turned to her and took a deep breath. "The woman has a knife to the girl's throat."

Lydima gasped.

"She insists she will kill the girl rather than give her up to us. We had to back off. Two of our best archers are skirting the clearing to try and find a clear line of sight."

"They are going to shoot her?"

Freosyd's grizzled sergeant nodded. "It is the only way. She has killed once already. There will be no restitution for this."

"He is right, Lydima," whispered Yoused. He kept his arm firmly around her shoulders as she put her head in her hands. "Saley will need you when it is over."

Lydima took a deep breath and stood up straight. She summoned all her remaining strength and looked toward the pocket in the rock where Saley was being held. She must know the exact instant she could go to her. It was only a few moments, but they seemed like an eternity. Lydima's heart pounded in her chest and her throat became dry.

Suddenly, there was a skull-cracking thwack, and the taller of the shadowy figures crumpled to the ground. Yoused let go of Lydima and she sprinted headlong toward the cleft, stumbling several times as she ran. When she reached the outcropping, she dropped to her knees in front of the stricken child and clutched her tightly. The woman's knife had fallen to the ground at her feet, and Saley had a tiny cut where the blade had pressed against her skin.

"Your brother and sister are safe!" Lydima knew this was what Saley would most want to hear. "Lord Yoused found them. They are safe, and they will be here tonight!"

The girl let out a sob and burst into tears. It was the first real emotion Lydima had seen from her.

"You are safe now, too. Valryn is a prisoner in Lord Yoused's custody. He can never hurt you again."

Saley continued to cry, and Lydima cried with her. Somehow she found the strength to lift the girl and carry her away from the dead woman. She was much heavier than baby Lylie, but Lydima carried her all the way to the goat path and would give her up to no one.

Only when they were met by men bringing horses did she finally relinquish her and hand her up to Byden when he had mounted. As soon as she let go of Saley, her legs turned to jelly and she collapsed in a heap.

∞∞∞

Yoused gently lifted Lydima up, and, for the second time in his life, he set her on a horse, but this time he got up behind her. Holding her tightly around the waist so she did not fall off, he guided the horse back to Freosyd.

The sun was nearly at its zenith by the time they returned, and both Lydima and Saley were asleep in the saddle. Half the castle had been up all night, and everyone was tired. Yoused himself was taxed beyond what he would have thought possible, but he managed to carry Lydima up to her room. She and Saley were laid next to each other, and Lydima stirred enough to put her arm over the girl before she fell back asleep.

Yoused bent over and softly kissed her forehead. Then, completely exhausted, he went and found an empty bed and fell instantly asleep.

∞∞∞

"My lady, the children have arrived."

The first thought that came to Lydima's mind when Nyla woke her was that she was extremely hungry. Then Nyla's words penetrated her brain and she sat up quickly.

"Saley, your brother and sister are here!" Lydima gently patted the girl's shoulder.

It took Saley a moment to shake her mind free of sleep also, but was wide awake as soon as she grasped the news. They jumped out of bed and hurried downstairs shoeless, with mussed hair and clothing.

When they entered the hall, one of Yoused's servants was standing with two small, scared-looking children. Their red eyes and the streaks on their faces showed they had been crying. Saley ran up to them and threw her arms around them. Once they realized who she was, they hugged her back and cried as well.

"Kanie, I miss oo," said the girl.

Saley kissed them both all over their faces. Lydima looked on happily.

Yoused entered the hall at that moment, blinking in the light and rubbing sleep from his eyes. He smiled when he saw the joyful reunion. Lydima walked over to him and put her hand on his arm.

207

"Thank you, Lord Yoused," she said with shining eyes, "for this, and for everything else. It means a great deal to me. It will mean the world for these children."

"It was my pleasure."

Lydima turned her attention to Saley and her siblings. She wasn't sure how the children would respond to strangers. "Saley, can you introduce me to your brother and sister?"

She whispered so softly that Lydima had to strain to hear her. "Tye," she put her hand on her brother's head.

The boy looked around four or five years old. He was so skinny, it was hard to tell.

"Mya." Saley stood up with her sister still hanging around her neck. The little girl was younger looking than Dzhon, maybe two.

Little feet slapped against the flagstones as Dzhon and Katya burst into the hall. Udmyla and Maygla had been getting them ready for bed, but they had heard the commotion and wanted to see Lydima and Saley. They ran to Lydima and practically jumped on her. Having suffered so much loss already, she could understand their need to be reassured that she and Saley were alright after being absent from them all day. They had not been allowed to see her when they returned so that she could rest.

"I was so worried about you and Saley," whispered Katya in Lydima's ear.

"Everything is fine. We are alright." Lydima kissed the girl on her forehead.

"Maygwa said 'no goats'!" Dzhon complained.

Lydima laughed. "I will take you to see the goats tomorrow, even if it is pouring rain. We will need to show them to our new friends." She gestured toward Tye and Mya.

Saley beamed as Katya came shyly over to say hello to Mya. "Is this your sister?"

Saley nodded.

"Wanna chase me?" Dzhon asked Tye, but Tye kept his head down and looked furtively around at all the people in the hall. He shook his head. "You wike goats?"

Tye nodded.

"We see dem tomowow."

The rest of the castle had already eaten, but more food was brought into the hall for the newcomers, and Lydima let Dzhon and Katya stay and sit with her and the other children while they ate. Dzhon chattered at the silent Tye the whole time, but Katya sat watching Saley and her sister eat. Mya was an extremely messy eater. Saley was very patient with her, and Lydima let her help her sister since it appeared they would not be separated. They would need to have baths before bed.

"You can tell they are related to Saley because they do not talk either," Katya observed to Lydima.

"Yes," Lydima affirmed hesitantly. She knew the children would have a serious adjustment ahead of them. She didn't know how she was going to help them other than providing for their basic needs. Safety and security would go a long way. So would love. She remembered her own behavior when Eemya had first tried to help her, and she shuddered. Hopefully it would be easier for Saley and her siblings since they were younger than she had been.

The nurse brought Lylie in to see Lydima as well. It was the longest she had gone without seeing her since she had been at the castle. Lylie had not slept well during the night, had not taken her naps, and was red-faced and petulant. As soon as Lydima took her, she calmed down, stopped crying, and started hiccoughing. Lydima patted her on the back and spoke soothingly to her until she fell asleep.

∞∞∞

Yoused sat apart from them at another table. He ate quietly and contemplated Lydima and her young charges. Her life had drastically changed in the last few weeks. It would not be right for him to introduce the possibility of another huge change at this moment by sharing his feelings with her. She would need time to settle into her new role as caregiver. The children would need time to heal and learn their new place.

It occurred to him that if he was ever able to persuade Lydima to marry him, she would want to bring them all with her to Sonefast. He hadn't really considered that aspect of the situation. It would be fine with him if she brought them. He enjoyed children. The way that Lydima interacted with them was endearing. During their long night of searching, he had admired her fortitude and selfless focus on Saley's well-being. Somehow he needed to court her without being overly obvious. A suitor was something she might not be open to right now.

When he had come to go over the accounts, he had been surprised that she had not tried to flirt with him again, or anyone else for that matter. She not only seemed to have given up that lifestyle entirely, but also to consider winning his affections an impossibility. 'I know you do not approve of me,' she had said. How could he explain to her that he disapproved of her past actions and former style of living, but he cared about who she was on the inside?

Only a very strong woman could fight for herself and others the way she did. When she felt something intensely, she let nothing stand in her way. He smiled at how quickly and fiercely she had come to love the small baby and the other children, even though she had been so reluctant at first. Holding Lylie now, with her frizzy braid and wrinkled dress, she was more beautiful than he had ever seen her. Her eyes shone with love and happiness. One day, he hoped those eyes would look that way toward him.

∞∞∞

"I am too excited to sleep!" insisted Katya.

"I wan to show Tye my bwocks!"

"It is time to go to bed!" Lydima declared in her firmest voice. She handed Lylie carefully back to Puriya, and fortunately she did not wake up. "Come, Mya. You must wash and dress."

Mya would hardly let go of Saley long enough to be cleaned after dinner and let a nightgown be pulled over her. Both she and Tye had to be treated for lice. At first, Tye wouldn't let anyone touch him, and he squirmed away. Lydima had to instruct Saley how to wash his long hair, and he reluctantly let her wash it.

A cot was brought in for Tye, and Mya got into bed with Saley. Lydima put a diaper on her, just in case, though she hadn't been wearing one before. Even though Saley had slept most of the day, once Mya and Tye fell asleep, she nodded off as well. Lydima decided to station a servant outside of the door, just in case they needed anything, but she knew that for Saley, at least, she no longer had to fear that she would run away.

After all the children were taken care of, Lydima went back to her own room. It was nearly impossible to comb all the tangles out of her hair, but she finally got them loose and braided it again. By candlelight she changed into a clean nightdress, then slipped under the blankets quietly so that she wouldn't disturb Katya who was breathing evenly in slumber. She knew it was important for them all to get back to a normal routine as soon as possible. Tye and Mya might have no idea what a normal routine was like, and she imagined it would take more energy than she possessed to mother all six youngsters.

She looked at Dzhon who slept peacefully in his cot with his mouth open. Lydima smiled to herself. She couldn't think of any better way to spend her life than caring for these sweet children.

∞∞∞∞

"No! NOOOO! Aieeeeeee!"

Mya screamed and refused to sit in the special chair with the attached tray. Youced had told Lydima some of what had been found at the inn, and she decided that any type of restraint was probably not a good idea. Saley held out her arms for her sister as Lydima removed her from the seat.

"Try to keep her from making too much of a mess," Lydima sighed, resigned, as Saley spooned food into Mya's mouth.

Tye ate nervously and put food in his pockets, just like Saley had done. When one of the male servants came in to help Maygla carry the trays back to the kitchen, he shrank into a ball, trying not to be noticed. Jayred came in shortly afterward, and Tye went so far as to hide under the table. All this worried Lydima greatly, but she hoped that time would be the best healer.

After breakfast, the nurse supervised Mya and Dzhon while they played, and Lydima gathered Katya, Saley and Tye around the table for reading and spelling lessons.

"We are learning how to read and write, Tye. You may join us if you like."

In front of him she merely set a slate and chalk pencil so he could try if he wanted to. He scribbled briefly on the slate, then got up and went to play on the floor. Lydima let him.

Nyla, who Lydima discovered was good with sums, came in to work with the girls for a while. Saley kept looking over her shoulder at her siblings.

"Come here for a moment, Saley." Lydima took her aside. "I am going to keep you, Tye and Mya together. You will stay with me, and you will not have to be apart again, I promise."

Saley nodded at her, and her shoulders seemed to relax a bit.

"Lord Yoused told me that he discovered your real name is Kandys. Do you want me to call you that?"

Saley shook her head vigorously.

Lydima patted her shoulder. A new name was a good way to begin a fresh start.

After lunch, Lylie went down for her nap, and Lydima took the rest of the troop out to the barn to see the goats. The new kid was now a sprinter, and kept the children busy chasing him around the yard. Tye and Dzhon climbed on the fences and hung on the railings of the pens.

"Stay away from the pig pen!" she warned futilely.

Dzhon slipped in some mud and sat right in it. At least he and Tye were giggling and having some fun.

When they returned to the castle, Lydima sent Udmyla to help Saley put Mya to bed while she took care of Dzhon. She didn't know if Tye would take a nap, but Saley could keep him busy once Mya was asleep. Normally Katya would go with Aylria during this time, but Maygla took her instead.

"I am going to check on Aylria," she told Maygla

213

and headed toward the infirmary. Katya had asked after her, and she had promised to let the lady know the girl missed her.

Yoused caught up with her on the way. "May I accompany you?"

"If you wish," she agreed, not really giving his presence much thought. Her mind was busy with many other things.

Aylria was lying in a cot with her head propped up. Her skin was pale and clammy, and her lips and fingernails had a bluish tint. It looked like she had been scratching her arms. Lydima came and sat by her bed while Yoused stood back by the door.

"How are you, Aylria?"

"How do you think I am?" Aylria replied with a surprising amount of anger for someone in her weakened state. Lydima sat back, unsure how to reply, but Aylria continued, "That girl just sat there and let that whore poison me! After all we have done for her!" she said viciously.

Lydima was shocked at her vehemence. "She was too frightened for her brother and sister to say anything, Aylria. It is not her fault."

"You care more about those worthless children than you do about decent, hardworking people. I suppose that is to be expected, since you were one of them yourself."

"You may say whatever you like about me," Lydima said, trying hard not to let her anger show, "but you must not blame an innocent child." She straightened herself. "I do not blame you for being angry. What was done to you was wrong. I hope that when you have recovered, you will return to yourself and not harbor bitterness against Saley for what happened."

She stood up. "Katya wanted me to tell you that

she misses you and hopes you will be better soon."

Aylria turned her head toward the wall and refused to look at Lydima.

Lydima spun around and left the infirmary. Out in the sunlight of the courtyard, she took a deep breath and blinked back tears. She felt emotionally drained from the encounter. A hand squeezed hers, and she looked up into the concerned blue eyes of Lord Yoused. He said nothing, but she appreciated his silent support.

Letting go of her hand, he said, "I will return to my holding tomorrow and prepare to take Valryn to Letina. I intend ask Lord Tomus to render judgment on him."

"And you will ask the council to consider changing the laws on indentured servitude?"

"Yes," he hesitated before continuing. "If you have a moment, I would like to ask your advice on something before I leave."

"Certainly. Shall we go to the study?" Lydima led the way inside. They entered the study and she motioned him into a seat.

"I hate to ask since you have so much to deal with already, but I have no idea what to do with the women who remain at the inn. Do you have any thoughts on what should be done to help them or provide for their futures?"

Lydima felt for these women, and she knew they needed help to escape the lives they had been living, even now that Valryn was no longer present. But, she couldn't help feeling upset that Yoused considered her to be the best person to advise him in this situation. She couldn't blame him for it. She was the obvious person to ask, but she wished she wasn't. For some reason, Lord Yoused's respect was something she thought was worth having. He was looking at her earnestly, and she closed her eyes so she could think.

"Unfortunately, I do not think there is an easy answer. Some of those women may have been there their whole lives. Do you know how old they are?"

"No." He thought for a moment. "Some of them looked very young, perhaps fifteen or sixteen. The oldest might be forty-something. It is hard to tell. Continued opium use can age a person prematurely."

"I am not sure I can be much help. I have never used opium, so I can give no advice about that. Whenever I find myself in a difficult position, I always have my cousin's generosity to fall back on. I doubt any of these women have a virtuous and wealthy family member willing to set them up in a respectable occupation," she smiled sadly.

"I am willing to do whatever needs to be done to help them myself, but as you say, I am not family. They may not trust me, and my real concern is that they will not want to learn a new trade."

Lydima squirmed a little in her seat. "That is likely. Change is scary, even when the change is positive. The unknown can be more frightening than the known."

"But change is possible."

"Of course." Lydima considered the women's plight. "It would probably be best to give them several options and let them choose what they would like to do, but do not pressure them. Let them decide when they are ready. In the meantime," she stated firmly, "they should all be taught to read."

"That is what Lady Eemya would say," Yoused smiled.

Lydima studied Yoused curiously. She wondered if he still cared for her cousin. She felt sorry for him if he did. Eemya and Darius were practically disgusting with how much they loved each other. It was hard not to envy them.

"May I ask what you intend to do when your cousin returns?"

The question surprised her a little. Why would he care what she did? Did he think that if she could change, there was hope for these other women? Was he afraid she would return to what she knew best? She almost decided to tell him it was not his business, but part of her wanted him to know.

"I plan to ask her if the children and I may stay on with her. Eemya has a huge heart, and I am sure she will be happy for us to remain here."

Yoused nodded. It might only be her imagination, but she thought he looked relieved. She excused herself to check on Tye and see if he had fallen asleep.

"By the way, when he was found, Tye was dressed as a girl. I do not know to what purpose."

Lydima could think of one, and it made her angry. She clenched her fists. "It is possible that he was being groomed to accept the same fate as the women." She stalked away leaving Yoused to marvel at the depravity of his fellow men.

CHAPTER SIXTEEN

The journey to Gabrishia was remarkably uneventful. In the princess' entourage, Talia was completely overlooked.

They travelled in a large, enclosed cart, like a giant box. There were plenty of carts in Berush, but they were covered with tarps when necessary. This cart had doors and curtained windows.

"I have never seen anything like this before. Is it a common form of conveyance?" Talia asked as she climbed in next to Bashalis.

"No, it was specially made for me so I could stay out of the sun."

The seats had thick cushions, but Talia could still feel the bumps as the vehicle lurched forward. She wished she could have tried the new spring-equipped carts on the island. They proceeded slowly through the crowded streets of the city until they reached the checkpoint barring the road between the two cliff faces.

"Halt!" commanded a harsh voice.

The driver gave a muffled reply.

A guard opened the door and scrutinized the passengers. "Your highness." He gave a slight bow to the princess after glancing around and then waved them on their way.

No one asked her name. They didn't even look at the rug tied tightly to the top of the cart with the luggage. Talia wanted to laugh at how easy it was. She hoped the Chief's plan for Stelan would be as successful.

The princess, though a little conceited in spite of her adverse circumstances, was not bad company. She described to Talia what she could expect to see at Chysh's palace, the key people she would encounter, and how she should behave.

"My brother likes a challenge, so keep your eyes down and be as meek and demure as possible, and he will be less likely to take an interest in you." She looked Talia over. "You are too tall for him, so hopefully that will be enough of a deterrent. Stay out of his way as much as possible."

Talia planned to do that already. As they travelled, she tried to scan the landscape for evidence of the strange explosion Bashalis had described. The wind turned colder, and the princess shivered.

"Close the curtain. It is becoming chilly in here, and the light is too bright."

Talia complied. She tried peeking behind the edges but eventually gave up. She thought about asking to sit on the bench with the driver, but decided that would be too suspicious.

Being a handmaid was a new experience for Talia, but she adapted quickly. In public, she was silently solicitous toward the princess, but never overly so. In private, she quietly performed whatever tasks the princess requested, but did not offer more than was absolutely necessary. Bashalis was grateful for this arrangement, and spoke to Talia more like a friend than a subordinate. Talia guessed she didn't have many friends. Probably there were even fewer people the princess could trust.

They stopped once in the middle of the day, and when Talia got out to stretch her legs, the driver pulled a canvas screen from a special slot and handed it to her.

"Make yourself useful," he grumbled.

"You hold it between me and the sun," Bashalis explained as the driver turned to assist her.

The princess was squinting at the sunlight, though she wore a hat and veil. Talia angled the large screen so it cast a shadow over the girl as they walked. Her long arms made it easy to hold, but they were sore when it was time to return to their seats.

At sunset, they pulled up to a tavern, and Talia followed the princess inside flanked by Bashalis' security detail.

"Y-your highness," the innkeeper scurried over to her and bowed ingratiatingly. "W-we are m-most pleased to serve you."

"The princess requires a hot meal, and your best accommodations," demanded the captain of the guard.

"Y-yes, immediately! Follow me, my lady."

Bashalis glided after him demurely and never said a word, while her host scurried around in obvious fear of his life. The innkeeper ushered them into a warm, well-furnished room.

"I h-hope this will be adequate."

"This looks satisfactory," pronounced the captain. "Now ale and food for my men. Be quick about it," he snapped, then turned back to the princess. "You will remain in this chamber, my lady, for your safety." He bowed and departed for the great room.

"My guards were all hand-picked by my brother," murmured Bashalis when the captain left. "They are here to 'protect' me, but I might as well be a prisoner. My wishes are never consulted."

"There is more than one type of prisoner, I suppose."

At Talia's tone, the princess looked up. "I am sorry. I forgot you have suffered also."

Talia thought of Shania and wondered how much pain she had endured before her death. She thought of Stelan and wondered how he was faring.

"At least, if you are suffering, it means you are still alive."

∞∞∞

In the slow-moving cart, it took three days to reach the Cerecian capital.

Each day, they passed several merchants on the road bringing grain and other goods from storehouses to sell in the port. They slept under their carts to protect their merchandise, so they didn't compete for rooms in the taverns. Even so, the second tavern they stayed at was full, and some unlucky tenants had to double up or sleep in the main room to make space for the princess.

"You should sit with the driver today," suggested Bashalis on the third day, to Talia's secret delight. "That way you will have a good view of the city, since you have never seen it before."

"Thank you, my lady," she replied as the driver grudgingly made room for her.

When they arrived in Gabrishia, Talia was surprised to see how crowded it was. Conditions didn't seem as bad as in Herida, where people had relied heavily on the fishing industry for food and trade. The streets were sparklingly clean, and all the gates and buildings were well maintained. However, many soldiers patrolled the streets, and the atmosphere seemed strained. In the center of the market, a newly erected statue of Chysh stood pompously surveying the citizens trading there.

For the sheer number of people in the town, it was amazingly quiet. Everyone spoke in hushed tones, and as the princess' coach went by, they grew completely silent and bowed low.

At the entrance to the palace, the cart drew up as close to the door as possible, and Talia screened Bashalis from the red light of the setting sun. Another servant took the screen from her once she stepped inside and returned it to the cart. Talia followed.

"That rug must be delivered to Princess Bashalis' room along with the rest of her luggage," she ordered authoritatively as the servant began to unload the bags. "Unpack nothing. I will do it myself."

"Less work for me," he shrugged carelessly.

Back inside, the king had arrived to greet his sister, and Talia tried to fade into the background while observing him at the same time. Without making herself smaller, she made her posture as unattractive as possible by relaxing her stomach muscles and rounding her shoulders.

Chysh was shorter even than Bashalis, but completely her opposite in coloring and vibrant personality. His hair and eyes were black, his skin darkly tanned, and he was thin and wiry. His hair was cropped short, eschewing convention. Every pore of his body exuded suppressed energy. He looked like a tiger ready to spring.

Nothing escaped his notice, and after the princess dutifully accepted his kisses on her cheeks, he turned to Talia who immediately lowered her eyes.

"Who is this?" Chysh's voice held the same jealous tone Tharch's had. Both of them were extremely controlling and didn't like the idea of Bashalis making a decision independently of them.

Bashalis repeated what she had told Tharch with the additional qualification that Tharch had agreed to the arrangement. Talia thought this clever of her. Tharch *had* tacitly agreed by allowing her to stay.

"She can join the rest of the household servants. I have already chosen another maid for you. This one does not look suitable."

"Thank you, my dear brother. You are so kind. I really need a second maid. I am sure Shania can find time to help the housemaids when she has fulfilled her duties to me."

"Very well. I will see you at dinner."

Bashalis gave him a curtsey, and Chysh walked off, but not before giving Talia a look that made her think he was trying to come up with a way to eliminate her without incurring his sister's displeasure directly on himself.

She followed the princess to her chambers, and they found the new handmaid awaiting them.

"Good evening, your highness," the maid curtsied deeply, almost to the floor. "I am Evash, your new maid."

Bashalis barely looked at her. "Draw me a bath, not too hot, but warm enough to melt butter."

Talia helped her undress while Evash rushed back and forth fetching the tub and trying to make the water the proper temperature.

"It is too hot," complained Bashalis after testing it with a finger.

Evash emptied some of the water and brought more.

"Spoon some butter into it."

"Yes, your highness."

The butter melted, but slowly enough to indicate it wasn't too hot, and Bashalis climbed into the bath and closed her eyes. Talia could tell she was suppressing a sigh of satisfaction.

"Shania, show Evash which bags to unpack.

"All of my dresses need to be washed an ironed.

"Air out my bedding.

"Store the rug under the bed. It was a wedding gift from Lady Parisha and will go with me when Lord Tharch and I are married."

Bashalis gave Evash one order after another. Talia saw what she was up to and smiled. The maid would be reluctant to hover around her mistress if she was constantly run off her feet. Bashalis had also come up with a brilliant explanation for the presence of the rug. She was definitely underestimated.

While the other servant was rushing around, Talia merely massaged the princess' hands. That was about all she knew how to do anyway. When the bath was over, Bashalis wisely had Evash dress her hair, and then asked her to leave so she could rest until dinner.

"The new maid will be useful for making up for your deficiencies in training, but she will report back to my brother everything I do and say. It will be a relief to have one person who is, if not on my side exactly, at least not on my brother's."

"I am on your side, as much as it is possible for me to be."

∞∞∞

Stelan passed the three days of the festival in an agony of boredom and worry. He paced around Janis' front room until she swore he was wearing the carpet thin. They practiced Cerecian several hours a day,

225

and Stelan acquired enough of the language to carry on simple conversations. Janis also taught him several curse words.

"If you cannot think of any reply, or do not understand the question, swearing may be a more convincing response than any other."

Stelan recognized some of the words as ones Talia had used with the pirates, and he smiled. The chief was supposed to get him in contact with her again once they reached the capital, but he wasn't sure that was a good idea. Maybe it was best to make a clean break. It might be safer to make their way back to Artylia separately. Plus, he didn't know if he could keep from kissing her once he saw her again. He missed her. Having to say goodbye again would be more painful than the torture he had received from Cush.

The afternoon of the last day of the festival, Zariana again knocked on the door. "It is time to go."

"Did Talia make it out of the city safely?" he asked the question that had been burning in his mind for days.

"Yes," Zariana gave him a gleeful smile. "No one suspected one of the fugitives to be in the princess' own company."

Strapping on his newly acquired sword, he turned to Janis. "Thank you for your hospitality. I will tell your granddaughter about you."

The healer nodded appreciatively. "Here." She equipped him with a small pot of salve and some extra bandages for the few wounds that still needed care.

"Take this also." Janis held out the miniature of Lydima's mother. "My granddaughter will have more use for it than I."

Stelan took it and placed it in the pouch Janis had

provided for him. He gave the healer one last glance of deep gratitude for all she had done, and her eyes misted over. He ducked quickly out of the door after the Chief's daughter and they set out across Herida.

"Where are we going?"

"Your Cerecian is much improved," complimented Zariana, impressed.

"Thank you, but where are we going?"

"To get you out of the city."

Stelan gave up and followed her submissively. They wandered purposely toward the northeast side of the peninsula and into an uninhabited area covered with boulders and scrubby trees. Zariana led him all the way to the rocky coastline where outcroppings of sharp stone jutted into the ocean from the steep cliffs.

A man stepped out from behind a column of weathered rock. "I will be your guide from here," he stated and turned and walked toward the edge of the water.

Stelan followed.

"Farewell, Lord Stelan," Zariana waved, grinning.

She had found out his name. Probably all of Herida knew it now that the news of his escape had spread.

His guide picked out a treacherous path along the edge of the cliff. The waves splashed at their feet, and it was hard not to slip on the jagged rocks. A crack in the rock between two spurs of the cliff was their goal. Stelan had to turn sideways to get into it, and the hilt of his sword scraped against the natural stone walls. Once they were through the crevice, Stelan found himself in a narrow tunnel, worn smooth from the passage of many feet. The walls bore evidence of slow toil to widen them. It must have taken years.

"You may not reveal the location of this tunnel to anyone," ordered the guide sternly as he lit a lantern.

"I will not reveal it."

The guide appraised him and seemed satisfied. "This way."

Deeper and deeper into the earth they went at a slightly upward angle. At one point, the walls of the tunnel changed from solid rock to a mixture of rock and soil. Support beams shored up the sides. The air smelled damp and earthy. Another shaft branched upward serving as an air vent. The lamp flickered. Stelan's hands became clammy and he began to sweat. Without knowing it, he stopped moving forward, and his heart began to beat faster.

The guide turned back to look at him. "We cannot linger."

Stelan shook himself. "Sorry. I was in a cave-in this summer."

The guide nodded as if he understood and waited for Stelan to continue. His feet felt like iron weights, but he forced them forward. Breathing evenly, he tried to keep himself calm. The smell and the structure of the tunnel brought back memories of being trapped beneath a mountain of rubble, barely able to breathe. The panic he had felt then, gasping for air with a punctured lung, was worse than the burns and bruises he had endured from the Cerecians.

He tried thinking about other things to keep the walls from closing in on his mind. Talia's face appeared before his eyes, but it was too painful to dwell on. He thought of the island and was overcome with homesickness. He hadn't known how much he missed it. They continued at a steady pace, stopping only for the guide to share some bread and a flask of water.

At one point, a dozen or so men carrying heavy packs passed them travelling in the opposite direction. The tunnel was barely wide enough to admit two, so Stelan and the guide flattened themselves against the side. The men tipped their heads at the guide as they passed, but did not slow down. They would have to take their packs off and drag them behind in order to get out the fissure at the other end. Briefly, Stelan wondered what they were carrying.

When they finally reached the other end, Stelan could see the dim light of dawn showing through a small opening. Two men waited for them inside the mouth of the cave and stood as they approached. One of them wore a bandage over his eyes and held a walking stick.

"How did it go?" the guide asked the men.

"They made me take off my bandage and prove that I was truly blind," said the man with the bandage. "As if they could not remember that they were the ones who put me in this condition in the first place."

"The Chief was right not to try and get him through the barricade in disguise, even with the festival going on," the blind man's companion gestured toward Stelan. "They would have found him out."

"Of course he was," said the guide impatiently, and he turned to Stelan. "Now that it has been established without a doubt that Blind Bari has left Herida, you can assume his identity without being questioned."

The simple genius of the plan was immediately clear to Stelan, and he and Bari quickly exchanged clothing. The blind man's height and girth was close enough to Stelan's that the clothes fit without alteration. The man must have some Artylian blood in him too, thought Stelan, for the man's skin was nearly as light as his own. Bari's beard was longer, but there was nothing to be done about that.

Stelan changed quickly, though he was sure all but Bari had seen his scars in the flickering light of the lantern. If they had noticed, they made no comment.

Stelan's sword was a problem, since the beggar didn't own one. The guide took it, and with some work, was able to adjust the belt to tie the sword to Stelan's back. Bari's long cloak could now hide it from view. A small pack over the shoulders helped to cover the unnatural stiffness of his back. It would only be a problem if he had to sit down. The bandage Bari had worn was meant to spare the public from the sight of the scarred recesses where his eyes had been, but it allowed enough light to pass through that Stelan would have some idea of where he was going.

"You and Bari go to the woodsman's hut and stay there until I return," directed the guide. "I will continue with our friend here to the capital."

The men cautiously crept out of the shelter of the cave and into a cold, foggy morning. The opening was hidden by immense rocks. Even with the gray fog obscuring their movements, they went silently from boulder to boulder, crouching as low as possible. The blind man's companion, who was a very large man, carried him across the rocks on his back. The absence of vegetation in the immediate area was a blessing. Broken leaves and trampled grass would leave an obvious trail toward the secret entrance.

At the bottom of the rocky hill, Bari and his friend followed a path leading east. Stelan and his guide headed north. During the descent, Stelan hadn't worn the eye covering. Navigating his way down the hill had required his full vision. Once they reached the bottom of the hill, however, his guide instructed him to put it back on.

"Whenever we meet anyone, it would be best to

close your eyes. That way you will behave more like a blind person. I will take your arm and lead you along. The rest of the time, we can walk normally and travel more quickly."

Though Stelan wished he knew his guide's name, the Chief's men did not seem prone to introductions, so he didn't inquire. Talia had only learned Zariana's name because someone else had spoken it. He supposed it was safer for them that way. There was one other thing he felt he *should* ask.

"Will we pass by the area where the army tests its fire?" He did not know the word for weapons.

"Our path will lead us close by it, but it is not in my instructions to take you there."

"I would like to see it."

"It would not be advisable. We could be discovered. I am supposed to deliver you to one of our contacts in the capital and return right away."

The guide's tone was firm, but Stelan thought he should make the most of every opportunity to learn about the enemy's plans. There was no telling how much Talia could have learned if she hadn't had to worry about him. Plus, he had heard of how devastating the Cerecian fire arrows had been. If they were allowed to develop more powerful and accurate weapons, the combined forces of Berush and Artylia might not be enough to withstand them.

"I must try to see it. If you will not take me there, bring me as close as you can and I will find my own way."

Stelan could almost feel the guide's frown of disapproval, even though he could not make out his features through the cloth bandage.

"I will not promise anything," he said finally. "We will see what we will see."

Stelan accepted this enigmatic response as the

best he was going to get. They walked mostly in silence, only speaking when necessary. The vegetation increased as they went, and by evening they were inside a forest. His guide led him off the path under the shelter of some large trees. A lean-to had been constructed against one of them, and the guide started a fire in a ring of stones in front of it. He had obviously been this way before.

With a pot from his pack, the Chief's man made a stew of dried meat with roots he had gathered along the way. They used the last of the dry bread to soak up some of the watery stew. Several berry bushes grew nearby and these provided some fruit for dessert. Stelan removed the sword from his back and tucked it out of sight under some leaves in the lean-to while they ate.

Their small shelter attracted another weary traveler. As dusk fell, a tired old man limped into the firelight.

"May I share your warmth this evening?"

"Certainly, friend," nodded the guide. "You are welcome."

The poor in Cerecia were the same as everywhere else, more ready to share or give what little they had than the richest king. In return for a place at the fire, the man shared a little cheese and an even more welcome flask of wine. He was on his way to Herida, looking for work.

"There is plenty of work to be done, but little in the way of payment right now."

"Even if food is the only pay, it will be more than I have. I bought this cheese and wine with my last coin. When that is gone, I will have nothing."

The guide had compassion on the man and mentioned the name of a merchant who was looking for reliable help. "When you find him, tell him Hashin sent you."

The man was extremely grateful.

Stelan wondered if Hashin was truly the guide's name or if it was a code word.

There wasn't much space inside the lean-to, but the three men managed to fit. Stelan crawled in on the side where he had hidden his sword. After hiking all night through the cave and all day on the trail, he was exhausted and slept more deeply than he had since he left home.

In the morning, he woke to the smell of fish. His companion must have been up very early fishing in some nearby stream.

"Our new friend has already eaten and headed on his way." The guide held out a tin bowl. "You sleep like one who has never been in battle, though you have more scars than any living man I have seen, save the one who gave them to you."

Stelan had no good reply to this, so he merely grunted and gratefully began to eat his breakfast.

"One of our men was caught and questioned by General Riash last year," continued the guide in an uncharacteristically talkative mood. "He did not survive."

"He did not have an ally on the inside, as I had."

"Even so, it is not something many would volunteer for."

The subject was distressing for Stelan to speak about, but he felt he had to correct him. "I did not vol-un-teer," he sounded out the word, inferring its meaning from the context. "It was not planned for me to be here at all."

"And you still want to risk being recaptured by scouting out the testing site?"

"Yes." Now that he was here, he would perform his duty as well as he could. Talia would be in the princess' company the entire way, and it was not likely she would get the chance to look it over. It had to be him.

The guide looked like he was mulling it over, then he made his decision. "Very well. We will go."

With that, he began to break camp. Other than stamp out the fire and rinse the pot in the stream, there wasn't much to do, and they were soon on their way.

The guide led him out of the woods and onto a more heavily travelled road. Stelan had to take Hashin's arm as they joined the traffic returning from the festival, and they progressed more slowly while he feigned blindness and used his stick to search out potential hazards. They changed their pace occasionally to avoid falling in with other travelers so Stelan wouldn't have to risk speaking in his limited Cerecian.

After walking for several hours, they took a path leading away from the main road and into some hills. There were few trees, and no other cover. The grass looked like it had been recently grazed, and there was evidence cattle had been in the area. This coincided with what the princess had told Talia. They came upon a small thicket of brambles under a low-branching tree.

"You should leave your sword and any valuables here in case we are questioned. If you are found with the sword, it will arouse suspicion."

Stelan obeyed and thrust the sword into the heart of the bushes. He removed his pouch as well, and hid it with the sword before continuing.

The path was narrow, but there were deep ruts on the sides indicating some heavy carts had passed that way. They followed it over the hill and found themselves looking at a wide, green valley. Or mostly green valley. Here and there were blackened areas of scorched earth and burned grass. On the far side of the valley were a couple of outbuildings and a large barn. No one was in evidence, not even the herd of cattle. The valley was strangely silent.

Stelan headed toward the nearest of the black circles. As he got closer, he smelled rotting flesh and noticed a cloud of flies swarming around the carcass of a cow. Slowly and methodically, he walked around in a circle examining the ground. He slid his bandage up just enough that he could see underneath of it. Here and there he saw small shards of iron.

After making several circuits, he was rewarded by finding a rounded piece of metal nearly as long as his thumb. He slipped it into his pocket thinking that a good mathematician should be able to calculate the size of the object from the shape of the curve. He paced back to the center of the circle to estimate the distance the shard had travelled.

Suddenly, five horsemen appeared on the crest of a nearby hill.

"Bari, cover your eyes!" the guide called, using his assumed name as a reminder of who he was supposed to be.

Stelan turned away from the riders and pulled the bandage back down. In no time, the riders galloped up and surrounded them.

"Who are you and what are you doing here?"

Stelan and his guide assumed appropriately humble stances and cowered before the horsemen.

"We heard there was fresh meat to be had. Thought no one would mind if we helped ourselves," explained the guide in a whiny voice. "It is far from fresh, however, so we will be on our way, if it pleases you."

"You most certainly will be on your way," sneered

another soldier. He urged his horse forward and slapped the guide on the rear with the flat of his sword.

The guide stumbled forward and fell to his knees. "Owww!" he cried plaintively.

Stelan whirled around waving his hands frantically and pretended to trip. He fell on his face and acted afraid, covering his head with his arms.

The guide crawled over to him and tried to help him up. "We are going! We are going!"

The soldiers didn't let them go without more fun at their expense. One of them grabbed Stelan's walking stick and beat the pair over the head with it. Another pulled off the guide's pack and dumped its contents everywhere. When they finally tired of their game, they rode off laughing.

The pair picked up the pack, retrieved the items that had been strewn around, and walked away as quickly as they could. In the shade of one of the few trees, they stopped to take a long drink of water from their flasks. Stelan let out a breath of relief.

The guide said what Stelan had been thinking, "If they had pulled off your bandage, we would have been done for."

Stelan nodded. He was glad he had not been carrying his sword or pouch. If they had found the miniature of Lydima's mother, it would have brought questions as well. "I am sorry I put you in danger by asking you to take me there."

The guide rubbed his head where he had been hit with the stick. "I just hope it was worth it."

"I think it was," said Stelan, fingering the piece of iron.

∞∞∞

If she had not been constantly on edge, afraid that someone would discover her identity, Talia would have been bored to tears. A day full of dresses, hair styling, baths, and elaborate dinners was her worst nightmare. Parisha's women had braided her own hair so tightly, that it had not needed to be restyled, but she had to spend time every day brushing Bashalis' hair and watching or assisting Evash in styling it. Talia had never known anyone to take a bath every day, but Bashalis seemed to greatly enjoy them. Either that, or she enjoyed making Evash work to prepare the bath.

The handmaid was painfully pleasant to the princess, but she threw Talia a nasty look whenever she could. Talia found burrs in her bedroll and pepper in her tea. She was careful not to eat or drink anything Evash brought after that, in case she upped her game.

The only truly interesting part of the day was when they had dinner in the great hall, or rather, when she served Bashalis dinner. Talia ate in the kitchen with the other servants when the meal was over. There were always enough fruit and vegetables, but the meat and bread were often gone by the time she got there.

Dinner in the hall was interesting because she was able to listen to the king's conversations. Bashalis sat directly on his left, and Talia stood right behind her. It was hard to remember, and uncomfortable to maintain, but she slouched as unattractively as she could and shuffled her feet unbecomingly. Chysh looked at her with disdain and gave her no more notice.

"A new shipment of weapons is scheduled to arrive at the testing site in a few days, my dear sister. Would you like to go and watch the demonstration with me?"

Talia knew, as did Bashalis, that this was not a request.

"If you wish it," she replied.

"Lord Tharch will be escorting it back personally, so you will get to see him again as well."

Chysh said this as if he thought he was fulfilling his sister's greatest wish. He must know the truth, thought Talia. Could he really be so blindly arrogant as to think that his sister liked that man?

The information about the weapons delivery was extremely important to Talia. She was vexed that she was so powerless to do anything. She didn't know where Stelan was or when he would arrive. She still didn't know the location of the testing site. If she stayed long enough to try and accompany the princess to view the test, it could put Stelan in more danger. Every day they delayed was more perilous than the last and increased the risk of exposure. What if General Riash was there also? None of this even mattered, as she still didn't know how she was going to escape from the palace.

That evening, after the dinner was over, Talia went with the other servants to the kitchen to eat what she could before returning to the princess' chambers. One of the male servants, a skinny, long-nosed fellow who had been watching her at dinner for the last couple of days, approached her.

"Hello, my name is Hatch. I was wondering if you would like to take a walk with me, some night when you are free?" he asked in a timid, but hopeful voice.

"No, thank you," she replied as she grabbed another bite of food.

The man held out the last piece of meat to her. "The kitchen garden is a nice place to walk," he persisted. "It is where I spend *the chief* of my free time."

The emphasis on the words 'the chief' captured Talia's attention immediately. "Indeed," she said with renewed interest. "Well, perhaps I may join you there sometime after all."

"How about tomorrow night, after your duties are finished?"

"I will look forward to it." She smiled at him.

He gave her a shy, lopsided smile in return, and everyone hurried back to their posts before they were missed.

Talia had to give the Chief credit for the skill and cleverness of his recruits. Not to mention brazenness in making contact with her in front of a roomful of people, and none of them the wiser. Allying with this audacious smuggling mastermind might prove to be the most valuable thing she would accomplish during this mission.

The next morning, she listened to Bashalis mutter complaints about viewing another demonstration of the new explosive devices.

"I hope, at least, that there will not be cattle involved," she sighed.

Talia tried to decide if she wanted to hint to Bashalis that she might be leaving, or if she should just go, without saying anything. If she had had time, she would have tried to turn Bashalis into an informant for Berush's spy network. Maybe it could still be done.

"Have you discussed your views with Lady Parisha?"

Bashalis gave her a sharp look. "Why do you ask?"

Talia had to proceed cautiously here. Bashalis preferred people to mind their own business. She also didn't want to say anything that could incriminate Parisha. If Bashalis ever wanted out,

Parisha could put her in contact with the Chief, who could put her in contact with Ashur. Somehow, they ought to be able to help her, or at least forward any information she had.

"I believe Lady Parisha is good at finding solutions to complex problems."

The princess narrowed her eyes at Talia. "I will keep that in mind."

Evash returned and the conversation turned to mundane matters. Somehow, Talia managed to get through the day. It was hard not to let her nervousness show. She was sure Bashalis suspected something.

After sending Evash off on a contrived errand, Bashalis confronted Talia. "So you are leaving?"

"Soon. How did you know?" Talia held her breath to see how the princess would react.

"First, you advised me to get in touch with Parisha if I needed help, which implies you will not be around to give it. Second, you are tighter than a drum skin."

"I had hoped I was a better actress than that."

"Oh, no one besides me would notice anything. I have nothing else to do but observe people, so I cannot help but notice if something is different." Bashalis hesitated, then blurted out, "I wish I could come with you."

Talia's heart went out to her. "I wish you could too, but it would be too dangerous."

The princess put her chin up stoically. "I know. I am too noticeable."

"If there is a way to do it, I will try to send help for you. I have contacts who are very good at that sort of thing."

Bashalis shook her head in resignation. "That is kind, but I do not think it is possible. Come; assist me at dinner one more time."

Chysh was, thankfully, absent from the hall this evening. The steward informed them that the king had ridden out to confer with the commander in charge of border patrols. Security was being tightened everywhere with the escaped spies on the loose. After dinner was over, Bashalis went to walk on the roof, while Talia ate her own quick meal in the kitchen.

With a promise to meet her contact in the garden in an hour, Talia returned to help Bashalis with her evening rituals. She and the princess reached her bedroom at the same time and opened the door to find Evash standing over Talia's leather armor on the unrolled rug. Talia quickly shut the door behind them.

"What are you doing?" exclaimed Bashalis indignantly.

"I might ask you the same, harboring a spy! The king will not be pleased to hear about this!"

"I do not know what you are talking about!" Bashalis replied.

At the same time, Talia interjected, "She knows nothing about it."

Evash sneered. "The king's dear little sister, a traitor. So sad." She turned to Talia. "I suspected from the first moment that you were not what you seemed."

Talia started toward her, but Evash awkwardly drew Talia's sword and waved it at her.

"Turn around!" Evash demanded. "We are going straight to the captain of the guard."

Talia pretended to turn around, but instead she grabbed a vase of flowers and threw it toward the treacherous maid. As she expected, Evash dropped the sword and tried to catch the vase. In two long strides, she reached the maid and had her hands around her throat.

The smaller woman was no match for the seasoned warrior. After a few gurgling noises, she stopped struggling and her eyes bulged unnaturally. When she was sure the maid was dead, Talia laid her on the floor on top of the carpet and turned to Bashalis, who was frozen in shock.

"I am sorry you had to see that. I could not leave her alive, for she knew you had helped me."

Bashalis hugged her stomach and looked as if she would be sick. Talia took her by the shoulders and gave her a shake.

"Listen to me! I have to go. You must tell the truth. Tell your brother that Evash found out I was a spy, and I killed her. Just do not do it right away. Pretend to faint, and call for help after a suitable amount of time. No one should come looking for any of us tonight. I will appreciate as much time as you can give me."

Bashalis nodded, staring vacantly. Talia made her repeat what she needed to say.

"Do not mention the armor, either, or someone may suspect that you knew about it."

Satisfied that the princess knew her part, Talia quickly removed her overdress and put her cuirass on. Bashalis fumblingly helped her with it. Talia had stashed her trousers with the armor, so she put them on as well. Then she put the overdress back on, though it was very tight now, strapped on her sword, and put a heavy cloak over everything.

"Anyone looking closely will notice you are wearing a sword," warned Bashalis, coming back to herself slowly.

"I will have to take the chance. There will not be many people about this time of night." Talia looked at the dead woman and then back at the princess.

"I will be alright," Bashalis visibly steeled herself for a night with a corpse. "My life seems like one morbid scene after another. This will be good practice for being married to Tharch."

Bashalis' biting humor was intact. Talia considered that to be a good sign.

"I am not who you think I am. My real name is Talia. Use it if you ever need it." She ventured to give the princess a quick hug, which was returned, and left quickly.

Avoiding the palace guards wasn't too difficult. If she had to pass one, she made sure to keep her sword on the opposite side of the guard. Walking purposefully deterred anyone from asking her business.

When she reached the kitchen garden, Hatch was waiting. He unlocked a small wicket gate that led into an alley used to pile refuse. They made their way through the alley and out an archway at the other end. The guards on duty let them pass without comment. Talia assumed they must have been paid off. Hopefully they had been paid enough to keep silent once the alarm was raised. It occurred to her that the Chief had invested a great deal in this enterprise. Perhaps, more than a lucrative trade agreement, he really wanted a means of communicating with the Artylian and Berushese governments. It bore thinking about, but not right now.

As they turned into another dark alley, two cloaked figures stepped out in front of them, barring their way.

∞∞∞

It took Stelan and his guide two more days, on

foot, to reach the capital. They slept outside again the second night, but the third was extremely cold, and they slept on the floor in the common room of a tavern. The wooden floor was harder than a bed of leaves, but it was warmer. He slept on his side, with his back to the wall, rather than try and sleep on his sword. He was beginning to think it was a mistake to try and bring it. Talia was better than two of him anyway.

Once again, they had to hike all day. Stelan had followed Janis' directions about the ointments and bandages, yet the constant movement chaffed the remaining wounds, and some of them had been rubbed nearly raw again. In addition, after ten days of bedrest, and a week of imprisonment before that, Stelan was having a hard time keeping up the pace.

By the time they arrived at the main gate of the city, Stelan was so tired that he hardly noticed any of his surroundings. Through the thin cloth over his eyes, few details were discernable anyway. As the sun went down, they wove their way across the city and skirted the walls of the palace. Around the back, they ducked into an alley and hid in a recess in the wall. For the first time in his life, Stelan actually fell asleep standing up, and his companion had to nudge him awake.

It was now fully dark, and he had no idea what time it was. Footsteps could be heard coming toward them, and two dark figures came around the corner. The guide stepped into the middle of the alley and held up his hand. Stelan stood next to him.

"Stelan?"

The taller of the two figures threw back her hood. It was Talia, with some elaborate mess of braids in her hair. He nodded back at her, afraid he would break down if he tried to speak.

The manservant next to her greeted the guide. "I did not know it was to be you. Good to see you!"

"And you. You are to see them on their way and inform the captain there," he gestured at Talia, "of our arrangements for the border."

"I have it from here. Farewell."

"Farewell."

"Wait!" called Talia. "You must warn Lady Parisha. I fear that she has risked too much by sponsoring me. My absence will not go unnoticed, and there will be questions. I had to kill one of the maids, a spy Chysh had set on his sister, in order to escape."

"This is an unwelcome, but not completely unforeseen development. I will inform the Chief." He bowed with a grim expression and was off before Stelan could even thank him.

"Who was that?" Talia asked the question Stelan had been afraid to ask for four days.

"That was the Chief's eldest son. Now, let us be on our way. We must have you out of the city before dawn."

CHAPTER SEVENTEEN

Lord Yoused returned to Lyliana with a much lighter heart. With the help of his son, Warryn, he had presented his case to Lord Tomus. Berushese law, he found out, did not allow for servitude without pay. This was considered slavery in Berush, and was illegal. Conspiracy to commit murder was punishable by death in either country. This, and the falsifying of documents, was clear enough under Artylian law that Tomus did not even need to convene the council to pronounce sentence on him.

In a vindictive rage, Valryn had named one of the Artylian lords as the customer who had paid for Saley. That lord had been summoned, and he had protested that the girl had escaped during transport so he should not be held liable. However, he had paid, and Valryn had refused to give him a refund, so he was guilty of purchasing a slave under Berushese law. The Artylian law was less clear in this instance, and Tomus vowed to convene the council for clarification.

The best news was that Tomus had received

confirmation through his spy network that Lord Stelan and Captain Talia were alive and in hiding in Herida. They were awaiting an opportunity to sneak out of the city. Tomus had assured Youseds that the entire border was on alert and being patrolled with as many soldiers as they could spare.

Youseds was excited to share everything that he had learned with Lydima, so he stayed only one night at Sonefast before riding for Freosyd. When he arrived late that evening, he was informed that Lydima was upstairs with the children, and he told Jayred he would show himself up.

In the passage, he heard angry screams, and he quickened his pace. At the doorway, he pulled up short to take in the scene in front of him. Lydima held a squirming Tye who was kicking and yelling at the top of his lungs. Saley was hitting Lydima with her fists as hard as she could. As Youseds watched, Tye leaned forward and bit Lydima on the arm, and she cried out and dropped him.

Youseds had seen enough. "What is the meaning of this?" He asked sternly.

At his voice, Tye scrambled to his feet and ran around behind the bed. Saley stopped hitting Lydima, and Mya ran over and hid behind her sister. Katya and Dzhon were crying in a corner. Lylie was not in evidence.

"I am not exactly sure," said Lydima breathlessly. "Tye threw Dzhon's ball in the fire, so I was going to make him sit on the bed while I explained to him why that was wrong, and he threw a huge fit, as you saw. Saley must have been afraid of what I was going to do and came to his defense."

"I see." Youseds would have given his own boys a whipping if they had thrown a fit such as this, but with all they had been through, that might not be the best way to get through to these children.

"I have to remember to explain everything I am going to do before I do it," she sighed. Her shoulders sagged, and she rubbed her bite mark.

Youshed walked over and crouched down in front of Saley. "Lady Lydima is trying her best to help you. She is not going to hurt you, or Tye, or Mya. She is going to teach you how to behave properly. It is not right for you to hit her. You will have to go to your room as a consequence. Do you understand?"

Saley nodded.

Youshed went around to the other side of the bed. Tye covered his face with his hands and would not look at him.

"Tye, taking something that belongs to someone else is wrong. That is stealing. It is mean to destroy someone else's property. You must go to your room as a consequence. Do you understand?"

Tye gave no response.

"You can walk to your room with your sister, or I will have to carry you there. I will give you a moment to decide," said Youshed, and he walked back around to the other side of the bed.

Tye got up and barreled down the passage to his room with Saley close behind. Mya, surprisingly, after watching her siblings leave, decided to stay and sat back down on the floor with the blocks.

Lydima went over to Dzhon and Katya and hugged them. "We can make you a new ball, Dzhon."

"But I wan dat ball!" He cried.

Lydima sighed again. "I know."

"Why was Tye so mean?" wailed Katya.

"I do not know. We will make him a ball of his own. Maybe he thought it was unfair for Dzhon to have one when he had none."

"Then I will throw his ball in the fire!" Katya

declared.

"You will do no such thing. You will be kind, like the sweet girl you are. We want Tye to learn to be kind also. He will not learn it if we do not give him a good example."

Katya sniffed. "All right. I will try."

"Good girl. I am very proud of you." Lydima hugged her again.

"C'mon, Dzhon. Let's play with Mya." Katya led her brother over to play with the blocks.

Lydima stood up and looked at Yoused. "Thank you for your help. Tye is afraid of you, though."

"That is well enough for now. He will obey me. Eventually he will learn that there are some people he can trust."

Udmyla came in, and Yoused asked her to stay with the children while he took Lydima for a walk. He told her to put on her cloak, and they strolled out to the kitchen garden in the moonlight. Yoused looked at Lydima and saw tears glistening on her cheeks. She put her head in her hands and wept.

"I . . . cannot . . . do this. I . . . do not have . . . what it takes . . . to be . . . a mother," she choked out between sobs.

Yoused put his hands on her shoulders and she leaned forward and cried on his chest. He held her in his arms and let his chin rest on the top of her head.

"You are doing a marvelous job. You love them. That is what they need the most. It will just take time."

Her sobs became less intense, and he stroked her hair. She looked up at him, and he bent down and kissed her. He couldn't help it.

Lydima pushed him away and stared at him, shocked. "What are you doing?"

Yoused tried to gather his wits for a reply, but

before he could say anything, she turned and fled back into the castle. As soon as he recovered, he ran after her. He had to figure out what was wrong and explain himself.

∞∞∞

Lydima ran through the hall and into the study and slammed the door. Lord Yoused had kissed her! Of all the men in the world, he was the only one with whom she had thought she would be safe. Now, it seemed, he thought of her the same way every other man thought of her. The sting of that realization made her gasp with pain, and it nearly brought her to her knees. She had hoped to earn his respect, and instead had achieved the opposite.

Footsteps sounded in the corridor, and she heard a gentle knock on the door.

"Lydima, are you there? I am sorry. I should have asked your permission before kissing you. Please open the door and let me explain."

Lydima sobbed and backed farther away from the door.

"Lydima, please. I must speak with you. I love you! I want to ask you to marry me."

Her jaw dropped. She wasn't sure she had heard correctly. She ran to the door and yanked it open. "You what?"

He started forward, but she held up her hand for him to keep his distance. He looked at her with a pained expression.

"I love you," he repeated simply. "I want you to be my wife."

"Why?" Lydima was incredulous.

Yoused chuckled softly, but with an edge of cynicism. "You are a strong and beautiful woman, and

251

these past weeks you have shown yourself to be a wiser, kinder, and more caring woman than any I know. You are a fierce defender of those you love, and I want nothing more than to be included in that small circle."

"But you sent me away before."

"And you assumed it was because I did not want you, but that was not it at all."

"Then why?" she demanded.

"I knew if we had come together then, it would have been merely lust on my part and avarice on yours. Nothing good would have come of it. I have known what it is to love deeply, and I want that again, not just some temporary satisfaction."

"What about Eemya?" She could not understand why he would have proposed to Eemya if he had been interested in her all this time.

Yoused sighed. "I greatly admire your cousin. She is a lovely woman and a good leader. Not to mention the fact that the consolidation of our two holdings would have been financially beneficial. I thought we could be happy together. However, I did not have the passion for her that I had for my wife, and I have for you. I had given up on finding it again. She could sense it. That is why she refused me."

"But you cannot marry me!"

"The only thing to prevent me is your refusal. I pray that you will give me your consent instead," he pleaded earnestly.

Lydima looked into his eyes and saw that he told the truth. She felt faint and had to look away. "Your children, your subjects—they will never accept me. You will be a laughingstock. I have been . . ." she blushed, and could not finish.

"You have not been with any of my sons, have you?"

She shook her head, grateful that she could honestly reply in the negative.

"Then I can deal with anything in your past, if only you will promise me your future." He got down on his knees and took her hand. "Will you marry me, Lydima?"

Lydima's thoughts swirled around in her head, and she couldn't think clearly. Already emotionally exhausted from dealing with the children, she had no idea how she felt about Yoused's declaration. She spoke the only thought that came to her mind.

"What about the children?"

"They may come with you. I would be happy to have them."

"I . . . I will need some time to consider."

"You may have all the time you need," Yoused assured her. "I must return to Sonefast tomorrow," he said regretfully, "but you may send for me whenever you are ready to see me."

Lydima nodded numbly.

Yoused rose to his feet and changed to a more light-hearted tone. "I actually came here today to share some good news with you."

First, he told her what he had heard of Stelan. Lydima was appropriately joyful to hear he was still alive. Then, he explained that Tomus held his views on the legal ramifications of the situation at The White Lily and that Valryn had been found guilty according to several points of Artylian law. No one would have to fear him anymore. Yoused also recounted how Saley had managed to escape.

"I knew she would never have left Tye and Mya! She was trying to get back to them! That makes sense now. She had probably never even left the inn before and did not know the way back," mused Lydima.

"Lucky for her, she made it to you," Yoused smiled.

"Your insistence in this matter gave me the impetus I needed to deal with a disagreeable problem. I had been avoiding it."

"You always do the right thing when you know what it is, my lord." She put her hand on his arm, and he covered it with his own.

Lydima felt her eyes mist over, and before she could cry again she moved toward the door and excused herself by saying, "I need to put the children to bed."

"Would you like some help?"

Lydima rested her hand on the doorframe and looked at Yoused over her shoulder. Not many men would volunteer to assist with wrangling a herd of wild children into their beds. She wasn't sure if his presence would be beneficial for Tye at this stage or not, but perhaps he could help with Dzhon. The one thing she knew for certain she could not be was a male role model.

"Yes, please."

Instead of offering her his arm, Yoused came and took her hand and held it as they walked back up the stairs. Walking this way made Lydima feel warm and tingly all over. Lord Yoused's proposal had come as a complete surprise, but the regard of such a man was not to be taken lightly. It was incredible that a man like him could love a woman like her.

Already she held him in high esteem. Her gratitude for all he had done for her and the children was boundless. Could she love him? Did it matter? Marriage to someone, anyone was all she had thought she wanted only a few months ago.

But now there were the children to consider. Would Sonefast be a good place for them to grow up? Would they have to listen to snide remarks about their adoptive mother? Would they be simply tolerated, or would their presence be resented?

People would look down on them. They were somewhat sheltered at Freosyd because of her relation to Eemya, but that tentative acceptance would not extend elsewhere. These questions plagued Lydima, but she knew right now was not a good time to make a decision.

When they reached her room, Mya was looking decidedly droopy, and when Lydima picked her up, she laid her head on her shoulder and closed her eyes. Udmyla had started getting Katya ready for bed, and she was already in her nightclothes.

"Thank you, Udmyla. Can you sit with Aylria for a while? I am worried about her. Katya, can you wash your face and get under the bedcovers? Dzhon, Lord Youth will help you get ready and tuck you in, and then I will come check on you."

She walked out of the room with Mya as Dzhon began chattering at Youth. She washed Mya's face and changed her diaper, then put her in her own small cot next to Saley's bed. Mya was still wetting the bed, and the cot was much easier to clean if the cloth diaper didn't absorb it all.

Saley and Tye washed their faces sullenly, but Saley hugged Lydima before getting into her bed and let Lydima kiss her goodnight. Tye pulled the blanket over his head, so she couldn't kiss him.

"I still care about you Tye, even though you did something wrong," she said to the lump under the covers. "Goodnight."

She hoped Youth was right, and that he would learn to trust eventually.

Next Lydima peeked in on Lylie, who was already asleep with the nurse, and then she returned to the corridor to see Youth quietly slipping out of her room.

"Dzhon is asleep, but Katya is determined to stay awake until you come in." The crinkles around Youseé's eyes deepened, and his eyes twinkled with humor.

"Thank you," Lydima said sincerely.

She remained standing in the passage, unsure of what to do or say. Youseé stepped closer to her, and she caught her breath, thinking that he might kiss her again. Now that she knew his true feelings, she almost wished he would.

"I must leave very early in the morning, so I will not see you to say goodbye." He took her hands in his, and his voice deepened with emotion. "Why did you run when I kissed you?" he asked softly.

"I thought . . . I was not sure . . . " she was afraid to say what she had thought for fear of offending him.

"Were you afraid that I would take advantage of you, that I had base motives?"

She nodded, staring at the floor. She was ashamed to have believed it, even for a moment.

If he was disappointed in her for thinking that of him, he did not say so.

"It is not because you think I am too old, or my gray beard disgusts you?"

"Oh, no! Not at all!" she looked up quickly.

Youseé looked relieved, but gazed at her with a serious expression. "I know that you have been hurt in the past, and the last thing I want to do is hurt you again. You will have to tell me what you need from me. How can I prove my love to you?"

"You have nothing to prove. You have done so much for me already. I just need time to ascertain my own feelings." Her heart started beating faster as she arranged what she wanted to say next, and she continued breathlessly, "I have never been kissed by someone who loves me before. Now that I know your intent, I would like it if you kissed me again."

Yoused sucked in his breath, released her hands, and placed his own around her waist as he drew her close. "Are you sure?"

"Yes," she answered as she wrapped her arms around his neck.

If she had any doubt of his devotion, it was completely erased when his lips met hers. She had been kissed many times before, but this was totally, immeasurably, earth-shakingly different. The love and warmth she felt flowing from him overwhelmed her.

In that moment, she also knew that she could love him back. She returned his kiss, pressing into him and parting her lips to cover his mouth more fully. Yoused's kisses became more amorous, and Lydima had to restrain herself from doing the things she would normally do to escalate a situation like this when she was expecting compensation. She was just as capable of taking advantage of him as he was of her, and she wanted to, badly.

It would be unfair to him, however, for her to let things go any farther when she didn't know how she was going to answer him. He desired a lifetime commitment from her, and she could hardly behave as she had not wanted him to behave only a short while earlier. Soon, all thought was driven from her mind, and she lost herself in his caresses. Enjoying this moment was enough for now.

Suddenly, Yoused's pace slowed. He kissed her once more, tenderly, and then stepped back. They stared at each other, panting, and trembling with passion.

"Are you . . . was that all right? Did I go too far?"

"It was more than all right." She placed her hand softly on the side of his face and slid her fingers along his jawline. "Goodnight," she whispered as she walked away from him.

Leaving him standing in the passage, she went into her room and closed the door. Much as she wanted to reassure him, she could not. Though she knew now that she loved him, she realized that she could never marry him. She would not allow him to disgrace himself by marrying her. But oh, how was she ever going to tell him?

∞∞∞

Yoused did not catch a moment of sleep that night. He was so confused. After a kiss like that, it seemed like Lydima must feel something for him, yet her goodbye had sounded almost mournful. Could she have kissed him that way and not felt anything? After all, she was experienced in arousing men's desires.

No, he would not allow himself to think that. She wouldn't play with his emotions that way, especially when she had been so upset at the thought that *he* might be insincere. Had he ever given her cause to doubt his sincerity? He didn't think so. Why would she doubt it?

The answer finally came to him as he tossed and turned in the middle of the night: every other man she had known had been insincere, or at least lacking in commitment. It would be hard to believe that he would be any different.

Jayred had told him a little more about Valryn's visit and the effect Lydima's uncle had had on her. Men like him had used her all her life, men who should have protected her. She had learned to use them in return, but that was no excuse. No wonder she was wary.

He had rushed things. He should have told her his

feelings first, asked to court her, given her time to get used to the idea. It had not been in his mind to propose yet, but circumstances had necessitated that he make his intentions clear.

Before dawn, he made his way to the hall, and the servant on duty brought him some cheese and day-old bread from the kitchen. His guards were waiting, and he mounted his horse and rode toward home. Not for the first time, he wished that Darius could have found someone else, anyone else, to be acting governor in his absence. Leaving Lydima right now was the last thing he wanted to do.

Yoused's thoughts were agitated, and his mount could sense it. The animal flicked its ears back and forth, and Yoused spoke soothingly to him. The uncertainty in his own mind remained, but one thing was very clear: he was not going to give up easily this time.

After a long day's ride, several urgent business matters had to be attended to. Tired as he was, before he finally went to bed that night Yoused wrote Lydima a letter:

My dear Lydima,

I would like to assure you that if I were so fortunate as to secure your affections, I would treasure your love above all else in this world. I want you to feel confident in your decision, so take all the time you need. If there is anything I can do for you, anything you need from me, you have only to ask.

Life offers many hardships and obstacles, and I would like to face them with you. Having someone you love by your side, from whom to draw strength, can mean the difference between perseverance and despair. I love you, and I would be your strength, if you will have me.

Your past makes no difference to me. I know if you promised yourself to be true to me, you would keep that promise, as I would for you. That is all that matters.

Yoused

When he had finished, Yoused sealed the letter and handed it to his steward to be sent first thing in the morning.

CHAPTER EIGHTEEN

Talia and Stelan followed Hatch to a small house in the city wall. Once inside, the owner of the house presented Talia with her bow and arrows. The Chief had kept his promise to deliver them to her. On inspection, she found that someone had added two Cerecian fire arrows.

"From now on, you will travel only by night," said the manservant, "so you may resume your own identities."

"I am glad to be able to wear Lydima's father's sword properly. I cannot think of it as my own." Stelan belted it securely around his waist. "I am not looking forward to another sleepless night of travel, but at least I do not have to do it blindfolded," he declared as he set the disguise aside.

Talia shed her overdress and used her dagger to shorten her underdress to her customary long tunic length. She still wore her fancy boots, which were not as practical for hiking, but at least they fit. Armed with her sword, her quiver and bow slung on her back, she felt normal for the first time in two weeks.

The owner of the house had left them alone. It was better not to know more than he needed to. Hatch unfolded a map and laid it on a table. It was very close to the map Janis had drawn, which Stelan had in his pouch.

"It will take you three days of steady walking to reach the mountains from here. Along the river is the easiest path, but also the most travelled. The shortest route is to travel due north. We have safe houses here and here," Hatch pointed to marks on the map, "where you can rest during the day.

"Chysh's soldiers are covering the foothills like ants. There are no good passes in this stretch of the mountains, but we have not had our first snow yet, so it should be possible to cross. The challenge will be to avoid the patrols. This area here is extremely steep and rocky and impossible for men on horseback to navigate, but a man, or woman," he smiled at Talia, "Can climb it."

Hatch started to fold up the map, but Stelan stopped him. He looked at Talia. "I know where the weapons testing site is. We stopped there on the way," he said in Berushese. He fished a metal shard out of his pouch and held it out to her. "I picked up this."

Talia's eyes lit up. "Chysh said they are expecting a new shipment soon. Tharch is supposed to deliver it himself. I would love to sabotage it, or at the least, watch the demonstration from a distance."

"Do you think it could be a trap? What if he suspected you to be a spy, if he did not suspect your actual identity, and said it to flush you out?"

"It is possible, but it might still be worth the risk. What do you think? If you think it unwise, we will not go." She had put him through enough already, and wouldn't force him into more danger.

Stelan's face registered surprised that she deferred to him. "I think it is very unwise, but the danger posed by these new weapons is so fearsome that any setback we can give them would be helpful to our side."

"You should not go," interjected Hatch, smiling when he startled them by speaking Berushese. "It is too risky. The area is completely exposed. There is no cover."

"He is right," mused Stelan. "What if we attacked the shipment in the woods, here, on the way?"

"If we could reach it in time, and if we could avoid detection until then."

Hatch sighed. "If you are determined to go, there is a dry rainwater cistern that we use as a hidey-hole where you could stay one day, and a farmer with an available hayloft for the next day." He pointed out their locations. "The patrols are concentrated in the cities and the border. It is not likely that they will be looking for you to retrace your steps."

With this information, Talia and Stelan decided to risk it. Hatch supplied them with food for the journey, and explained the stone markings the smugglers used to identify their safe havens. Then they prepared to set out. The city wall was not as high as the palace wall, and they were able to lower themselves carefully from the roof and drop the remaining distance to the ground below.

∞∞∞

All night they ran, keeping to the trees and the fields, running low along the stone fences to keep from being seen by the rare night traveler or farmer checking on his animals. Just before dawn, they found the cistern Hatch had described. It was next to the foundation of a burned-down farmhouse. The narrow opening was covered with a weathered board. When they moved it, they saw a large space meant for storing water.

With no building to funnel rainwater into it, the cistern was dry. It was dug deep into the ground and lined with mortar. The mortar was made from quicklime produced by burning a fire on limestone and turning it to powder. Combined with volcanic ash and water, the resulting mixture was powerful enough to melt glass. Dry, it formed a hard, watertight surface.

Hand and footholds had been cut into the side, and they descended into the large, wide hole at the bottom. Talia came in last and pulled the cover back over the entrance. Exhausted, they removed their swords, put their packs under their heads and fell asleep.

∞∞∞

When Stelan woke, it was late in the afternoon. The sun was still shining, but the small amount of light filtering through the cracks in the cistern's wood cover was barely enough for him to discern Talia's outline. He estimated he had slept nine or ten hours. Feeling round the dark space, he discovered a lamp left by the smugglers and lit it.

Talia was still asleep. At first, he thought she was shivering from cold, though the daytime temperature underground was quite tolerable, but then he heard her whimpering and figured she was dreaming. She was frowning in her sleep, and Stelan became worried that she was having a nightmare.

"Talia," he called softly, squatting down and patting her shoulder.

As she woke up, she made a strange, silent scream and sat up quickly, pushing Stelan roughly away from her. He rocked backward onto the floor. She reached for her sword, and before he could blink, he found himself staring at the point of her blade for the second time.

"I know your skill with the sword is far superior to mine, but you do not have to constantly remind me of it," he said jestingly, but it was hard to keep an edge of fear out of his voice.

Talia blinked and returned her sword to its scabbard. "Do not do that," she said shakily.

Stelan couldn't tell if her voice shook from anger or from something else. He rolled onto his side and sat up. "I am sorry. I thought you were having a bad dream."

Talia sat back down and put her head in her hands without speaking. She gulped in air and blew it out several times.

"What is wrong, Talia? Please tell me." Stelan scooted over next to her.

"Get away from me," she replied harshly.

"Not until you tell me what is the matter."

"I killed a woman with my bare hands yesterday!" she yelled at him. "I have never done that before."

Stelan didn't know what to say, so he just sat quietly, ready to listen.

"I did not have to kill her. I did it to protect Princess Bashalis. I could have tied her up and run, but I was afraid of what Chysh would do to his sister when she was found. That is what happens when you let your feelings get in the way."

"Chysh has killed at least an uncle and a cousin that we know of. It is not hard to believe that he would kill his sister, too, if he learned that she betrayed him by helping you. You probably saved her life."

Talia shook her head. Her eyes stared vacantly. "Do you know how many people I have killed now?" She turned to look at him. "Fourteen. The first time was three years ago. Tomus and I were riding with Prince Darius in a scouting party near Mount Barus.

"We were tracking an Artylian raiding party, and they ambushed us with a hail of arrows. Tomus was shot in the shoulder and fell off his horse. I defended him and dragged him to safety while Darius and his men quickly rooted the bandits from their hiding places and slaughtered them.

"I killed two men who thought it would be easy to finish my brother off with only a woman guarding him," she scoffed. "The first I shot with an arrow, and the second I gutted with my sword. I was so jittery afterward I could barely stay on my horse, but I did not get sick. I had Tomus to look after, so I would not let myself be sick.

"We took Tomus home to recover, and that is where he met Onia for the first time. Queen Sashia was visiting my mother, and Onia was with her. She has her mother's gift for nursing."

"Tomus is lucky to have a sister like you."

Talia looked up at the opening of the cistern and appeared not to have heard him. "The sun has set. We should be on our way." She began to climb up the short shaft to the exit.

"Wait, you should let me go first. I am more dispensable than you are."

She glared down at him and looked like she wanted to argue, but she descended. "Go," she motioned upward.

Stelan put out the lamp and climbed to the top of the cistern. Then he cautiously removed the cover from the opening. Peering out of the hole, he saw the faint glow of light on the western edge of the sky was fading quickly, but the area seemed deserted. It was well away from the road, and there were no houses nearby. After looking and listening for several moments, he gave Talia the all clear.

The nights were getting longer and colder, but their constant movement kept them warm. Talia did not seem to tire. They stopped only to eat a few bites from the provisions Hatch had given them, or to relieve themselves behind a tree or stone wall. Every time they stopped, Stelan wanted to scratch his scabs. They were at the point in the healing process where they were constantly itchy, so it was just as well they didn't stop often.

They travelled much faster than they had on the journey to Gabrishia. By the end of the second night, they had covered nearly the same distance that had previously taken three days. The barn they were to sleep in was very close to the forest where they planned to wait for the caravan.

"We are in the right place," Talia said as she studied an arrangement of stones in the yard.

Hatch had told them what to look for. One configuration meant safety, another meant danger. It appeared that all was well.

Stelan climbed gratefully into the hayloft just before dawn, but Talia told him she was going to do some scouting.

"I need to find try and find out when the shipment will be passing through," she reasoned.

The farmer, who had come out early to milk his cow, had been persuaded to give her the name of a contact in a nearby village who might have information. Stelan was too tired to argue, and he fell asleep almost immediately.

∞∞∞

The sun was setting again when Stelan awoke. He was relieved to find Talia asleep nearby. She had put her overdress back on under her cloak for warmth, and for reconnaissance into the village. She stirred and sat up, rubbing her eyes. The red glow of sunset flooded through the window of the loft and bathed her in its soft light. Stelan felt a strong urge to kiss her, and do more than kiss her, and he had to look away.

"Who did you, what out find did you? I mean . . . ," he cursed uncharacteristically and slid off the hay toward the ladder. "I cannot do this," he muttered as he climbed down from the loft.

Talia stared after him with a bewildered expression, but he didn't enlighten her. Stelan walked over to the rain barrel at the corner of the barn and dipped his head in it. The chilly night air on his wet hair cooled him off quickly. He rubbed his scalp vigorously until his hair stood up on end. He felt his beard. Janis had touched it up with more dye the day before he had left. It was now the length of the nail on his pinky finger.

He sighed and took a deep breath, leaning over the barrel with his hands resting on either side of it. Behind him, he heard Talia's footsteps approaching uncertainly. He didn't think he could even look at her, much less talk to her right now.

"I have changed my mind," he heard her say timidly.

It took a few moments for her words to sink in. Even then, he was not sure he could trust his own ears. He turned to look at her.

"What did you say?"

Talia took a deep breath. Her eyes were shining

and she gazed at him earnestly. "After this mission is over, I will return with you, if you want me."

"*If* I want you!" He closed the distance between them, put his hands on her shoulders, and studied her intently. "I want you so badly it is all I can think about! But what about being a soldier? Are you sure you are not just feeling morose after what happened in Gabrishia?"

"I have had a lot of time to think the past few days," her voice broke and a tear ran down her cheek. "I feel like I am losing myself. I do not think I can continue to deal out death anymore and still keep my humanity. It is time for me to do something else."

Stelan reached up and wiped her tear away with his finger. "I will gladly be the something else," he said as he pulled her close and covered her lips with his. His yearning for her was so strong that he all he could feel was her body and his heart pounding in his ears. All other senses were drowned out.

Talia slipped her arms around his waist and clung to him. He held her tightly, kissing her tenderly. He could tell she had spoken the truth, and she needed him right now. She needed him to care for her and to support her in spite of everything she had done, even though she had done it for her country and her people, and, he hoped, to get back to *him*. And he would do anything for her. But they were still a long way from home.

She pulled away. "Not yet. We have a mission to complete."

Stelan let go of her, knowing she was right, but he was relieved he no longer had to deny his feelings. It had become nearly impossible. He wished he knew how to say everything that was on his mind. He felt so awkward and unsure of himself around her, but his heart soared at the thought that she would return with him. Somehow, when this was over, he would find the words.

They gathered their things and prepared to search for the enemy shipment. And to destroy it.

∞∞∞

"I found the Chief's contact in the village. She said the caravan is due to pass through tomorrow. They are camping in the other end of the forest tonight. If we can sneak up on them while most of them are asleep, it will be our best chance."

Stelan nodded. "I am ready. Let's do it."

The evening was clear, and the moon was bright, but the forest was very dark. The overdress went back into the pack again. They dared not follow the road, so they followed a stream that would take them close to their destination. Talia tried to stay alert and not let her thoughts distract her, but she couldn't keep her mind from wandering to the man behind her. She hadn't planned on telling him about her decision yet. She had barely made it herself.

One's duty in open warfare was usually obvious, but this particular mission had asked a lot of her. She had had to make choices that she was not completely comfortable with, even if they were the best ones available. When she had brushed the princess' hair and thought about how easy it would be to kill her, she hadn't been pleased with herself and who she had become.

Seeing Stelan again had made her feel so happy, but then she had felt unworthy to be with him. He was so pure, so good. He wouldn't want to be with her when he knew what she had done, she had thought. But it hadn't fazed him. He had tried to comfort her, and he put her safety before his own, though she had to agree tactically that was the best strategy. No matter how hard she had tried to push him away, he still cared for her.

All last night while they ran, she had tried to run from her feelings, but could not escape them. When she'd returned from the village, she had sat and watched Stelan sleep, and she'd admitted to herself that she loved him. She could no longer deny it.

She had almost woken him and told him right then and let him make love to her. She wanted it as badly as he did. But she had been afraid it would distract them from their mission and make it more difficult to get home safely. Then it had become evident Stelan was already so distracted and off-balance from trying to keep his emotions in check that telling him might be more helpful than harmful.

They stopped briefly to drink from the stream. Before she could start walking again, Stelan took her hand.

"Talia, when you said you would return with me, did you mean to the island?"

"Unless you plan on going somewhere else?"

"No," Stelan smiled, then hesitated, "but does that mean . . . ?"

"I will have to learn Artylian," Talia teased.

Stelan chuckled softly. "I mean, will you go as my wife?"

Talia had thought about this. Marriage was not a mission with a definite end. This was the rest of her life. If she was no longer going to be a soldier, there was nothing to stop her from marrying and having children, but there were so many unknowns. Talia did not like unknowns or variables. The island was unknown, Stelan's domain was unknown, the people were unknown, and the language was unknown. She would know nothing and no one there but him.

But Stelan, she felt, was a constant. Under the worst of conditions he was kind, understanding, and supportive. With him, she could face any unknown.

"Yes," she replied.

He kissed her again. She struggled to remember they had somewhere to be.

"Come on, we have to keep moving."

As they drew closer to the reported location of Tharch's camp, Talia left the stream and picked her way carefully through the undergrowth with Stelan following. They went slowly, testing every step, listening for any unnatural sounds, not wanting to make any noise of their own. If it was a trap, sentries or patrols might be posted farther out than normal for this type of shipment.

The moon was halfway through the sky by the time they spotted the enemy campfire. At least two dozen men were sleeping around it. A wagon filled with wooden crates sat well away from the fire. They could see two sentries inside the camp. Several horses were tethered at the edge of the woods. On one side of the clearing, there was a tent. She assumed that was where Lord Tharch was sleeping. She wished she had enough arrows to set it alight too.

Talia touched Stelan's shoulder and they crouched down. Silently she pointed out the sentries.

"We mutht wait until the watch changeth. I want to know for thure how many thentrieth there are, and where they are hidden," she whispered in his ear, slurring her 's'es so the sound wouldn't carry.

They waited for some time. Her legs started to cramp. At last, one of the sentries went and roused several of his fellow soldiers who got up and prepared to take their turn at watch. Stelan and Talia carefully counted them and observed where they were stationed. One of them melted into the forest on the far side, and they couldn't see where he went, but Talia counted slowly to fifty-four before she saw a man return from the same direction.

Another man, armed with a bow and quiver of arrows, came into the woods very near their hiding place. He stopped below a tree and waited while another archer climbed down, then he went up into the tree. Tharch was taking precautions. Talia watched the archer closely to see where he perched. She would have to take him out first. Two men disappeared down the road on each side, and two new sentries patrolled the camp itself.

Stelan had told her how far he estimated the shards from the explosive devices would travel when they burst. The only problem was, she wasn't sure how accurate she could be with the fire arrows from that distance.

The Cerecians had improved their design since the battle in the channel. They were now affixed to a normal arrow, so she assumed their flight would be truer, but there was still a fuse that had to be lit. She didn't know how it would affect her aim. If the fuse didn't ignite the fire until after it had hit the target, that would be best, but there were only two arrows, and she wouldn't have an opportunity to test them.

The man in the tree was straddling a branch about three horse lengths above the ground. Talia's vision was very sharp, and she could just make out his outline. Occasionally, the firelight reflected off of something shiny. When she hit him, he would most likely fall. That meant they only had a few seconds to light the fire arrows before someone sounded the alarm and started searching the woods for them.

Talia handed Stelan her tinder box, took her dress out of her pack, and held it up to screen him. The guards might hear the noise of the flint striking the steel, but if they couldn't see the spark, they would not discover their location until it was too late.

"Now," she whispered.

As soon as the tinder had caught, she dropped the dress, nocked an arrow, and loosed it at the man in the tree. He had nocked his own arrow and was searching the woods for the source of the noise, but he didn't find it in time. Talia's missle found its mark with a soft thud.

Swiftly she nocked a fire arrow, Stelan lit the fuse, and she shot it at the wagon. As soon as it hit, the fuse reached the magic fire, and it showered sparks everywhere. It wasn't exactly where she had aimed, but it hit a crate, nevertheless.

Talia readied the second fire arrow as the men on watch started shouting. The archer had fallen at the same moment the first arrow had hit the wagon, so his demise went unnoticed. The second arrow stuck in the canvas covering the top of the wagon, and it quickly went up in flames. Rather than try and put out the fire, the men ran down the road in the opposite direction.

Tharch emerged from his tent just as the shower of sparks began to increase. One of the fuses inside a crate had caught. The weapons stored in the wagon might be bait to draw out the spies, but they were real. In moments, they would explode. Tharch held his hand up to his eyes, then turned and ran after his men. No one ran into the woods.

"Go," hissed Talia, as she stuffed her dress quickly back into her pack. She didn't want to give Tharch any clues as to who did this, though he would probably guess. They didn't pick their way quietly this time, but rushed headlong into the forest.

When the wagon exploded, they were both thrown to the ground. Talia had a brief moment of intense pain before darkness engulfed her.

∞∞∞

Stelan turned to look and saw a huge ball of fire and debris flying through the air. Not all of the weapons burst at once, and a few minor explosions quickly followed the first. Some of the bombs were blown farther from the wagon before they detonated, an effect he and Talia had not anticipated.

Stelan hadn't factored the wagon itself into the blast radius either, and pieces of it fell all over. His ears were ringing, and everything seemed to be moving in slow motion. He turned to check on Talia, and she was still lying face down on the ground. A section of heavy board lay next to her.

"Talia!"

Stelan couldn't see well enough in the dark to tell where she was injured. He felt her over carefully and his hand came away from her head covered in blood. He tried not to panic. They had to get out of there quickly, before they were discovered. He didn't know if Talia was still alive, but there was no way he was going to leave her.

He looked around and tried to think of what to do. Most of the horses lay dead or wounded in the camp. One had pulled loose from its tether and bolted down the road, but one reared and whinnied and strained against the rope that held it. Quickly, he retrieved the dress from the pack and ran over to the horse.

Speaking calmly in Cerecian in case anyone heard, and because the horse would be more familiar with it, he was able to get close enough to throw the fabric over the horse's head. The horse stood still enough for him to cut the tether and lead it into the woods.

With its eyes covered, Stelan led the horse next to

where he had left Talia. He was now thinking clearly enough to check for a pulse and was relieved beyond measure to find one. Behind him, Tharch's men were beginning to venture back to the camp. Once the smoke cleared, they would fan out and start searching for the saboteurs. Fortunately, the horse was dark, and the flames licking the remains of the wagon were crackling loudly enough to cover the little noise he was making.

After considering how best to get them both onto the saddleless horse, he gently picked Talia up. They were the same height, and although she was slimmer and weighed less, it was a still a great effort to lift her. First he had to remove her pack and leave the bow. They were too bulky. Their only chance now was not anonymity, but speed. Next he unslung her sword and strapped it over his own. Then he rolled her over, sat her up, pulled her over his shoulder from a squatting position, and then stood. To get her on the horse, he had to slide her over its back, feet first.

Once he had taken charge of the horse, it remembered its battle training and waited patiently. It was used to the danger of combat, but this was the first time it had experienced an explosion of this magnitude. Stelan noticed it was bleeding from several gashes in its side.

Speaking softly, Stelan removed the eye-covering and put it in his pack. Grabbing a handful of mane, he pulled himself onto the horse's back and swung his leg over. Briefly, he let go of the mane and adjusted Talia so she straddled the horse right behind its withers. Conscious, it would be a very uncomfortable way to ride.

Putting one arm around Talia's waist, he grabbed the mane again with his other hand and sat forward. The horse responded and began to walk. War horses were trained to carry fighters who had to use both hands for defense and attack and didn't need reins.

They hadn't gone far before he heard a shout. They'd been spotted.

Stelan might not have any battle experience, but he knew how to ride. He had ridden almost every day of his life for as long as he could remember.

He urged the horse faster and angled it toward the road. They could not travel quickly enough through the dense undergrowth and low branches. He would have to risk an arrow in the back to avoid being surrounded in the woods.

As soon as the horse's hooves hit the packed dirt, Stelan leaned as far forward as he could and squeezed the horse's sides with his legs. The horse quickly sped into a gallop. Stelan heard an arrow whiz by his ear, but then they went around a bend in the road and were out of sight of the camp.

CHAPTER NINETEEN

Lydima went through the day after Yoused's proposal in a state of numbness and complete inattention. Mechanically, she went through her routine and cared for the children, but they noticed her absence of mind and took advantage of it. When Tye managed to drink a goblet of wine at dinner while no one was looking and made himself sick, Maygla finally spoke to Lydima.

"My lady, you must rally yourself. The children need you."

Maygla's words brought Lydima to herself briefly, and she noticed how cranky the children were. Dzhon and Mya had missed their naps since she had let them play right through them.

Yula took a subdued Tye to the infirmary to give him something for his stomach, while Nyla and Udmyla helped her take the rest of the children upstairs. Saley helped with Mya, who fussed and cried through the entire process of getting ready for bed. Mercifully, she could not keep her eyes open and fell asleep as her sister carried her to her room.

Dzhon was no better, and he squirmed and thrashed while Lydima tried to help him into his nightclothes. Finally, she gave up trying to dress him and just laid him in his cot. Katya sang him a sweet, nonsensical lullaby she had composed. His eyelids soon became heavy and he was fast asleep.

Then the nurse came in with a fussy Lylie. "I cannot get her to calm down."

Lydima sighed. "I have been neglecting her too." She held out her arms and took the baby, who instantly stopped crying. She took several shuddering breaths, and her little hand grasped a loose lock of Lydima's hair and held on tightly. Lydima felt guilty about how self-absorbed she had been. "Go on to bed," she told Puriya. "I will keep her tonight."

She walked around the room with Lylie until she also fell asleep. Lydima was exhausted when she finally laid the baby down and climbed into bed. Katya was still awake. She turned and patted Lydima's hair. That simple action broke the dam Lydima had built around her feelings, and tears began to stream down her face.

"Do you miss Lord Yoused? Is he going to be our new daddy?"

A laugh caught in Lydima's throat. "Why do you say that?"

"Only daddies tuck children into bed," replied Katya with logical certainty. "And he sent Saley and Tye to their room when they were bad."

Lydima smiled as she wiped tears off her cheeks. "He has had practice with three of his own sons."

"Oh." Katya thought about that for a while. "But could he do it again?"

"Lord Yoused has his own castle and lands to take care of. We would have to move to Sonefast."

"I would not mind."

"I would."

"Why?"

"Katya, it is time to go to sleep. Sing one of your lullabies for me."

Katya complied, and Lydima drifted off while she was still singing.

∞∞∞

The next day offered more trials. Tye still looked queasy in the morning, and ate little of his breakfast. A couple of the ladies had taken Saley and Katya for sewing lessons yesterday, and helped them to start piecing together new cloth balls for Tye and Dzhon. After breakfast was cleared away, they continued working on them. When they were finished, and the girls presented the toys to the two boys.

Dzhon squealed happily and started playing with his right away. Tye looked at his for a moment and promptly threw it into the fire. Lydima was surprised, but held her tongue and watched to see what would happen next.

Saley's eyes started to tear up, but then she stiffened and turned away to work on her spelling lesson.

Katya gasped and looked at Tye in disbelief. "Your own sister made that for you! How could you?"

Dzhon picked up his ball and held it close, afraid that it would be Tye's next victim.

Tye glanced at Katya's shocked face, then at his sister's straight back, and ran from the room.

Lydima reached the passage in time to see him slam the door of his bedroom. She summoned a manservant and posted him outside the door. Tye could be heard yelling and throwing things inside the room.

"Only interfere if it sounds like he is becoming a danger to himself, or he breaks the window," she instructed quietly and returned to the other children.

Mya and Dzhon were playing happily, Tye's outburst already forgotten. Katya's sensitive nature was still disturbed, but she sat next to Saley and worked on her lesson. Nyla came in for a while to help them with sums, and Lydima took another turn with Lylie. After lunch, Udmyla came to take the girls to practice embroidery.

"Udmyla, can we make a dolly for Mya?" Lydima heard Katya ask as they went down the hall. She smiled. Katya's aunt had not known what she was giving up when she let her go.

Lylie and Dzhon went down for their naps, and Lydima put Mya down on her own bed. Then she went to check on Tye.

"I think he wore himself out," said the servant. "He started crying and then was quiet. I checked on him and he had fallen asleep."

Lydima fetched a tray of food, then returned and opened the door of the room. Tye was asleep on his bed. All the blankets and pillows had been torn off the beds and thrown on the floor. One of the pillows had been ripped open and feathers were strewn all over the room. Tye stirred and woke as she entered the room.

"Would you like some lunch?" She picked up the side table, which had been tipped over, and set the tray on top. Then she sat on Saley's bed on the other side of the room.

Tye sat up and blinked, looking remorseful. Instead of getting something to eat, he slithered underneath of his cot.

Lydima decided it would be hopeless to expect him to clean up his mess, at least at this point. It was a battle she did not want to fight. She began picking up the bedding and talked to him while she was doing it.

"I know what it is like to be angry and frustrated, Tye." She shook as many feathers as she could out of the blankets, yet they continued to swirl around and settle over everything. "But your sisters love you, and they need you to be strong for them. Can you help me pick up the feathers, so Mya and Saley can sleep without being tickled by them? Then I will fix the pillow for you."

Tye didn't move, so Lydima kept working and talking. She picked up everything except for the feathers on the floor. Tye snuck out and snatched some of the food from the tray and took it under the cot.

"If you decide to clean up the feathers, put them in the pillowcase and bring it to my room. I have some things to see to, and then I will come back and check on you."

She left the room and asked the servant to remain outside, just in case. Byden had asked to see her when she had time, so she went looking for him. She found him in the courtyard overseeing routine maintenance on the portcullis.

"I have discovered Valryn's source of information about the cavern," he stated grimly.

"Oh?" Lydima had completely forgotten about this security issue.

"An elderly man in a village on the border between here and Sonefast had not been seen for some days. When his neighbors went to check on him, they found him stabbed to death. A man matching Valryn's description had been seen in the area. It would have happened shortly before Saley was kidnapped."

"Oh dear. What did this man have to do with it?"

"He had worked on the castle in his youth, nearly seventy years ago, when it was first built. When I started working here, he was still working at the castle as a mason. He was one of the few still living who might have had knowledge of the cavern and its secrets. He will not tell anyone anything now."

Lydima shook her head. So many people had fallen prey to Valryn's schemes. They would probably never know how Valryn found out about the man or got him to talk. Through one of his customers, no doubt, or perhaps the man had been a customer himself.

Lydima left Byden and put the problem from her mind. There was nothing that could be done about it now.

Dzhon and Mya were just waking up when she returned to her room. Katya and Saley returned from their needlework shortly afterward. To her surprise, Tye entered the room with the torn pillowcase full of feathers. He handed it to her silently. She thanked him and he went to the floor to play with the blocks. Dzhon eyed him suspiciously, but shared the blocks.

Lydima stitched up the pillowcase while she watched them play. Dzhon had taught Mya his game of stacking the blocks and throwing the ball at them. Tye sat to the side and made his own stack of blocks. Dzhon took his ball and walked over to Tye. Lydima froze mid-stitch.

"Trow it at you towew," he instructed Tye.

Tye took the ball slowly and looked at his tower. Saley and Katya turned from their drawing to watch. He threw the ball and knocked over the stack of blocks. Dzhon and Katya cheered.

"Me!" called Mya who picked it up and threw it at her tower. She missed and tried again.

"Good trow!" said Dzhon when she hit it on the

second try.

Lydima was amazed. Dzhon had been the one throwing fits when he first came, and now he was exhibiting magnanimity she would not have suspected possible for one his age.

Maygla came to help her take the children to dinner. Lydima carried Mya downstairs since it took her forever to navigate them herself. She didn't want Saley to try and carry her down the steps either. Incredibly, they managed to get through dinner and bedtime without any major incidents.

When Lydima tucked Dzhon in, she praised him for sharing his ball with Tye. "Lowd Oosed towd me to."

"He told you to share your toys?"

"No," Dzhon's tone showed exasperation at her denseness. "To be a man."

"Really?" Lydima wondered what Dzhon understood by the idea. "So how do you do that?"

"By doin' fings dat awe hawd."

"Ah. I see. And sharing your ball was hard?"

"Yup. A'cause Tye's so bad."

"He has had a very difficult time. People were bad to him. We have to show him how to be good. How to be a man."

"Like shaewing my ball?"

"Exactly like that." Lydima kissed him goodnight. Sweet boy. How was she going to teach him to be a man? She was about to begin getting herself ready for bed when there was a knock at the door. When she opened it, Jayred was there.

"My lady, there is a messenger from Lord Yoused to see you. He has a letter that he says must be placed into your own hand."

Lydima followed him downstairs with a heavy heart. She dreaded to read it. She took the letter from the messenger and went into the study. Almost, she decided to burn it without reading it, but she could not. She broke open the seal and read the letter.

Lydima thought she couldn't possibly cry any more than she already had, but as she read over Yoused's words, tears rained again. His letter was so perfect. He didn't beg, he didn't bribe her with gifts, he merely expressed his love. The idea of having someone to lean on appealed to her greatly. She needed it after a day like today. It would be good for the children to have a father figure. He had already made quite an impression on Dzhon and Katya. Her resolve wavered.

Then she imagined him the object of ridicule, losing the respect of his subjects, the respect of his sons for marrying her. She could not stand to see that, could not stand to be the cause of it. Things couldn't go on as they were. She must let him know her answer right away, so he could start to get over her. She called for Jayred.

"Tell Lord Yoused's messenger to convey to his master that I will see him at his earliest convenience."

There was no way to write what needed to be said. She had to tell him in person, if she could find the courage.

∞∞∞

Yoused arrived at Freosyd two evenings later. Lydima had asked Byden to give her advance warning of his approach so she could await him in the study. Normally she was an expert at masking her emotions, but not this time. She knew, try as she might to prevent it, her expression would give everything away as soon as he saw her. It did.

Lord Yoused entered the study with eager steps,

took one look at her, and his face turned ashen. "So your answer is 'no'?" he asked softly.

She nodded sorrowfully. She knew this would break his heart, but her heart was breaking as well.

"There is nothing I can do to change your mind?" His eyes pleaded with her, trying to understand.

"I am sorry. I cannot take the children to Sonefast. I am not sure that being in a castle at all is good for them. When Eemya returns, I may ask her to give us a small farm to live on."

Some light returned to Yoused's eyes as she said this. "Is this your only objection?"

Lydima hesitated.

"What else is there?" Yoused persisted. "Tell me."

"You do not know what you are about in marrying me. You would lose the respect of those closest to you. I will not be responsible for that," she said firmly, standing as tall as she could, but her knees wobbled.

Yoused stepped nearer to her. "You have never been one to give place to the opinions of others. Why now?"

Lydima broke. "Because I never cared about anyone before now!"

"Are you saying," Yoused rasped, "are you saying that you care about me?"

"Yes." The word wrenched itself from her lips without her consent.

"You are refusing me because you care for me?" he was incredulous, but his tone was joyful.

"Yes!" She turned away from him, but he placed his hands on her shoulders and gently turned her around. He lifted her chin so she would look at him.

"Do you love me, Lydima?"

She closed her eyes so she could not see his face.

"Yoused, please do not make this harder for me

than it already is."

"I will take that as a 'yes'." His voice was both tender and triumphant. "Do not worry, my dear. It will take some time, but I know what I must do. Have faith. I will not abandon you for long." He kissed her forehead and left while she stood gaping after him.

Her breath went out in a whoosh, and she sat down, drained from the effort it had taken to maintain control of her emotions. Perplexed, she tried to understand Yoused's response to her refusal and failed. She had obviously not been convincing enough. He had hope of changing her mind. What in the world was he going to do?

CHAPTER TWENTY

Stelan's dominant thought was to put as much distance between himself and Tharch as he could in the shortest amount of time. This meant staying on the road. Horses had excellent night vision, and there was no one else travelling this time of night. It might be some time before Tharch and his men could equip themselves with new horses, so they should be able to follow it safely until dawn, at least. However, the road went almost due west, and they needed to head north.

After they had travelled what seemed like a considerable distance, they came to a place where a stream ran across the road. Stepping stones had been arranged for those travelling on foot, but horses were easily able to wade across. It was a perfect spot to leave the road without leaving an obvious sign of their departure from it. After letting the horse stop to take a drink, he headed it northward up the stream.

He did not let himself dismount until he had found a place where they could safely stop and rest. Without rest, he didn't think he would be able to get them both back on the horse. The sun rose, and he left the stream as it wandered east into a village. Most of the land they rode through was used for farming or grazing cattle, and there wasn't much cover.

Stelan remembered Janis labelling some swampy areas on the map, and he headed in that direction. Soon, the soil became marshy and wet, and it was no longer suitable for farming. It was not conducive to habitation either, and would be a good place to hide. The cooler weather meant they would be free from mosquitos as well.

He spied a small island of dry ground surrounded by cattails and guided the horse onto it. Carefully, he slid off its back and pulled Talia down after him. She was still breathing, and didn't seem feverish. He covered her with his cloak and turned back to the horse. Before he could see to Talia, he needed to take care of the animal and get it out of sight.

While talking with a soothing voice, he rubbed the horse down with a section he tore from the spare dress, inspecting the wounds to make sure there was nothing still in them. Stelan rummaged around in his pack, and in the bottom of it was an apple. That, and a crust of bread, was the last food they had. Using the apple as an incentive, biting off bits of it at a time, he coaxed the animal into lying down. It was a well-trained horse, and appeared to have been taught to lie down for just such situations.

As soon as the horse's head was below the top of the rushes, Stelan turned to Talia. He had assisted Lady Eemya in the infirmary at Freosyd on several occasions, and he tried to imitate her calm detachment. Talia had a deep gash in her head that was nearly as long as his index finger. The skin had parted down to the skull. Part of her ear had been sliced off. Initially, there had been a lot of blood, but the bleeding seemed to have stopped. The injuries did not appear to be life-threatening.

Stelan used a clean section of the remains of the dress and soaked it in the cool, clear water that surrounded their marsh island. Gently he washed off Talia's face and dabbed her forehead with the cold rag. Her eyelids fluttered, and he gasped with relief.

"Stay still," he directed as she started to thrash around. "Do not move. We have ridden all night and will stay here until it is dark again." He remembered he still had some of Janis' ointment in his pack and took it out. "I am going to treat your wounds and bandage them up. This might hurt."

Talia tried to say something, but closed her eyes with a sigh. The effort was too much. Stelan put some of the salve on her ear and in the gash on her head, and then he tied a strip of the fabric around it. The only sign Talia gave that she felt anything was a quickening of her breath and flared nostrils. He helped her sit up enough to sip some water from his leather flask, which she promptly vomited up. He wiped her face again and helped her to find a comfortable position in which to rest. Then she was able to fall into a natural sleep.

Stelan lay down next to her and held her close to keep her warm. The horse would either stay, or he wouldn't. He pulled the cloak up over their heads to shield them from the sun and slept also.

∞∞∞∞

When Stelan woke, all he could think of was that he was cold, and it was dark. Then he heard the horse nicker. Talia was shivering in her sleep, and he tried to wake her. She made a startled cry, and he quickly reassured her.

"Everything is fine. It is time to move on. Can you put your arm around me? I will help you up."

Talia groaned and stood to her feet with Stelan's assistance. The horse was already standing, and with a boost from Stelan, Talia was able to pull herself onto its back. Then Stelan pulled himself up after her. The horse found its way carefully through the marsh, and they had to travel more slowly than the previous night. Talia leaned back against Stelan and didn't speak.

As they went further north, the landscape changed, and became hilly. The vegetation changed to low trees and shrubs. Stelan had been worried about what they would eat, but the horse sniffed out a crabapple tree, and they stopped to rest and let the gelding eat. Talia's head hurt, and Stelan noticed she had a hard time eating the apple he gave her, so he took his dagger and sliced it for her. They ate the last crust of bread and drank some water from the flask. Stelan filled his pack with crabapples since he didn't know when they would find more food.

Before he helped her back on the horse, Talia turned to Stelan and held his face in her hands. "I am not sorry."

Stelan blinked back tears and put his forehead to hers. "No matter what happens, I want you to know that I love you."

"And I love you."

They rode until dawn, feeling nothing but their love for each other and concern over the other's safety. Stelan's emotions went from euphoria to despair to intense happiness to fear in a regular cycle. The terrain turned to badlands as they got closer to the mountains, and Stelan figured it would only take them two more nights on horseback to reach the pass Hatch had spoken of.

After sleeping through the day in a hollow between two hills, they continued their journey north. The horse evidently viewed them as its new 'herd' and had stayed with them, finding a few tufts of grass to graze while they slept. When she awoke, Talia was more alert and behaved like her normal self. Stelan returned her sword, and she strapped it back on.

Stelan's stomach was rebelling from eating only apples, and he and Talia were both sore from riding bareback, but they were alive and getting closer to home every day. For two days, they had seen no one, not even a goat herder. They had passed far to the east of the weapons testing site, deliberately avoiding it. As they approached the mountains, their chances of encountering a patrol increased with every step.

Close to morning, they stopped at a spring and refreshed themselves with the cold, sweet water. There was enough soft grass and clover for the horse to eat and to provide a comfortable place to rest. The trees and shrubs were taller around the spring and would hide them from anyone passing by who was not stopping to use the spring. Stelan knew he should keep watch this close to the border, but the wind from the south was cold, even during the day, and he did not want Talia to catch a chill in addition to her injury.

As they lay down, the feel of Talia next to him was nearly driving Stelan mad. Even blood, sweat, and dirt from days on the road did nothing to cool his desire. She must have been feeling the same because she turned to him, pressed her body against his, and began to kiss him ardently. He responded to her, and she began to loosen her sword belt.

Stelan knew what was about to happen, but it didn't feel right. It took all his willpower, but he grabbed her hands. "Wait."

"I cannot wait. I want you now!"

"Talia, I cannot look your father in the eye and ask for your hand if I have already taken you. As difficult as it seems, we should do this the right way. Back at the barn, you told me to wait, and you were right. Now I am telling you the same, but for a different reason."

"But what if we never make it home?" she whispered.

"It does not matter. I will not love you any more or any less than I do at this moment. No one can take that away from us."

"I am afraid," she choked out a sob and buried her head in his chest.

Stelan had never seen her like this. He stroked her cheek gently. "All the more reason not to give in and let fear dictate our actions." He held her securely. "I cannot promise that we will make it back safely, but I can promise that we will face the future together, whatever it holds."

∞∞∞

Talia squeezed Stelan tightly.

"You always say the right thing, even if I do not want to hear it."

She had wanted the physical intimacy as a means of escaping their circumstances, if only for a little while, but it wouldn't change anything. Instead, as she nestled into his arms, she felt his love and strength enveloping her, and that was what she needed. Calm began to wash over her and the tightness in her chest began to relax. Her breathing slowly returned to normal.

"Sleep now," soothed Stelan. "Tonight we will

reach the mountains."

∞∞∞

The sun was low, but had not yet set. Talia woke to the horse's loud whinny. She heard hoof beats in the distance. Stelan heard them also and jumped to his feet. Several horsemen galloped through the trees toward them. They had been discovered. The two of them wouldn't be able to outrun fresh horses on their tired mount, so they drew their swords and stood back to back as the riders surrounded them.

"Well, well. I will enjoy learning from my betrothed how a spy came to be her handmaid. I must admit, you are very resourceful. I am glad to see that you have taken care of my horse."

It was Lord Tharch.

By changing to fresh horses every day and riding on smooth roads, he could easily have caught up to them. Somehow he must have deduced that this spring would be a likely place to stop before attempting to cross the mountains. Tharch motioned to four of his men who dismounted and drew their swords.

"Remember, Chysh wants them alive." To his quarry he said with a chuckle, "I assure you, the king does not delegate his interrogations to others. He will do the job properly."

This speech had the opposite effect on Talia than Tharch intended. The advantage was hers if her attackers were hobbled by trying not to kill her, and they had nothing to lose if capture resulted in torture and death. She took her stance and was ready to counter their onslaught.

Talia's skill was known to the Cerecian soldiers, but they knew nothing about Stelan other than his ability to withstand torture. As a result, the four

295

swordsmen hesitated as they came within range.

"Take them!" demanded Tharch.

The soldier on Talia's right lunged forward, and rather than meet his blow, she sidestepped and stabbed him through the heart as he tried to recover his balance. Too easy. The second soldier learned from the mistake of the first and was more cautious.

Behind her, Talia could hear the ring of steel against steel but could not turn to look. This time, she began the attack, and her blade moved with fury. Her current opponent was burly and strong, but like the pirate captain, he lacked finesse. She was easily able to work her way inside his guard and dispatch him.

Before the second man hit the ground, she turned around and ran to help Stelan. He was holding his opponents at bay, but barely. The rest of Tharch's men began to dismount as she drew away one of Stelan's attackers.

With only one man to face, Stelan swiftly defeated his enemy, slicing through the soldier's throat with the tip of his sword as he avoided a swing from his opponent's blade. Blood spattered from the wound, and some landed on his face.

Talia killed the fourth man, and they stood back to back again, panting. The remaining men unsheathed their swords.

"Enough," roared Tharch, and his horse pawed its hooves, channeling his rider's anger and impatience. Possibly Tharch was feeling nervous as his guard had been reduced by half in only a few moments. He turned his horse a little to the right, unslung Talia's own bow from behind his back, and nocked an arrow to it. "Alive does not mean unharmed. Throw down your weapons, or I will stick you with arrows thicker than a porcupine's quills."

The four enemy soldiers stepped back to give

Tharch room to shoot, but were still close enough to contain the spies. Tharch closed the circle around them on one end, but Talia didn't give him time to draw. Before he even raised the bow, she ran toward him with a yell. The soldiers on either side of him were not close enough to stop her. When he tried to draw the bow, she did a barrel roll and the arrow struck the ground behind her.

Angrily, Tharch threw down the bow and reached for his sword, but it was too late. Tharch's mount was a seasoned battle horse and stood still for the whole scene waiting for his master's command, but it never came.

Talia cut the horse's throat, and it fell as Tharch jumped clear. He had trouble freeing his feet from the stirrups and landed heavily. The horse was between him and his men, and before they could reach him, Talia thrust her blade between his ribs. Fleetingly, Talia was glad that Bashalis would no longer have to marry him, if she survived her brother's wrath, that is.

She turned just in time to block the swing of a blade, and her strength waned as she began to feel the effects of her injuries. One of her knees buckled, and she feared this might be the end, but then the soldier facing her crumpled to the ground with an arrow in his back. It was a Berushese arrow, but not hers.

Stelan had just slain a second man, but another was set to stab him from behind when that soldier, too, fell with an arrow sticking from his back. The last soldier turned to run, but was struck by an arrow before he could take two steps. Talia and Stelan walked toward each other as they gazed northward and saw three men on the crest of the hill. As the newcomers approached, they recognized one of them.

"Lord Stelan," said Prince Darius, "I do not remember sending you on this mission."

CHAPTER TWENTY-ONE

Darius and his men had crossed the mountains on foot, so after retrieving their arrows to avoid leaving evidence, they borrowed the riderless Cerecian horses and rode them as far as they could for the return journey. When the climb became too steep, they set them loose.

Talia was exhausted. The fight with Tharch and his men had spent every last measure of her strength, so they made camp on a wide ledge on the side of the mountain. They couldn't risk a fire, since it might attract a patrol, but they passed around a flask of wine and ate stale biscuits and dried meat. The food tasted like a banquet after days of only sour apples.

Talia leaned against Stelan's shoulder and fell asleep, but Stelan wanted answers. "How did you come to be here?" he asked incredulously.

"Eemya was worried about you. She had had a dream that you were in danger and insisted I find out if all was well. When you have a pregnant wife, you do whatever she asks you to do. I had business to attend to in Letyna anyway, so I went to see Tomus.

There I found out that you were missing, and it was reported that you and Captain Talia were in hiding in Herida. We have been patrolling the border for over a week, trusting that you would find your way back.

"A couple of days ago, a man came over the mountain claiming that he had seen you and that this was the pass you were going to be taking. We are not ready to make a full-scale invasion, so I picked a couple of my best men to come and look for you. Effan is leading another small team, and they should catch up with us tomorrow."

"Who was the man who told you we were coming this way?"

"He did not give his name. He only said that his chief had sent him and that you would explain when we found you," Darius looked at Stelan curiously. "I did not think that Cerecians arranged themselves by tribes."

"They do not," Stelan grinned.

"It looks like you will have much to tell me," Darius said, observing Stelan's arm around Talia, "but not tonight. Now it is time to rest."

Stelan closed his eyes. "I see their faces," he said quietly. He remembered the taste of the blood and shuddered. "They were just doing their duty."

"And you were doing yours."

"I know," Stelan sighed, "but it seems like there must be another way."

"Sometimes there is, sometimes there is not. With Artylia, we were able to find another way. With Cerecia . . . ," Darius shook his head.

"King Chysh loves violence for its own sake."

"You have taken out one of his staunchest supporters in Lord Tharch. Who knows what will happen now? Leave the worrying to people like Cyrus and Yarin. Take your rest. You have earned it."

Stelan nodded and tried to sleep. With Darius on watch, he felt safe for the first time in weeks and was able to let go of the tension that had been with him constantly. Eventually, he drifted off, but his dreams were disturbing.

∞∞∞

The steepness of the ascent made it nearly impossible to carry on a conversation while climbing the mountain, as did the biting wind, but by the time Effan's group caught up with them the next night, Darius had finally heard the whole story.

". . . so he stole a horse, saved me from death in the forest—"

"And when Tharch caught up with us, Talia slayed three men in the blink of an eye—"

"You killed two."

"Only because you helped me."

Darius chuckled.

"What?"

"I am proud to have had a hand in your training, and I am profoundly happy for both of you." He smiled benevolently at them.

It took them more than a week to travel over the southern range and across Artylia to the capital. They stopped in a village on the way for Talia to see a healer. Stelan took the opportunity to take Darius aside.

"As governor of Lyliana, do I have your permission to marry Talia?"

"Son," Darius put his hand on Stelan's shoulder, "I owe you more than my life, and I would give you anything you could ask for."

Stelan blinked as his eyes became moist. "Thank you, my lord."

"I imagine," he said with a twitch in the corner of his mouth, "that the transition from an elite soldier to the lady of a manor will be a challenging one for your betrothed. You will need to be patient with her."

"I will. You think, then, that her parents will give their consent?"

Darius grinned. "That is something you will have to discover for yourself, but you will not have to wait long to find out. They are visiting Tomus and Onia and will be waiting for us at the palace."

Stelan wondered what Darius found so amusing, but he went to find out the healer's analysis of Talia's injuries.

"Fortunately, the wounds are not infected and seem to be healing properly," observed the healer as he examined the patient. "The gash on your head will scar, and the hair will probably not grow back, but it could easily be covered by pulling another section of hair over it. How do you feel?"

"My ears ring."

The healer nodded. "The impact of the debris, combined with the shock of a blast such as you describe, could produce that effect. It may make it harder for you to distinguish words in noisy settings."

"Will it diminish with time?" asked Stelan.

"Possibly. Probably not. The missing piece of ear, of course, will have little effect on her hearing and is merely a cosmetic issue."

Talia absorbed all of this quietly. None of it was a surprise. Both she and Stelan had returned quite a bit different from when they started. Stelan's skin had almost completely renewed itself by now, but there was some slight discoloration and scarring over most of his body. The scars in their minds would be the most difficult to deal with.

"I love all of your scars," Stelan whispered in

Talia's ear when the healer left them alone for a moment, "but I love this one the most." He touched her sleeve in the area where Cush had burned her.

Talia threw her arms around him, and they both wept silent tears.

∞∞∞

Darius and his men had left their horses at the castle of a nearby lord. They spent the night there to wait out a winter storm of cold, driving rain. This gave Stelan and Talia a chance to get a bath and a clean change of clothes, after which they felt refreshed and rejuvenated. Stelan also shaved his beard and trimmed his hair, which was starting to show its blond roots.

The next morning, they borrowed a couple of extra horses for the returning spies and headed to Letyna. When they finally rode through the gates of the capital, Stelan turned to Talia and asked, "How do I address your father? Is he a chieftain or a lord?"

"We do not have lords in Berush. He is the head of our tribe, which means the same as the Cerecian word for chief. His name is Rolind." She looked sideways at him. "Are you nervous?"

"A little," he admitted.

Talia's face held the same amusement he had seen on Darius'.

"You think it is funny? You do not have to ask anyone for my hand."

"I could ask him for you," she teased.

"Oh no, you will not. I will do it myself!"

Talia laughed and spurred her horse ahead while he raced to catch up with her. Darius, Talia and Stelan dismounted in the courtyard and made their way to the great hall. The prince had sent word ahead of their arrival, and Tomus and his parents were waiting for them.

"Oh, my baby! What has happened to you?" exclaimed a woman Stelan assumed was Talia's mother. She rushed forward and took Talia in her arms. Talia rolled her eyes, but returned her mother's embrace.

"I am fine, mama, really."

"Fine? You are most certainly not fine. Look at you! You are missing half an ear!" Talia's mother broke down and started crying. Talia sighed and looked at Stelan for sympathy, and he gave her a small smile.

Darius took over and approached Tomus and Rolind. He summarized the information the pair had gathered about the production of 'magic fire,' the important contacts they had made with the Chief and his organization, the damage they were able to inflict on the Cerecian supply line, and ended with the news that Lord Tharch had been eliminated.

Rolind looked proudly at Talia and put his hand on her shoulder like he might with a son. "Well done, daughter."

"You have no idea how relieved I am to see you," declared Tomus with emotion. "Though I was the one to recommend you for the assignment, the responsibility was nearly unbearable. I have not stopped worrying since the day you left."

"All is well, brother. The mission was a greater success than we could have hoped."

"The mission! Who cares about the mission? What about my poor Talia? What is to become of her now? She cannot continue to be a soldier after this, can she?" Talia's mother looked at Prince Darius hopefully.

Stelan had been waiting for an opportunity to

speak his piece, and now seemed as good a time as any. "Actually, I have something to say to that." He turned to Talia's father.

Rolind was a tall, heavyset man with bushy black eyebrows and a long, grey beard. He had a formidable expression, but Stelan gathered his courage and refused to be intimidated.

"Chief Rolind, I would like to ask your permission to marry your daughter."

Talia's mother gasped and was momentarily speechless.

Rolind appeared surprised and looked at his daughter. "Do you wish to marry him?"

"I do, father."

"Give him your permission, before he changes his mind!" exclaimed his wife, finding her voice. "I never thought I would see this day! My eldest daughter is finally going to be married!"

Rolind looked at Darius.

"I have already given my consent," the prince informed him. "Lord Stelan is the worthiest young man I know."

Rolind turned back to Stelan and smiled. "I know from experience that once my daughter has set her mind on something, she will not be turned from it. If you know that and still want her, you can have her with my blessing."

Stelan grinned. "Thank you, Chief Rolind." He held his hand out to Talia and she went to him and took it.

"Talia, we must discuss a date for the feast, and invitations, and you will need to be fitted for a dress!"

"Mother," said Talia firmly, "You know I do not want any of that. I am taking this man to bed right now, and I will not be wearing a dress! You may eat what you like." She grinned widely at Stelan and left the room, dragging him willingly after her.

"But," her mother pouted and looked at the men, who all smiled and shrugged. None of them would dare risk Talia's wrath by coming between her and her new husband.

"Think how much cheaper it is this way," said Rolind with satisfaction.

∞∞∞

The newlyweds stayed in Letyna for a week. Talia's mother fawned over Stelan and gushed about her pride and happiness in her married daughter. When Lord Yoused's pleasure yacht arrived to take them to the island, Talia was more than ready to go.

Tomus went with them to the pier to see them off. "I am so happy for you, sister. I love you!" He hugged her tightly. "I am glad I asked you to sail with her," he said to Stelan.

"As am I," Stelan grinned.

Tomus gazed at his sister intently. "Being a soldier was exciting for me. Invigorating. An adventure, but with hard, long days and many harrowing moments. Being a husband and a leader has been demanding, but even more fulfilling. It calls for a different kind of strength, a deeper strength. Strength of character. I know you will rise to the challenges your new life will offer you."

"Thank you, Tomus," Talia held his face in her hands and then turned to let Stelan help her into the yacht.

For a long time, she had insisted on doing everything herself, without a man's help, but she knew that whatever Stelan did for her, he did out of love, not from any idea that she was weak or needed his assistance. She waved once more to Tomus and then coaxed Stelan into the cabin with a smile.

"I went to Cerecia in search of 'magic fire,' but I found something much more magical than that," she said and closed the cabin door.

CHAPTER TWENTY-TWO

Lydima walked out to the courtyard to meet Stelan and his new bride. She had received word that they were coming and had a room prepared. They were going home the long way, after visiting his family at Sonefast, so he could show his wife where he had spent half of his life.

The younger children were still down for their naps when the guests arrived, so only Saley and Katya were with her. It was an unusually frigid afternoon for this early in the winter, so they all wore heavy cloaks. Lacy tendrils of frost still covered the inside of the northern wall. The girls blew out long breaths of air and watched as the moisture froze into visible clouds while the visitors rode through the gate.

Lydima had heard that Lady Talia had been a warrior, so she was not completely shocked to see her misshapen ear, but she did wonder why she didn't style her hair differently to cover it up. She was also wearing trousers under her dress. Other than that, Talia was a tall, strong, beautiful woman.

Lydima could understand why Stelan had fallen in love with her.

"Welcome to Freosyd, Lady Talia."

She introduced herself, and Stelan interpreted since his wife knew little Artylian. Talia studied her with a strange expression, but Lydima marked it down to her foreignness and did not regard it.

"We have something to show you," said Stelan once the introductions were over.

"You do?"

"Shall we go into the study?"

"Certainly."

Lydima noticed Stelan carried an extra sword and thought it strange. She sent the girls to find Udmyla and showed her guests into Eemya's office. Once inside, Stelan took a miniature out of his pouch and set it on the table.

"Where did you get this? I do not remember sitting for it."

"It is not you," said Stelan. "It is your mother."

"What?" Lydima stared at it.

Stelan related the story of how they had acquired the small portrait from Lydima's grandmother, and then he presented her with her father's sword. Lydima was at an utter loss for words. She clutched the sword tightly, with tears streaming down her cheeks, and listened while Stelan explained how her parents had met and what had happened to them. When he had finished, he and his wife quietly excused themselves and left her alone.

Her parents had been married! They had loved each other! They had wanted her! It was overwhelming. She must have been born almost immediately upon her mother's return, and she had died before telling anyone the story. Or else no one had bothered to repeat it to her daughter when she was old enough.

Lydima sat in the study and cried for nearly an hour. Hearing her parents' history was something she had been completely unprepared for. She felt sad and happy at the same time, but more than anything, she felt free. Free of a weight she had carried for her entire life. The weight of shame for her very existence. Now she had pride. Pride in who her parents were and who she was as a result. She stood up and walked out of the study feeling like a new woman.

∞∞∞

Months passed. Winter turned to spring, and spring turned to summer. Freosyd was prospering. There had been no new outbreaks of fever, the fields were planted, the rainfall was normal, and Artylia would not need another loan.

"Lord Yoused has forwarded an order for grain from Letyna," Jayred informed Lydima as they met to determine the yearly obligation to the capital. "They will pay for what they need in addition to the tribute, and repay the loan next summer."

"I hear Artylia is smuggling goods into Cerecia for huge profits," grumbled Byden. "If they are reselling our grain, they should pay us more than this."

International intrigue was of no concern to Lydima. "Lord Yoused is not coming to check our records?"

"No, I believe we can handle it ourselves," answered Jayred.

Lydima voiced her agreement but felt absurdly deflated. She left Jayred and Byden to iron out the details and returned to hear the children's lessons.

"Katya, you are reading better and better every

day!" she exclaimed when the girl read aloud a poem she had been studying.

"Listen to Tye say his alphabet!"

Katya beamed at a bashful Tye, who dutifully recited the letters with secret pride. He was still sullen occasionally and would not talk to the men, but there had been no more conflagrations like there had been the first week. He'd even let Lydima cut his hair the last time Dzhon got his trimmed.

Lydima clapped and laughed with delight. "You did it! I am so proud of you!"

"No, Lylie," Lydima heard Saley admonish the precocious baby from across the room, "you will hurt yourself."

Lylie had crawled over to the table, pulled herself to her feet, and was reaching for a bowl of fruit.

"Come play with Mya."

Saley picked her up and placed her on the floor. Mya held out a block. The temptation of the toy overrode the desire to pout, and Lylie and Mya were soon entertaining each other.

Lydima marveled at Saley. It had happened slowly and gradually at first, just a couple of words here and there, and then a torrent of speech had begun pouring forth. Lydima rejoiced to see her progress.

"I want to learn too," insisted Dzhon, and Lydima gave him a pencil and slate and began showing him how to form letters. He looked at Tye's work and copied it with intense concentration.

"Katya, Saley," called Aylria from the doorway.

"Are we going to do more knitting?" Katya asked eagerly.

"We surely are," smiled Aylria.

It had taken some time, but eventually Aylria had started helping with the children again. It was Katya who brought her back. She sought Aylria out for her sewing lessons and chattered away like nothing had happened. The older woman couldn't help but respond to the young girl's concern and enthusiasm.

Lydima sighed in satisfaction. With six growing and happy, healthy children, her heart was full. Almost.

Youshed had written once, to inform her of how the women from The White Lily were faring. They had lost one. In the throes of withdrawal from her opium addiction, one of them had hung herself. Lydima grieved over her, and wished she could have done something.

The rest were availing themselves of the opportunities provided for them. One of them, as soon as Valryn was out of the way, had received an offer of marriage from a long-time admirer and had accepted it. The remaining seven were learning to read, write, sew, and cook, and a few had already found gainful employment. One had a debilitating disease and would require constant care. Others had various physical ailments that were being treated, but overall, the outlook was positive.

Lydima couldn't help but wonder what Youshed had meant when he had said that he knew what he must do next. What was it? How long was it going to take? She tried not to worry about it, but she remembered how she had felt when he had kissed her, and she had to shake herself to keep from having regrets.

Before she knew it, fall had come again, and Eemya and Darius returned. Lydima had kept her apprised of the state of her holding and the increase in the household via letter, but Eemya was anxious to hear everything firsthand. She was excited to greet all the children, and eagerly showed off her own son, Darius, named after his father but called Dari for short. He was barely older than Lylie had been when Lydima started caring for her.

"He is lovely, Eemya. He has his father's dark hair and eyes."

Eemya was absolutely glowing with love and pride. "He is amazing, Lydima. I love him so much! But tell me, how have you been, really?"

"I am well. I was grateful when you asked me to stand in for you, but intimidated and unsure of myself, and angry. I do not know why. But these children . . . " she looked around at the boys and girls playing happily on the floor, "these children have given me a purpose. I wanted to ask you if there was a small farm or house available somewhere. I do not want to crowd you here."

"Lydima, you know it would be no trouble for me at all."

"I know, but I think these children would be better off outside of a castle."

"There is a vacant farm that would be suitable, if you are sure that is what you want."

"I am sure."

"What about Lord Yoused?"

"What about him?" Lydima became inexplicably defensive.

"There is talk that he had declared an interest in you."

Lydima looked away. She should have known Eemya would find out. Nothing could be kept secret inside a castle.

"Do you have any inclination to return his feelings?"

"My feelings do not matter. I cannot marry him."

"Whyever not?"

Lydima started to answer, but as she thought over her reasons, they did not have the same weight as they did before. Her objections sounded petty and unreasonable. She stared at the floor.

Eemya didn't press her. "You once counseled me to take a risk, and it has paid infinite returns," she smiled. "Just be sure that what you choose is what you want. Do not decline his offer out of fear. That is all I will say. The farm is available for you, but you are always welcome here, dear cousin."

∞∞∞

Lydima and the children moved to the farm the following week. The nurse had been spoken for by one of Eemya's guards, but Aylria accompanied them instead. She had surprised Lydima by requesting to go with her.

"My life here is one meaningless embroidery pattern after another. I want people to say more about me than 'she sewed the neatest stitches.' I feel like I can offer something to these children if you will have me."

Lydima had accepted her offer gratefully.

Eemya had arranged for a boy from the village to come when needed to help with some of the chores, and a woman to help weekly with baking, at least until Lydima could learn it for herself. In the spring, arrangements would be made for someone to help with the planting.

When they arrived at the house, Dzhon ran straight to the barn.

"Wydima, there's goats!"

"There are?"

"Lots of goats! Come see!"

Lydima followed him to the barn. There was a note tied to a post, and half a dozen goats stood in stalls, including a couple of nannies in dire need of

315

milking. Katya found a pail and started milking right away while Lydima read the note.

My dear Lydima,

I hope you will accept this offering towards your new endeavor. Since half of the children under your care are originally from my holding, you cannot deny me the opportunity to assist in providing for them. I know how much Dzhon would miss his goats, and Lylie could still benefit from their milk.

Yours ever,
Yoused

Lydima's eyes stung and she blinked back tears. Yoused was as thoughtful as always, but did this mean that he was not going to dissuade her from her plan? Had he given up on winning her? What was he up to? She had wanted him to leave her alone, but when he did, she was disappointed. She chided herself for being so fickle.

The other children called for her attention, and she was soon busy going over the rest of the yard and the house. The barn had several stalls, a hayloft, and a pen, although the fence was in need of repair. The farmhouse was unusually large. There was a porch, sitting room, more than ample dining room, kitchen, and four bedrooms upstairs, plus attic space.

Lydima and Lylie would share a room, Aylria would have her own for now, the two boys would bunk together, and the other girls would share. Lydima had worried extensively over the room assignments. She hadn't been sure how it would go over, but Tye and Dzhon were already arranging their toys as Eemya's men brought in their luggage. The older girls were talking about how they would decorate their room with curtains and drawings.

When evening came and they were left to themselves, Lydima and Aylria prepared a simple meal with provisions Eemya had sent, and everyone had goat's milk to drink. By the time dinner was over, all eyes were drooping, and the children went straight to bed. Lylie had been sleeping through the night for a few months, when she was not cutting teeth, but Lydima was restless. She still felt like there was something missing.

∞∞∞

Farm life was keeping them all busy. Caring for the goats and a few chickens, cooking, baking, cleaning, and doing their own laundry took up most of their time. Lydima had a new respect and appreciation for the castle laundress after having to clean a week's worth of soiled diapers. At least they had a well and did not have to go far to fetch water. It was hard work, but after a month Lydima was getting the hang of it. It was liberating not to have to answer to anyone but herself.

The children spent more time outdoors than they had at the castle, and they were all rosy and hale. They had chores and lessons to do, but it was easy to turn the work into play. Even Aylria was actually looking happy and had become an agreeable companion.

One sunny, crisp morning, shortly after breakfast, Lydima heard the pounding of a mallet out by the barn.

Aylria pushed open a shutter and looked out the window.

"There is a man working on the fence around the goat pen. Lady Eemya must have sent someone to

317

repair it."

Lydima grabbed her cloak. "I will go and see who it is." A cool breeze blew in her face as she opened the door and stepped outside.

As she grew closer to the pen, she recognized the figure standing next to it, and her heart leapt into her throat. The man heard her approach and turned and put down the mallet. It was Lord Yoused. She met his eyes and saw intense pain and longing.

"Lord Yoused, what are you doing here?"

"I am not Lord Yoused anymore."

"What do you mean?"

"I am just Yoused. Only myself. I have abdicated my holding in favor of my son, Warryn. Prince Darius has approved the transfer of lordship. I come to you with nothing, nothing except hands that can work and a heart that can love, if you will take me."

Lydima could hardly believe what she had heard. "You gave up your lordship for me?"

He nodded. "I love you, Lydima. I want to be near you, whatever it takes, even if it is only as a farmhand."

As he said this, Lydima fell to her knees, weeping uncontrollably.

"My dear, why are you crying? Tell me!" Yoused sank down in front of her and put his hands around her shoulders.

"Because I love you!"

Yoused gave an uncertain laugh, and Lydima slipped her arms around his waist and kissed him. Yoused remained uncertain no longer and kissed her joyously as they knelt on the cold, damp ground.

A child's voice whispered excitedly in Lydima's ear, "I thought you said Lord Yoused was *not* going to be our new daddy! Does this mean you changed your mind?"

"Yes Katya," Lydima laughed. "Yes it does."

AUTHOR'S NOTE

Human trafficking is modern-day slavery and involves the use of force, fraud, or coercion to obtain some type of labor or commercial sex act. For more information, to make a report, or to get help go to:

https://www.dhs.gov/blue-campaign/what-human-trafficking

National Human Trafficking Hotline: 1-888-373-7888 or text HELP or INFO to BeFree (233733)

If you witness, suspect, or are being abused in any other situation, you should contact your state's Department of Child or Family Protective Services.

Post-traumatic stress is a diagnosable condition that can develop after a person is exposed to a traumatic event. Symptoms can include disturbing thoughts, feelings, or dreams related to the events, mental or physical distress, difficulty sleeping, and changes in how a person thinks and feels. If you or a loved one is suffering from PTS, there are many resources available to help you including:

https://www.ptsd.va.gov/public/where-to-get-help.asp

WWP Resource Center: 888.WWP.ALUM (997.2586) or 904.405.1213

https://www.woundedwarriorproject.org

Please note: the author is not affiliated with or endorsed by any of these websites. They are listed for your reference only.

BEHIND THE SCENES

If you do not like it when people tell you how the magic trick works, or you never watch the deleted scenes or interviews with the director because it spoils the effect of the movie, then you do not want to read this part.

Talia gave a final, shuddering breath, and then her body relaxed as the life flowed out of her. "No! No, Talia . . . " Stelan sobbed with tears running down his face as he—

"Wait! Hold on, you cannot do this to me! Author, I am talking to you!"

"Hey, you're not supposed to talk to me. You're supposed to say what I tell you to say."

"I cannot let this pass. Have I not suffered enough? I already bear the guilt of my mother's death—"

"You're supposed to be over that."

"Whoever really gets over something like that? I have survived a cave-in, collapsed lung, capture, torture, been dragged all over enemy territory, and I have done everything right! You gave me this amazing woman, whom I love more than anything, and now you want to take her away! I cannot bear it!"

Talia, being dead at the moment, thankfully can't express her opinion.

"You think marrying her will make you happy? You two are not good for each other. She's going to give you hell."

"What is hell?"

"Never mind. Marriage with Talia would be extremely difficult. It will only bring you more heartache."

"Are you basing this on my character and Talia's or on your own past experience?"

Ouch. "That's low, Stelan."

"Is it the truth?" he persists passionately.

I don't want to go there with him.

"You and Talia fell in love during a high-stress adventure. Part of that time, you were her captive. There's a psychological term for that, you know. Day-to-day life is not the same."

"That does not mean that our love is less real!"

I admire his devotion, but he's so young and inexperienced. He doesn't know what he's getting into. Nevertheless, I begin to feel a little guilty. There have been many times when I made mistakes and didn't know what I was getting into, but I wouldn't take any of it back.

Stelan looks at Talia, forgetting about me, cradles her limp body in his arms and kisses her tenderly. Then he clutches her tightly to himself, rests his head on her forehead, and weeps with abandon.

I sigh.

Fortunately, my first drafts are written in my head while I lie awake between sleep cycles accelerated by narcolepsy. All I have to do is rewind to the beginning of the chapter and start over. I can't help giving

Stelan what he wants. He's such a good kid. Maybe it will work out. Man, I really wanted to write a death scene.

DISCUSSION QUESTIONS

1.   Whose responsibility is it to stand against injustice? List all the people who were involved in closing The White Lily Inn.

2.   Both Talia and Lydima had other priorities they put above their personal desires. What were they? What takes priority in your life?

3.   How did Youse deal with difficulties in his life? How did Lydima help him move forward in these areas? Do you have situations in your life that you are reluctant to deal with?

4.   How did Lydima's views on children change during the story and why?

5.   What difficult decisions did Talia have to make, and why did they bother her? How do you decide what is the right path to take when faced with important decisions?

6.   What were two results of Stelan's decision

not to keep watch at the spring? What are some areas in your life that you need to keep watch over, literally or figuratively?

7. Talia, Lydima, Yoused and Stelan all had different ideas of what they wanted out of a relationship, or if they wanted one. How did they differ? Did their goals and ideas change?

ABOUT THE AUTHOR

Ever since I was a little girl, I have loved to read. One of the first books I remember reading was a Wonder Book version of *Cinderella*. It was in the reading station in my kindergarten class, and I loved the illustrations. I would pick that book out every time, so my teacher finally removed it from the shelf to force me to expand my horizons. Now I have my own copy.

Another book that influenced me very early on was Richard Scarry's *Busy, Busy World*. It told a story of two creative painters who painted a mural of a large sun inside someone's house. I thought the idea was genius, so I drew a large sunshine on my wall with crayon. It was scrubbed off, but I continued to have a desire to express myself artistically.

In middle school, I enjoyed writing, and my English teacher told me I would write a book someday. I still loved to read, sometimes reading late into the night. When I was not reading, I was making up stories in my head for my own amusement, but I never wrote them down. I was more interested in drawing and painting than writing. I have since painted numerous works of art, including some very large outdoor murals.

Over the years, I have had a lot of trouble with insomnia. I had heard that if you write down your ideas, it will help you to be able to go to sleep. That didn't help, but I did end up writing some complete novels. Finally, I was diagnosed with narcolepsy, and understanding my sleep patterns, along with scheduling at least one nap during the day, has greatly improved my quality of life.

The line between dreaming and wakefulness for me is sometimes blurred, and some of my ideas come straight from my dreams. Others are worked out while I'm lying in bed unable to sleep. It was fun to type them out, and I am planning to continue writing. I hope you enjoy my stories and characters as much as I do.

Visit me online at www.facebook.com/ambergabrielauthor

Made in the USA
Middletown, DE
07 November 2021

51571646R00205